Universal Extinction

Michael Bradley

Copyright © 2022 Michael Bradley
All rights reserved
First Edition

Fulton Books
Meadville, PA

Published by Fulton Books 2022

ISBN 978-1-63985-546-9 (paperback)
ISBN 979-8-88731-002-2 (hardcover)
ISBN 978-1-63985-547-6 (digital)

Printed in the United States of America

Acknowledgments

I am indebted to my editor, Joyce Magnin, for all her excellent work in bringing this novel to a level which makes me proud to be the author. With her help and that of my wife, Anita, and input from our sister, Peggy Laurance, the manuscript has become something we can all offer as testament that our collective efforts have produced a book worthy of publishing. A special thank you to my wife for putting up with me throughout this entire odyssey.

Prologue

Their defeat was absolute. The fleet of Drezil warrior ships had descended on their planet with a sudden vicious attack that left nearly all the population of their home world dead. The alien ships spewed an energy plasma which ignited everything it touched. Even the dirt that made up the crust of the planet dissolved and turned into a flowing molten river of death to all who were caught up in its parade. From the invader's viewpoint, the planet seemed to shudder under their onslaught, with the atmosphere turning a dull shade of brown.

The leader of the invaders, Bordeth, felt a burgeoning sense of pride in his forces' killing rampage. Addressing his second-in-command, he said, "Once this planet has cooled, the atmosphere will contain all the gasses we need for survival. Our weapons have burned all the oxygen and nitrogen from the planet, and the rotting vegetation and decaying bodies will provide the additional methane we need to balance the atmosphere to support our species. Only a few of the inhabitants appear to have escaped, but they will not present any threat to us. They have entered deep space beyond this galaxy and are of no concern to us any longer."

The few Azdawn who survived the Drezil onslaught had taken their ships and set a course which would take them out of their galaxy and, hopefully, out of the grasp of the alien invaders. Having destroyed all evidence of their own advanced scientific discoveries, the defeated Azdawns took their formidable weapons and defensive technologies with them, hoping to be able to find another race capable of implementing a strategy for defeating this caustic force. The Azdawn leader, Rotan, had mapped a path across the cosmos which led to the outer reaches of their galaxy. After roaming the universe for what seemed like an eternity, a small blue orb appeared on their sensors which, on closer examination, they found to be a planet which was made up mostly of water but had many land masses that were populated by humanoid life-forms.

Rotan knew this planet and said to his crew, "If you are called upon to have any contact with the inhabitants of this planet, be warned. This planet's past is linked directly to our own. Our future and theirs will be determined by what we do now. We need to be extremely cautious when dealing with any species which is found here. Any contact we have with them can result in a change in our timeline that could not be repaired. Be careful to remain as undetectable as possible."

It appeared the inhabitants had long ago reached the level of development which allowed them to forge weapons out of metal. They seemed to be a warrior race that was accustomed to wars, fighting, and death. Rotan pondered, *Could their evolution bring a kinder, gentler race who could assist in the overthrow of the aliens? As our species is not allowed to wage war against any other race, we need to find a surrogate to utilize our technology to regain our place as masters of all who reside in this universe.*

After giving instructions to his crew to land their craft in as uninhabited a place as possible, he retrieved the container which held one of the most powerful forces currently found in all the universe. It was in the form of a small stone but was, in fact, a life-form which could make decisions on its own. It radiated a soft glow when at rest and could, however, become extremely powerful when stimulated in the appropriate manner. As their ship came to rest, Rotan directed his executive officer to take the stone and place it in the foliage at the edge of their landing site. A small group of dark-skinned humanoids noted their presence and disappeared into the jungle. Once the artifact was hidden in the vegetation next to their ship, Rotan gave the order to resume their voyage in the hope of finding another planet that might be suitable for them to inhabit.

His executive officer, Soute, offered a suggestion, saying, "Rotan, if we are to have any assurance that our artifact finds an entity which

UNIVERSAL EXTINCTION

will be able to utilize its power, we need to leave a guardian who can monitor it. It possesses so much power that we cannot leave it unattended. It will protect itself from falling into the wrong hands using its own self-preservation mechanisms. Only the individual who has been selected will be able to touch it. All others will become ill when they approach it. I will volunteer to stay on this planet to ensure our technology does not fall into the wrong hands. Although this may take a great deal of time, I think it is necessary."

Rotan responded, "You have defined your own future, Soute. You will remain here and take on the appearance of the local inhabitants so that we will be able to monitor the artifact's discovery and use. You will contact us when it has been found, and follow it until we can determine if it will be the catalyst for our return to our home and the destruction of the alien empire known as the Drezil. We wish you the best luck. We will contact you regularly to assess your situation."

As the ship rose, Soute began the painful process of changing his physical appearance to that of the natives he had viewed leaving the area as they landed. His ability to take on any physical appearance would be put to the test many times in the upcoming centuries. The need to connect with another species was paramount in the Azdawn's goal to once again become a driving force in this universe. Soute knew that his species had once been inhabitants of this small blue planet from which, eons ago, they had jumped to the heavens, leaving the humans to fend for themselves. Both he and Rotan were surprised that they had survived until now. The intent was not to enslave this species but rather to subtly direct them to take on the task the Azdawn could not do. They intended to use whoever first made contact with them as pawns in their campaign to forcefully take back all they had lost. They would then become, once again, the masters of the entire universe. Even though this would mean deceiving all who had placed trust in them and accepted their assistance, their agenda was total domination over all humanoid life-forms and the elimination of all other species who were non-humanoid.

Chapter 1

The day began as all others in the past many years with a slow entry back into the consciousness. Swinging my once powerful legs over the edge of the bed, I felt the familiar aches and pains which had become increasingly aggravating as I aged. Standing on the oak floor, I felt the cool smooth surface beneath my feet and wondered how many more mornings I had in my future. As a disabled veteran, I knew that my military experiences had been laced with exposure to any number of harmful chemicals and life-altering physical injuries. I was now paying the price for my dedicated service to my country.

I finished my routine morning bathroom activities—brushing teeth (still my own), shaving, combing what was left of my thin gray brown hair, and scanning my face for any new wrinkles that seemed to magically appear each morning. The water delivered during my morning shower was warm and soothing and seemed to dull the ever-present familiar aches which accompanied my seventy-years of life as it cascaded over my body. I was still in relatively good physical condition mainly because of my daily exercise routine. My hair was combed carefully to cover the baldness which had creeped back from my forehead. As I looked in the mirror to shave, I noticed my piercing blue eyes were calm now, but they could stop anyone with a singular glance if they challenged me. At six feet one, 185 pounds, my weight was distributed evenly to make me appear quite masculine and healthy. Having stumbled through my day's entry tasks, I found that it was all so boring and normal. I was begging for something completely different.

I had a nagging feeling that something was in the wind, something different, tangibly out of the norm. Without any audible cues, I could sense that a sound of some sort was invading my mind. It seemed like a shadow had crossed my path and left behind some message that I could not decipher. It was not a tone nor a buzzing but was more like a wisp of wind. It was there again, or maybe it wasn't.

I left my house via the large sliding glass door in the kitchen. The porch attached to the house led to some steep wooden stairs. At the base of the stairs was an embossed concrete pathway that terminated at a door. It provided entry into my shop. To the left of this door was another door which provided access to my two-hundred-square-foot office, where I started to plan my day's tasks.

I suppose every man needs a hobby, and mine was cars. The faster the better. Over the years, I had built many specialty cars and pickups. The Ford Model A was a nasty-looking beast with a 472-cubic-inch Cadillac engine, enough power to blow the rear tires completely off. The Bonneville Salt Flats racing roadster my friends and I had built and campaigned sat unobtrusively in a back corner, waiting for another chance at setting a land speed record on the slippery salt. The old 1927 Ford Model T was patiently awaiting its appointment with the upholstery shop. I had painted it a deep black cherry color and polished it to a mirror finish.

Although I was extremely proud of my work, I could not seem to get enthused about continuing to build more antique automobiles. Some other new experience seemed to be calling me. In most past cases, changes on my life's direction or my avocational interests had come about slowly. Now, however, an altogether unfamiliar feeling grabbed my attention. It was so crystal clear that it was impossible to ignore and seemed to bring me back to my high school days. My newly acquired direction deviated acutely from my current pool of interests and had nothing to do with cars or breaking land speed records, but seemed to have gravitated towards space travel.

It had all started when I was in the ninth grade. We had been given an assignment which entailed researching some subject which held our interest. I chose rockets and space travel. I spent many hours browsing through our family's *Encyclopedia Britannica*, learning all I could about this subject. I drew pictures of rocket ships which were dart shaped and stood on their tails, preparing to be launched into space. Although this design of a spaceship was archaic by current standards, at the time, the picture of the German V series rockets drove my imagination. I received a grade of A on this project, and the knowledge I gained from this experience stayed with me throughout my entire life. Now it seemed to have become an important new challenge for me to investigate. Something was driving me to set this new direction in my life.

Although incomplete, my latest project was a 1932 Ford three-window coupe. I had acquired this car through some skillful trading activities. It was anything but complete, and I set aside some time today to work on the exhaust system. The mufflers I had just received from my online supplier were laying on the floor next to the bench. I pulled the packing tape off and removed the muffler from the box. I had not specified any color, so I was not surprised to see that it was painted a pastel lavender. Something clicked in my head, as though I had some memory or connection to this color. My initial reason for coming into my shop was to work on the new car, but now I seemed to be drawn in a new direction, that which involved some association with lavender.

Some unknown force or entity was prodding me to set a new direction in my life. My interest in prior activities seemed to wane, and I felt that I was being pushed in an entirely new direction. I knew that our planet was suffering from a decaying environment, so it was not a total surprise that I felt the need to investigate technologies which might lead to sources of energy that could offer clean limitless power to the entire Earth. I walked to my office, which was attached to the shop to give me a chance to get myself back on some firm footing. The mirror on the north wall across from my computer workstation came into view as I entered. The same image which appeared in my bathroom mirror this morning gazed back at me. Although I appeared to be unchanged in any physical way, I saw something in my eyes which had not been there when I awoke. In addition, my mind had begun to fill with new thoughts that seemed to be based on my prior studies at California State University, Fresno, that identified all the current successes and failures of research into the subject of cold fusion. A fusion reaction had never been successfully initiated. These thoughts led to a speck of an idea that solving this problem would give me a method of powering a spacecraft. It was as though my own research in high school had been coupled with this new direction in my life to form the nucleus of a totally new passion. Why this reoccurring thought kept creeping into my mind was totally unknown to me. I would soon have the answer to this question.

Having previously studied all the materials on cold fusion available during my college years, I felt the need to at least try to apply my own solution to the generation of a cold fusion reaction. Moving forward in a direction which had shown promise in experiments conducted by Professor Martin Fleischmann and Professor Stanley Pons in 1989, it seemed to me that even after all the experiments that had been completed, something was missing in the scientist's approach to the problem as no real usable solution had been found.

The hydrogen and palladium mixture just didn't seem to be viable for releasing massive amounts of power. For a reason I could not define, the cold fusion dilemma kept tickling my mind, turning my attention away from my normal day's subjects. My need to pay almost total attention to this issue became stronger with each passing minute until ignoring it was no longer possible. Although not thunderous, the speck of an idea I had experienced earlier burst forth as an actual script. It came first as a small murmur, then a physical voice, and finally a fully blown plan to implement. The thought was now complete, and some unknown force was leading to an alternative solution that was becoming embedded into my mind.

I became totally confused by all the thoughts and stimulus which were bombarding my mind. I was mentally sorting through all the chaff swirling through my mind, and my eyes began to focus on the set of double doors on a cabinet situated high above the workbench. I opened the doors, and my eyes settled on a small gray wooden box which had remained hidden in the back of the cabinet for many years. The rickety ladder I placed in front of the cabinet began to sway dangerously as I placed my foot on the bottom rung. The nag-

UNIVERSAL EXTINCTION

ging feelings I had experienced earlier returned and seemed to grow stronger as I moved upward. Each step brought a more powerful sense of dread which abated if I paused for a moment before moving to the next step. I climbed high enough to reach the top shelf and stabilized the shaking ladder and opened the cabinet door. I reached into the cabinet and removed the box from its hidden location.

I slowly moved back down the ladder. I placed the box on the workbench and studied its exterior. A large brass padlock secured the lid, so I could not immediately gain access. I had placed the lock on the box sometime in the past, so I dug deeply into my memories to ascertain where I had placed the key. Normally, I could hardly remember what happened a month ago, but in this case, I had a vivid picture of the large key holder hanging on the side of the kitchen cabinet. All the keys used throughout the house and in all the cars were hung on this key holder. I rushed into the house and went to the cabinet.

All the keys were silver except for one small key hanging behind all the others. It was brass colored, and I knew immediately that it belonged to the box which I had taken from the cabinet in the garage. I rushed back to the shop and prepared to open the wooden box. The key slid into the keyhole with little effort. With a quiet click, the hasp on the box popped open. Little force was required to lift the lid and reveal the contents of the box. After many years hidden from view, I saw a treasure of artifacts which I had gathered during my military service. Hidden among the many relics which occupied the box was the rock I had found in Africa. I grabbed the stone, which immediately triggered a rush of memories from the time I first encountered the artifact. Its smooth texture sent a tingling sensation up my arm and into my brain. It seemed to attach itself to my psyche, and I became acutely aware that all my senses had been enhanced. The nagging force that had accompanied my entry into this scenario grew stronger, and my memory was rocketed back to my first sight of the glowing lavender stone.

Chapter 2

May 1961

In the era of the Mercury space project, I had been attached to a Naval anti-submarine patrol squadron. My memory brought back a vivid mental picture of what had occurred during that period. Once again, I was there, living it as though it was yesterday. I had been directed to keep any classified elements of this mission to myself and never discuss it with anyone.

Our preparation for this flight was a total departure from any normal mission we might have undertaken. A fellow crewmember, Barry (nicknamed Bear), had the same questions as me.

"Durell, what in hell is going on?" he asked. "This mission looks like a real shit fest that will most likely end with us getting wet." Rolling his eyes, he let out a roar of frustration. "Ya know, we have crewed together for several months, and this is the first time we have been left in the dark. This really sucks."

"Well, Bear," I replied, "I have learned that questioning missions assigned to us is not the wise thing to do. I'm sure that those who schedule the missions probably know what they are doing, so it's best to just follow orders and not become overconcerned about why we were chosen for this assignment. Let's just move forward with our preflight duties."

With a shrug of his shoulders, Bear began his preflight routine.

Beginning my own preflight, I moved to the open bomb bay and shook the storage racks to ensure that they were securely attached to the dropping lugs. I ducked out of the bomb bay and set about my inspection of the exterior of the aircraft. I ensured that the external

14

UNIVERSAL EXTINCTION

ground power cable had been attached to its receptacle under the fuselage. I switched the mobile power unit attached to the far end of the cable on and noted the subtle sounds that indicated that the aircraft had come alive. At the same time as the onboard gyros began to spin up, the rotating beacon on the top of the tail began flashing. These visual and auditory clues assured me that a normal startup had occurred. I was reminded of my own discomfort because my orange flight suit was becoming damp from perspiration because of the heat and humidity, which were a product of the climate of the Azores. I completed all my duties, which involved the exterior of the aircraft. I found no discrepancies, so I entered the aircraft through the open hatch in the rear.

A thorough operational check on all the electronic equipment went without identifying any issues that might impact the airworthiness of the aircraft. Gathering in front of the aircraft, the entire crew, beginning with Keith and Banky, gave their verbal report to the plane commander, Lieutenant Evans.

Following the complete report from the remainder of the crew where no problems were reported, Lieutenant Evans said, "It appears that we are good to go, so everyone board and go to your takeoff positions. We will start engines in ten minutes and should be airborne within the hour. All I can really tell you right now is that we will be heading directly south."

South, I thought. *There's nothing in that direction but empty ocean, with maybe the remains of some foolhardy idiots who challenged the Bermuda Triangle.* I wiped some sweat from my brow. *I think we're screwed.*

Having given the crew their orders, Lieutenant Evans finished the briefing, saying, "All our fuel tanks have been topped off, so we should have plenty of fuel for this flight. Make sure you all have your survival gear available to you because this flight will be entirely over water. Now let's get this mission going."

Our aircraft was a Lockheed P2V-5FS Neptune submarine hunter. Its gray body was painted with a white top. There were many blisters protruding from the underside of the aircraft. They were used by the submarine detection electronic devices that could detect sub-

15

marines that were well below the surface of the ocean. A large round radar antenna was housed in a radar dome attached to the bottom of the aircraft between the wings. It was used by the onboard search radar located on the flight deck and had a long range because of its two-megawatt power. We had a crew of nine highly trained Naval airmen, and our assignments varied from pilot to equipment operations and maintenance.

An antenna had been attached to the nose of the aircraft sometime in the previous night and covered with a shroud to keep it from view. Once the cover had been removed by one of the unknown ground maintenance crew members, we could see that it composed of four separate arrays arranged at forty-five-degree angles from each other. The aircraft identification number, LB11, signifying aircraft number 11 in the Navy Antisubmarine Squadron Seven along with the squadron symbols, had been removed by the maintenance crew.

"Oh, oh," I said to our ECM operator, Ringo. "I have a feeling we have just been dealt a real shit fest of a hand on this one."

The entire sequence of events led me to believe that some top secret activities were about to take place, and I was to be a part of this new adventure. I had never seen an antenna like this before. We had no idea of the antenna's purpose, but my senses were heightened by the prospect of becoming involved in something as undefined as this appeared to be. We were told that we would not be given any information concerning the antenna's purpose until we were airborne. Once we were in the air, we were finally informed by Lieutenant Evans that we would be using the newly acquired equipment to communicate with a Mercury space capsule when it was in the mid-Atlantic region. I now realized why the security had been so tight. The United States and Russia were involved in a race to determine which side would be the leader in space travel. I scanned the interior of the aircraft, cataloging each of my fellow flier's reaction to this news.

"Durell, are you aware of how important this mission is?" Keith asked. "Not only have we become part of the space race, but we're also doing it with our lives on the line. I know how much fuel was crammed into this ship and know that any issues which may arise might impact its performance and will likely put us in the water."

UNIVERSAL EXTINCTION

"Keith," I said, "you worry way too much." Turning away from my skeptical friend, I began to walk toward my station. "This aircraft is as trustworthy as any in our fleet. I have no doubt that we can deal with any issues that may arise. Now settle down, Keith. This leg of the flight will take at least eight hours."

Our mission began in the Azores, and our flight path led south toward the equator. Communication with Astronaut Alan Shepard Jr. was to be short, and we were required only to relay his status to Cape Canaveral. Our eight-plus hours of flight time placed us near the equator. The fuel usage we had experienced during the flight was well above normal but was not so high that our reserves would need to be tapped. Our radio operator, Ringo, had been given the correct frequency which would allow for us to reach the Mercury spacecraft. The Freedom 7 spacecraft atop a Mercury-Redstone rocket had successfully launched and was quickly approaching the communications blackout which would impede its ability to communicate directly with the Cape. Our small part in the leap of the United States into the space race was approaching.

Ringo dropped our trailing wire antenna and waited for a cue from Alan Shepard which would be required before he opened the comm link. "Lieutenant Evans," he said. "I have transferred voice communication to you and am just waiting for a channel to open with the spacecraft. As soon as I establish the link, you can speak directly with Alan."

Lieutenant Evans responded, "I have the script that I was given, so just get your end of this job done. We need to get started toward home as soon as possible."

The radio crackled as it came to life with the calm voice of the experienced astronaut. "LB11, this is Mercury 1," he said.

"Glad to hear your voice," responded Lieutenant Evans. "We are awaiting your message for the Cape."

The message followed: "All systems are normal, but I have experienced a small failure in the pitch program. I will deal with that issue if it becomes necessary during reentry. My speed is 5,180 mph, I am at an altitude of 116 miles, and I am approaching 1,300 miles from the Cape. The reentry phase of this mission will start shortly, so I am transitioning the ship to start my descent."

Lieutenant Evans relayed the entire message to the Cape using our high-power radio. Having completed the transfer, he radioed to Alan. "Your message has been delivered. We are going to head home. Good luck and God speed."

The response was "Thanks to you and your entire crew. It was really refreshing to hear a familiar voice out here. Communication link broken."

Our communication with Astronaut Alan Shepard Jr. had been short, and we were required only to relay his status to Cape Canaveral. After communicating with the capsule, we were set to return to the Azores. Our trek north toward the Azores was barely into its first ten minutes when a loud bang shook the aircraft. This was followed by a series of backfires coming from our right engine.

"I am going to shut our starboard engine down, and you all know what that means," Lieutenant Evans said. "We will not have enough power to stay in the air for very long unless we take some extreme measures. Stay at your stations and await further orders."

This P2V Neptune aircraft could fly very easily on one engine, but because of the distance from our current position to our destination, aircraft fuel was at a level where we would soon find ourselves in the ocean. I knew what the loss of one of our main powerplants meant. We would have to lighten our weight significantly to stretch our remaining fuel as much as possible. Even then, we all knew that our chances for survival were extremely low. The aircraft was equipped with two jet engines in addition to the two powerful 3350 Pratt and Whitney reciprocating engines. The jets consumed more fuel than the main engines, so they would only aggravate the problem if they were started. So options were few.

We declared an emergency, and the radio operator sent out the SOS which alerted all aircraft and ships of our situation. The emergency procedures were well-defined, and the Morse code—dot dot dot dash dash dash dot dot dot—was sounded as the first alarm utilizing our high-powered HF radio, which was configured for CW (continuous wave) only transmissions in Morse code. Our radio

UNIVERSAL EXTINCTION

blasted out our emergency: "This is LB11. We have lost our starboard engine and will not have enough fuel to return to the Azores. Our intention is to stretch our fuel as far as we can until we are forced to bail out. The closest land mass to us is the coast of Africa, so we intend to head east from this position. All aircraft and ships at sea, please assist in any way that you can."

Once the alert had been sent, search and rescue (SAR) aircraft were scrambled out of Bermuda and the Azores, but with little hope of reaching us before we got wet.

Rafik, a radio operator in Morocco, heard our distress call and began considering an alternative plan. He knew of several abandoned airstrips left over from WWII that were close to the Western Atlantic coast of Africa. Rafik radioed, "Aircraft in distress, I know of a couple abandoned airfields left over from World War II which may still be serviceable. I have sent their location to the Port Lyautey SAR group, and we feel you may be able to use one of them as a landing spot. I have relayed this information to Bermuda, and I will try to direct you once you reach the coast."

We made our turn toward the coast. It was a move of desperation with not much hope of a positive outcome. Although this thin straw did not carry much hope, I knew that if it were at all possible, this crew would make the impossible happen. We were all committed to doing our part to enhance our chances for survival.

I keyed my microphone and said, "Rafik, we appreciate your assistance. You may have just saved our lives, so we want to express our eternal thanks to you. The entire crew now has some hope that we will survive this situation."

The drone of the single engine was reassuring, but the snail's pace of their progress was maddening. As we attempted to squeeze as much distance out of our remaining fuel supply as possible, our plane captain, Dave, said, "Okay, guys, we need to lighten this bird up or we have no chance of staying in the air much longer. Our altitude continues to go down, and we will never be able to make the coast if this continues. So ditch everything that is not necessary for flight. This means all the electronic equipment except for the main radio and the radar. Lieutenant Evans, we will need to discard the bomb

19

bay racks and all the sonobuoys, tools, and personal articles. If we are to check this altitude loss, it all must go. Let me know when all this is done, and I will recheck our altitude and fuel consumption."

My position as first technician gave me the responsibility of determining which equipment we could discard. The inventory I had compiled was moved aft and positioned next to the after hatch. Opening the hatch caused a flood of noise and blast of air to enter the aircraft. Each heavy piece was shoved briskly down through the open hatch. A great amount of force was needed to make sure that nothing hit the fuselage. The remaining equipment was moved to the after hatch and thrown into the ocean below. We felt a lurch as the bomb bay doors opened and the racks were released.

Following the disposal of all the unneeded equipment, Dave came back on the ICS, saying, "Our altitude has stabilized, and our fuel consumption has been reduced significantly. You know, we may have a chance after all. If any of you have any other suggestions, let us know."

Lieutenant Evans followed Dave with his orders. "I need for you all to get into your survival suits and have your flotation gear close at hand. Your parachutes should be strapped on, and you should be ready to abandon this aircraft as soon as I direct you to do so. I'll keep you updated on all that occurs. There is a possibility that you may have to jettison more of the equipment to get this aircraft even lighter."

We were all aware that the chances of surviving a ditching were almost zero and were not prepared to give up on our current plan unless it proved impossible. I pulled the heavy rubber survival suit over my flight suit and zipped myself into this lifesaving straitjacket. I knew that without this protection, I would never survive in the chilly Atlantic waters. This was assuming, of course, that I would survive the parachute descent and was able to surface once I was in the water. This was all beginning to become way too real. I may very well die today. I thought, *Maybe ditching this aircraft might still be a better option than jumping.* We were all aware of our limited chances of surviving a ditching and were not prepared to give up on our current plan unless it proved impossible.

UNIVERSAL EXTINCTION

The bright sun was behind us, which gave a perfect twenty-mile visibility. The navigator, LTJG Wright, began to click off the remaining miles to the coastline while the flight engineer continued to recalculate the remaining fuel. The intention was to wait until the last drop of fuel was used and then for all of us to bail out. The fuel remaining numbers began to indicate that we were about to get really wet very soon. When all hope was beginning to evaporate, the radar operator began to paint land on the scope. We peered into the haze to the east, and a dark band of land began to materialize. It was the coast. The anticipation we experienced was overwhelming. Even though our resurrection was in sight, solid ground would only reduce the chances for any of us to drown.

Lieutenant Evans said, "As soon we are over land, I intend to order you all to abandon this aircraft. I am not willing to bet our lives on finding some mythical airstrip which may or may not be usable. So cinch up your parachute straps and prepare to jump."

"Lieutenant Evans," Dave said. "I think we have enough fuel to at least find some clearing that will give us a better chance of surviving this jump without any injuries. As soon as the engine starves, we'll just have to jump and take our chances."

Following the directions supplied by our new Moroccan friend, we turned north and began scouring the ground for anything that appeared to be a landing field or good spot to bail out. My only thought was that at least if we had to leave the airplane, I wasn't going to get wet. Maybe eaten by a native animal, but not wet. Intently studying the landscape, our ordinance man, Willy, called over the ICS (intercommunication system), "I see the field off to our right! It's that straight strip of land inland to the east."

As we were all eagerly investigating this sighting, the remaining engine backfired twice, indicating loss of fuel. *Damn*, I thought. *We are committed.* As the aircraft straightened out, the field that appeared in front of it seemed viable, short, covered with vegetation, but usable. With landing gear lowered, flaps extended, all crew in our stations, engine backfiring, we settled onto the hard surface of the old runway. It was like landing on a washboard. The grooves from years of erosion rattled the aircraft, testing every rivet in her

21

structure. It was amazing how this old relic could take that amount of punishment. Every loose piece of equipment, as well as some that had been thoroughly anchored, began flying around the cabin.

As the short runway was gobbled up by our slowing aircraft, all we could hope for now was the safety of silence. Finally, it came. We had stopped just short of the large trees that rose over one hundred feet at the end of the runway. No shouts of joy, no tears, no back slapping, just a stunned silence. I felt the pounding in my chest as my heart reacted to the stresses of the past few hours. I thought, *I suppose it was something like what one might experience after being brought back from death.*

I slowly unbuckled my harnesses and belts, freeing myself from the constraints of what could have very well been my metal coffin. I began to make my way toward the rear hatch which led to the outside. I noted that all my fellow crew members had exited the aircraft through the stairs inside the front wheel well. When my feet touched earth, I was totally overcome by the entire ordeal, kneeling to make sure that what I just experienced was, in fact, over. This fleeting relief was soon followed by the crushing heat and humidity of the jungle vegetation around me. We all gathered in front of our aircraft to assess our location and the aircraft's condition.

Although there was a real need for haste in assessing our next move, we all just sat on the ground, trying to flush the reality of what had just occurred out of our systems. In my mind, I could only recite the old saying about getting back on the horse after one was bucked off. I was not too sure if I could continue to function without some extended period to put this experience behind me.

"You all know that luck was with us on this trip," I said. "If you all are feeling the same as I am, maybe our best course of action would be to lean on each other for support and try to get everything done that will allow us to get out of here. We have no other choice. So I am going to spend a few minutes facing the reality of our current situation and start finding options which will get us home. Maybe things will be clearer in the morning."

Lieutenant Evans added, "Our aircraft batteries had a full charge, which will allow us to maintain contact with the SAR aircraft that is homing in on our position. I have inspected the aircraft and have not found any substantial damage from the hard landing, and I believe we could be airborne again if fuel were available."

The condition of the engine was extremely important, but as Lieutenant Evans wiped the sweat from his face, he noted, "Whatever the issue is with the engine, it may be remedied with a bit of work by Dave. The runway was serviceable when we landed, so we could most likely use it to take off if we give it a bit of maintenance. This is all dependent on our assumption that the problem which had caused the engine to fail in flight can be remedied. So we need to take a step back, get our heads clear, and take a night to decompress."

Dave nodded in agreement. "There was no fire or other outward signs of a serious engine problem, so I am relatively certain that I can find the problem and most likely get that engine fixed. If the issue is more serious, we will have to reassess our options."

"Our immediate need is to assess our location, the dangers around us, and develop some sort of escape plan," Lieutenant Evans said. "Check and make sure you all have your pistols, food packs, and knives. You can either shelter in the aircraft where you will be extremely uncomfortable or find some suitable location close to the aircraft to spend the night."

Our current situation, although not all that good, could have been much worse. The entire crew was concerned by the variety of deadly creatures around them, including any number of insects, snakes, large animals, and the imagined dangers which we collectively dreamed up because of the never-ending noises coming from the jungle around us. Even the odors seeping out of the foliage surrounding the runway conjured up visions of large panting creatures who could do us harm. Therefore, the entire crew decided to make their home in the aircraft, no matter what the temperature might be.

No one was surprised when the SAR aircraft arrived, buzzing over us to indicate that we had been located. I set the radio frequency to 121.5 MHz, the distress channel. Keying the radio, I said, "SAR aircraft, we have made it down safely. All crew members are unharmed, and our aircraft is not too damaged to become airborne if we can get some fuel and determine what made our engine fail.

Our engineer is an excellent mechanic and is currently assessing the engine to see if we can get it running again. If not, our intention will be to use our jet engines to get airborne."

I was relieved to hear the comforting voice of the SAR aircraft commander acknowledging my call. "We have already contacted a crew who may be able to bring fuel and oil to you. They will not arrive until tomorrow, so you need to secure your site for the evening. Just sit tight while they prepare for their drop to you. Our fuel state is at bingo [very low] level, so we will mark your position and head for Port Lyautey Naval Air Station. Good luck for your evening stay."

As night came, we settled in for an evening of hot, humid sleep. Although the other crewmen had decided to spend the night in the aircraft, I took my place outside, resting against the left landing gear. My curiosity concerning our surroundings led me to begin scanning the area for any movement. Twilight began to turn the entire area to a soft golden brown. In the half-light of dusk, I observed a very low intensity glow coming from the edge of the runway. Not too eager to be surprised by any of the possible surrounding population, I slowly crept over to find the origin of the glow. I approached the site and noted that an object emitting a lavender glow appeared to be a half-buried piece of metal or possibly a stone of some sort. My military training told me that I should be cautious when exposing myself to any unknown material, especially the glowing kind. Of course, with my curiosity, being alive and well, and feeling no heat, radiation, or other mysterious emanations from the object, I touched it. I felt a sudden rush of energy course through my body. My senses were immediately heightened, and I heard a subtle sound that could have been a voice or a low-level mutter. Although it was extremely warm outside, a cool wash of air seemed to envelope my entire body. I entered a state of consciousness that was not unlike suspended animation. I kept hearing the same sounds which I finally understood as speech, just not in English. I, however, seemed to understand what was being said. How could this be?

Chapter 3

From the time the Azdawns arrived on Earth during the reign of the Pharaohs, stories of both male and female disappearances abounded. The aliens attempted to breed with the women but were unsuccessful because of the DNA differences between their species. Men were utilized as donors whose sperm was altered to contain the foreign DNA of their captors. Nothing seemed to produce the results that were required to reestablish a new generation of their species. After many attempts to breed with humans, all unions had failed. The Azdawns moved on to find another species compatible with their own. Had they remained for a short time longer, they would have found that one of the women who took part in their experiment had conceived. She would become my distant relative.

Soute's vigil was coming to an end. The person who had just picked up the artifact was not like the other natives he had seen at this site. This person was very light skinned and seemed to be extremely curious about the stone he had just acquired. Soute had put him into a trance, which would allow him to converse telepathically with him in his own language. He knew that this would be the start of a journey which would take them both across the cosmos.

Soute spoke. "You will go many years without any thought of what has just occurred. Years in the future, you will solve a puzzle which will lead you to discover the power of this stone. When the time is right, we will again contact you. The survival of your species will be determined by how you respond to our next contact and what you do with this artifact."

MICHAEL BRADLEY

Durell

As I returned to consciousness, I found myself holding the glowing rock. It emitted no heat, just a cool feel which was unexpected because of the outside temperature. The previous conversation ebbed from my mind, and I seemed to forget that I had just experienced some unusual sensations. All that I was left with was a sensation of wonder that the glowing object was so inert. As I had already picked it up, I decided that it wouldn't be very dangerous. Nothing, just a rock that glowed. *What the hell,* I thought. *I'll just pocket this as a reminder of our stay in the tropics.* With that, it went into the thigh pocket of my flight suit.

Returning to the aircraft, I found my fellow crewmates milling around under the wings. We heard the drone of the powerful radial engines overhead as the rescue aircraft made a pass over our location. It was immediately recognizable by the twin booms which jetted from the fuselage toward the rear of the aircraft. The radio crackled to life, indicating that we were now in communication with the aircraft overhead.

"LB11, this is Lieutenant Bangston with the SAR group out of Port Lyautey Naval Air Station. We have fuel and rations which should tide you over until you either get airborne or are picked up by another crew."

Lieutenant Evans released a sigh of relief. "It looks like we will survive this little adventure," he said. "We all need to start our planning to get the hell out of here. I am open to any suggestions any of you might have to help speed up our departure from this hellhole."

"Our initial intention is to do a low pass and drop the palletized cargo directly on the runway. However, damage to the runway might occur, which would make it difficult, if not impossible, for you to use it. In addition, our clamshell rear doors were not designed for this type of drop, so we will jettison the cargo with chutes and hope it does not get damaged when it lands. If this plan meets your approval, we will begin the drops on our next pass."

26

Our only reply was "Drop at will. We will stand clear of the east end of the runway. Whatever happens, thanks for your assistance. The drinks are on us tonight."

As the pallets drifted slowly down from the aircraft, the entire crew gave a collective sigh, knowing that we had a chance to get airborne again. The provisions touched down with no damage, and we made our way to the bundles to inventory what the SAR aircraft had dropped.

Our reprovision continued without a hitch. The US Air Force C119 had dropped ten fifty-five-gallon drums of aviation fuel and a hand pump to us. After rolling the drums to the side of the aircraft, we laboriously hand cranked the precious fuel into the dry tanks. Dave, our flight engineer, had assessed the engine that had quit and found that a broken connector which routed the wiring to the engine's magnetos had come loose, and the engine was not getting any spark. He made the repair and started the engine, which came online without any problems. With the fuel we were supplied safely in our tanks, we cleared all the debris we could off the runway. We were successful in getting airborne and turned toward Port Lyautey Naval Air Station.

Looking back on all that occurred during that mission, I could only marvel that I had survived that adventure and the many other missions which I was fortunate to be involved in. After completing my service time, which included involvement in the Cuban missile crisis, an assignment with the Airborne Early Warning Barrier flying from Midway Island to the Aleutians for over a year, and several tours in Vietnam, I retired to what I felt was a well-deserved rest.

Chapter 4

Without knowing why, I now found that the object I picked up so long ago entered my mind. It was as if a silent whisper was urging me to find the stone and put it to use. Not knowing what it was, I had placed it in a metal box which held other trinkets I had acquired during my many adventures. I removed the stone, which was still in the exact state that I had initially noted when I first found it. As I still had no idea what it was composed of, I decided to ask a knowledgeable professor at the local university what he thought it might be. I made the short trip to the university science building and sought a knowledgeable scientist to assist me.

"Dr. Frei," I said. "Would it be possible for you to analyze this stone and help me determine its composition? I believe your lab may have all the tools necessary to get some answers concerning the source of this artifact and find some possible use for it."

Having served as a professor in the computer science division at the university, I knew that Dr. Frei was a very talented scientist who might have some insight into the behavior of the stone that I had witnessed. Dr. Arnold Frei spent the better part of every day in his unkempt laboratory in the science building. The physics lab was littered with equipment and long-ago abandoned class projects. He was short in stature, had pure white hair, and walked with a discernable limp. His back curved forward, which gave one the sense that he was always falling. He spoke with a slow Southern drawl that might lead some to think that he was not very intelligent. This was far from the truth, as he was respected throughout the scientific community for his many theories concerning the physics discipline.

28

UNIVERSAL EXTINCTION

I could think of no one better to provide me with the assistance I needed, so I put my trust in Dr. Frei, who would direct me in the assessment of the stone fragment. To allow for a closer examination of what I had brought to him, Dr. Frei asked me to open the container that held the object which I wished to have examined. Strangely, as Dr. Frei approached the stone, he became extremely distraught and felt forced to retreat from it. His reaction was so bizarre that I decided to take the lead. Neither Dr. Frei nor I could discern what the object's composition might be.

After extensive analysis, Arnold noted, "Even considering my own reaction to it, all I can determine is that this substance appears to be quite benign and will not react to any stimulus you offer or react to any resistance to the pressure you applied. The only evidence I can document is the low-level glow of lavender light it is emitting. In addition, I have amplified the low-level sound it is emitting and find it to be pulsating in tone and strength. I have absolutely no idea what this might be, but I can assure you that it didn't come from this earth."

Having produced no usable information from the experiments with the material, I returned to my shop with no idea of what to do next.

My past was filled with many different interests, among which was a driving curiosity in the research that had been done on cold fusion. For reasons I could not define, I had begun to study the documented research of Professor Martin Fleishmann and Professor Stanley Pons, which documented their research in the cold fusion arena. I was intrigued that the only elements they ever reported that had been used to create a reaction were hydrogen and palladium atoms, which were marginally successful in initiating a cold fusion reaction. Where this idea originated, I did not know, but I assumed that I had thought it up myself.

I was able to separate a small sample of the material from the body of the artifact. I placed the material in a small lead container which had a tube attached to inject different gasses into the vessel. I began to consider the possibility that the use of a different element might offer different results in a sustained cold fusion reaction. Not being faint of heart, I exposed a miniscule amount of the material I had recovered to a measured amount of hydrogen. A reaction immediately took place, causing the vessel which contained the two parts to heat up very rapidly. Reducing the amount of hydrogen which entered the chamber caused the temperature to decrease. Completely depriving the chamber of hydrogen stopped any further heat production. Could I have discovered a new and powerful energy source? The possibilities for use of this device could be endless. No more fossil fuels contaminating the Earth's atmosphere. Endless clean power. The possibilities were staggering in their limitless applications. The results could be summarized as no appreciable loss of weight of the base material and no measurable amount of hydrogen consumed. Could it be?

I reported my findings to Dr. Frei, who suggested that we go to a full-fledged experiment that used a larger amount of the substance with a greater concentration of hydrogen. I provided a small sample of the material for Dr. Frei to test. As before, I had no problem removing the small piece from the large sample I had, and there was no resistance to my chisel as I skimmed a piece from the artifact.

"Arnold," I said, "I have already witnessed the outcome of my own experiment, so if you wish to engage in another trial, feel free to do so." Taking the sample from the leather pouch I had placed it in, I presented it to Arnold as if it were a highly prized jewel. "I am going to proceed on the assumption that the mixture is indeed the cold fusion reaction that everyone has been looking for."

Although Arnold had no idea what my real intentions were, I assumed that he would be better off left in the dark to do his own investigation. My leather pouch was now empty, so I folded it and shoved it into my jacket pocket. I thought, *If he knew I was looking for some method to build an engine that can utilize its power, he would most likely refuse to go forth with this testing.*

"Arnold," I said, "let me know as soon as your testing is completed. Remember to stay a safe distance from the sample. We need to gather all the information we can before we commit to anything further."

UNIVERSAL EXTINCTION

With that, I left the laboratory and made my way back to my own workshop to gather my thoughts. About an hour later, I felt the ground shake, followed by a shock wave that hit me and a tremendous thunder of noise. I raced back toward the university, only to find that the entire end of the physics lab had disappeared. Only smoke and rubble remained. A huge cloud of debris had risen thousands of feet into the air with a top that resembled the mushroom cloud from an atomic explosion. Streaks of fiery red penetrated the cloud, and a low moaning sound could be heard emanating from the cloud. As the sound began to dissipate and the red glow disappeared, the sky began to rain disintegrated pieces of the building which had once housed the physics lab. As the firemen arrived, I found a lab assistant sitting behind the fountain that was a short distance from the building.

"Rachell, where is the professor?" I asked.

She seemed dazed and could only reply, "He was in the lab the last time I saw him. I don't know what happened." She hung her head. "I think he may be dead."

I touched her shoulder. "I'm so sorry. I—"

"As I left the lab," Rachel continued, "I noted that Dr. Frei was just beginning to start his experiments on the material you had given him. I was able to get out of the building in time to save myself, but I am sure my eardrums have been perforated. Whatever that substance was that you gave him is extremely dangerous and should be disposed of immediately."

I knew exactly what had occurred. The explosion was because of the unrestrained reaction within his test chamber. It appeared that once the reaction was started, there was only a limited amount of time to reverse the escape of the energy it was producing.

There was no doubt that government agents and investigators would soon arrive and quarantine the area to test for hazards. Professor Frei could not have survived the explosion. I calculated that the small amount of the artifact I had given him must also have been destroyed, leaving no trace for the government representatives to find. But that didn't matter. Once they arrived, I knew I would be

31

barred from the site and brought under intense scrutiny to find out what had occurred. I knew that Professor Frei had just gone too far.

As Rachell had been involved in the initial studies of the material, I asked her, "Rachell, I know you have some serious reservations about conducting further tests on this material, but it must be done. Would you be willing to assist me in building a vessel that could safely house the reaction which killed Dr. Frei?"

Rachell tilted her head and gave me a knowing stare. I had a feeling that she knew exactly where this was headed, but she was having some reservations about my request. "I intend to try to gain enough control over the reaction I have initiated." I extended my hand and helped her stand. "If we are successful, I want to build an engine that can power a ship of some kind. The purpose of the engine would be to provide the power needed to lift the ship beyond the Earth's gravity.

"If we wait long, the government will close our research before we can get control of the reaction. We cannot wait even though there may be every reason to considering what has just occurred. The difficult part is building a throttle system which I can use to control the power produced." I took a breath and smiled. "I know you had some deep feelings for Dr. Frei, but considering what has just happened, are you willing to help?"

Rachell tried to hide her tears. "It is too soon to make any commitments concerning the use of this artifact. It has already taken one life, and I suspect that is just the beginning. If I agree to help you, I will come to your workshop tomorrow evening." She smiled, but it was half-hearted. "I need to go home. Gather my thoughts."

I nodded. Of course she did. I watched her walk off through the gathering crowd.

"Okay, dummy," I said to myself. "Any chance on getting her to help is out the window. Maybe this is all just a pipe dream, and I should start acting my age. No one in their right mind will partner with you on this one."

To my utter amazement, Rachell arrived at my workshop the next evening, seeming very upbeat. I pulled open the door, and she didn't waste a moment on pleasantries. I liked that about her.

"Although I know how dangerous this artifact might be," she said, "I am willing to help you, if only to carry on with Professor Frei's work. However, if I ever think we are putting more people in danger, I will terminate my involvement in the building of this engine and inform the government of your research."

I grabbed her and gave her a real man hug. She seemed to be completely caught off guard by my actions but returned the hug. "I respect your position, Rachell, and I totally agree with you. I do not ever want to see this device spin out of control and end more lives, and that includes us. If you agree, let's begin our construction."

Shaking her head, Rachell said, "I might live to regret this, but I have no idea where to start. Do you have any experience that will assist us in the construction of this chamber?"

I couldn't come up with any response, so the time had come for me to put up or shut up. "I have built so many hot rods in my life-time that I think I can come up with a plan that will get us started. I have over a thousand pounds of lead left over from the ballast we used in our Salt Flats race car. That should give us enough material to build the capsule and provide some level of radiation protection. We'll need some protective gloves and aprons to handle the stuff, but at least it's a starting point."

Rachell gave me a darting look that did not convey any confidence that my starting point was all that inventive. "You drag your junk out and I'll try to help you put something together. If you sense that I am not all that thrilled about this, you are correct."

Even though many issues were yet to be resolved between Rachell and I, we set about building a chamber that could hold the reactive pair. We first invented a way to direct the reaction in a sin-gle stream, which could then be used to provide directional control. When completed, it looked like an oversized basketball with legs pro-truding from the bottom and sides. Each leg had a small opening which was attached internally to the engine within the device.

During the three weeks it took to construct our enclosure, I carefully monitored all my sources to see if there was any reference to our work. Hearing none, we initiated a test to determine the level of control we had over the actual force which was being created. As

I moved the joystick Rachell had built and attached to the chamber in several directions, a purple vapor jetted from several of the tubes. When the vapor changed from one tube to another, the chamber responded by moving in a direction opposite to the stream of gas. Although the vessel containing the experiment weighed over thirty pounds, we were able to move it in all directions and throttle the reaction to provide lift control. Amazingly, it appeared that only a miniscule amount of hydrogen was necessary to move the entire thirty pounds with ease.

Whatever the plasma was that provided the thrust exiting the system's nozzle, it seemed to be extremely hot, emitted a very low growling noise, and appeared to ionize the air around it.

Now that we had scared the hell out of ourselves, we decided to allow plenty of time to adapt to the system's peculiarities and conducted the experiments at very low power levels.

The temptation, of course, was to build a much larger chamber and see how much power we could produce with considerably larger amounts of the base atoms. "Rachell, I can only play with this small toy for a limited span of time. We have proven the concept, have throttle control, and know the proper ratio of hydrogen/element mix which produces a known amount of power. I think it is time to push the limits of the reaction."

So without further testing, and with Rachell still offering little resistance, we began to build a vessel which was large enough to contain all the material responsible for the generation of the power we had observed. Although the vessel which contained the cold fusion reactive pair weighed only a few pounds, the entire engine, which was only about two cubic feet in size, still weighed several hundred pounds. We knew it needed to be attached to something for our experiment to proceed.

Late in the afternoon, I called Rachell into my kitchen. I poured a couple of stiff shots of Crown Royal, which we both downed in one gulp. I said, "I think we have to move ahead with this entire project. I have a concept in my head, which is to build a large cylinder-shaped metal container which could conceivably carry a person."

UNIVERSAL EXTINCTION

Rachell knocked back a second shot. "Durell, I think I know where this is headed. If I am not mistaken, we are approaching this entire project as a prelude to providing a man or woman with a vessel and engine which will be the essential requirements for survival in an outer space environment. Am I correct in this assumption?"

"You're right, Rachell. I intend to test our invention as a lift vehicle to safely and cheaply move heavy loads from here to Earth orbit. The capsule must include air, heat, food, water, radiation shielding, viewports, and a complete set of controls for the engine we have designed. I hope this revelation does not duly concern you."

"I'm still with you. But I don't think we should test this concept with anyone onboard the capsule. Not until we have proven its stability." She looked at me, and I could see the concern on her face. "If you agree," she said, "then let's get started."

With a wave of my hand, I indicated my approval. The task ahead of us was daunting, so I knew that the earlier we started the sooner we would be ready for a real test. I knew it would take our maximum effort to build this ship so anything else we might have planned would have to take a back seat to this project.

As day turned to night and repeated this cycle for what seemed like an endless number of times, our design seemed to take on a life of its own. Progress in developing the basis for a viable spacecraft was agonizingly slow, spanning several months. What had initially started out as a half-hearted attempt to construct a life-sustaining outer space capsule began to take on the shape, size, and structure one might associate with a professionally built spacecraft. As we assessed our progress on the entire project, we found that the possibility for an actual flight as part of this set of experiments was inevitable.

Chapter 5

After months of constant labor, we had produced a vehicle which, if the engine worked correctly, could be capable of launching me into a low earth orbit. That was our thought process. But as untested as all our hypotheses might have been, at age seventy-five, I saw nothing to lose given the end of the tape measure I was crowding. So I initiated testing of a sort. Our first attempt at control of such a large heavy object was not all that promising or, in my own terms, a complete disaster.

Taking the control module in my hand, I eased the throttle a miniscule amount, and the vehicle rose from its perch, but it seemed to be extremely sensitive to lateral movement. Thinking the sensitivity was a product of my own inability to control the reaction, I handed it to Rachell.

Rachell began to slowly move the module, but her ability to have any effect on the devices were no better than mine. Setting the module on the table next to her, she said, "We need to go back to the drawing board on this entire system."

After much deliberation between the two of us, an idea surfaced. Pointing to the engine, I said, "If we install four side-facing nozzles and feed them with some of the thrust we have scavenged from the main thrust we might get the level of control we need."

We spent the next few days fabricating the side control jets and tying up the loose ends which were needed to complete the interior of our vehicle. On the fifth day, we revised the nozzle project. We again started the plasma motor and, to our surprise, had full control. As we remotely moved the vehicle around the shop, it became abundantly clear that we were very quickly approaching a full-scale manned test of the system.

Although I was still not clear on how the actual test started or how the decision was made, but I became the test subject who would try to fly this rather hideous piece of space junk. I gathered several items from my house which were precious to me and stored them in the box we had welded to the floor of the capsule. They included, of course, two flasks filled with Crown Royal whisky, which were intended for use as celebratory drink after our successful test. For some stupid reason, I also included my passport, as though I would be visiting another country.

I climbed inside and settled in for what I had envisioned as a short test session consisting of a flight that involved hovering the craft a few hundred feet off the ground. The lead-impregnated glass ports gave me a good 360 degrees of view around the ship, so I didn't have the claustrophobic feeling of being encased in a sealed shell.

Watching the round entry aperture close, I had the passing thought, *You stupid jerk. What possessed you to think there was any chance you could make all this work? I am about to die. Well, screw it, time to do something as dumb as I have ever attempted.*

Suddenly, I broke out in a cold sweat, shaking at the thought that I was totally unprepared for what was to come. I began to question my decision to try this rather dangerous trial without further testing. But like so many other decisions I had made in my life, the "throw caution to the wind" mentality overrode any common sense, and I strapped in for what I envisioned to be a short well-thought-out session which would either prove or disprove our entire experiment.

"Durell." The radio crackled. "Are you sure that this is a wise thing to do? Although our testing has gone extremely well, any number of things can go wrong. Please wait until we have had time for further assessment of this entire project."

"Rachell, nothing to worry about," I said. "We have studied all the possible negative aspects of this test, and I see no reason to back out now. If I feel there is any danger, I will abort."

With that, I grasped the joystick which controlled the fusion reaction and the lateral control nozzles and slowly began to move into the unknown realm of fusion-powered flight. As the craft broke away from its gravity tether to Earth, I began to feel a strange sense of floating and felt I could control this untested power and fly our metal sphere for at least a few seconds. I supposed that it should not be a huge surprise when things began to unravel as I tried to set the power to a level which would only sustain the craft's position above the ground.

It felt as though my weight was growing as the craft accelerated and the ground began to fall well below the ship. Pulling the throttle all the way back to what I assumed would be an idle setting had absolutely no effect on the acceleration of the craft, and I felt myself being pushed increasingly further back into the seat.

"What in the hell are you doing, Durell?" Rachell screamed through the radio. "Your altitude is way over what we had discussed as appropriate for this test. Are you still in control?"

Frantically moving the control from side to side and forward and back, I found that my inputs had absolutely no effect on the craft's direction or speed. Attempting to dislodge myself from the ship proved impossible. The fear I was experiencing was worse than the pain I was beginning to feel.

"I have lost all control over this machine. I can feel the g-force on my body increasing, which means that this craft is accelerating at an escalating rate. I cannot control the engine."

"Durell," Rachell pleaded. "Get out of there. You are disappearing into a strange cloud of some sort. I can't—"

The link severed.

I knew from previous experience what was going to happen next. The g-forces on my body would lead to a blackout. The light which had previously shown through the portals began to change. There were now extremely bright shafts of colored rays surrounding the entire craft, changing to a varying intensity of hues which seemed to include the entire visible spectrum of light. An extremely intense low moan began to fill the cabin. It had no actual source but seemed to be coming from the entire dimension which the ship had entered.

My whole physical world was dissolving into the pulsating light source that was beginning to absorb my entire psyche. As the effects of the acceleration of the ship began to cause the g-force on my body to exceed my maximum threshold of endurance, a gray curtain descended on my body. I knew that my bones were beginning to surrender to the massive forces which were pushing me into my seat. I had a passing thought that I was going to be crushed by the effects of the acceleration which were increasing by the second. Thankfully, I finally lost consciousness.

Chapter 6

The Drezil ship which was designated to map the DNA of all the inhabitants of the planet Earth had just established an orbit around the planet's sole satellite. It was a small moon that easily hid their presence. Bordeth, the Drezil leader, had placed this planet on the list of the next to be invaded.

Antok, the commander of this mission, told his crew of eight, "We need to complete our survey of this planet and build the list of survivors who will remain after we have purged all of those who are of no use to us."

Antok moved to the communication console in the center of the control bridge. Pressing a small blue button to key the transmitter, he said, "This is a final recall for all of you who have been studying this planet's social structure. Please report to your assigned departure points immediately."

The assignment for each of the members of the preinvasion team was to study the planet's population and determine who was to be spared during the initial DNA-based slaughter. Their DNA would then be entered into the system to exclude them as their occupations were considered critical for the planet's survival. "Our catalog of those marked for survival must be completed before we call in our ships."

Many of the planet's inhabitants had taken notice of the subtle changes which were occurring in the atmosphere. The changes were referred to as global warming, and any reference to this was dismissed by the majority of the population. No alarms were sounded, and the planet's atmosphere became more and more stressed.

UNIVERSAL EXTINCTION

"It appears that the introduction of the technologies we have given them has already begun the terraforming process. As soon as the atmosphere is suitable for our needs, we will do away with all remaining humans."

Bordeth had informed Antok that the planet was broken up into many separate geographical areas which were referred to as continents, each having several nations with separate governances. His instructions were clear. "Our intent will be to enslave all the leaders of these nations and utilize them to control all the others we have spared. Our DNA mapping process will only take a small amount of time, after which you are to call the strike force in to complete our takeover."

As the crew went about their assigned duties to begin the mapping process, Antok's attention was drawn to a bright lavender flash which seemed to be streaking outward from the planet itself. As he started to train his instruments on the light, it disappeared in a brilliant cascade of colored scallops which left a trail of material that appeared to be a plasma of some kind. Not knowing what he had just witnessed, Antok made no notation in any of his logs concerning this apparition. Rather, he reasoned out loud, "Best not report this as I cannot prove it actually occurred. If I screw this mission up because of some activity that I cannot define, Bordeth will have my head when I return home to Andop. Whatever it was, it could not possibly have any importance or effect on this mission."

Chapter 7

Atina was a strikingly beautiful woman by any species' standard. She had long golden hair that cascaded down her back to her waist. She wasn't quite 5'5" tall, had an hourglass figure, bronze skin, and deep blue eyes which turned slightly green when she became upset. It was obvious that she had either preceded the human species on Earth or was a product of it. From outward appearances, it would be impossible to separate her from any human group. Her keen mind had grasped all the technical knowledge that was presented to her by her mentors. She never had time in her maturing years to form any kind of relationship with the opposite sex and found males to be mostly boorish and undisciplined. She had no idea that she held the key that would be called upon to help map the future of the human species.

She was almost to the midpoint of her journey from Alpha2 to Habordiz in her ship, the Pentemor, with a load of salt in the belly of her freighter. Atina's home planet, Habordiz, was once considered the jewel of all planets in their solar system. Before the use of carbon-based fuels, the atmosphere had been a clean mixture of oxygen and nitrogen with a small amount of water vapor. As a result of the extensive use of carbon-based fuels, the air had turned into a brownish haze which contained methane, carbon dioxide, and an ever-increasing amount of corrosive acid vapors. The oceans, once teaming with aquatic life, were becoming void of any life, including the algae which had been the root of the food chain for many of the extinct species of fish. From space, the planet was quickly taking on the appearance of a garbage dump. It was as though the entire planet was being readied for a future that did not include the indigenous popu-

UNIVERSAL EXTINCTION

lation. The Drezil agenda had been met, and they attacked the planet in one vicious onslaught that totally overwhelmed the Habordizites' defensive capabilities. The planet was now a Drezil outpost.

The long trip had not produced anything for Atina but a numbing sense of boredom. The ship she was piloting was massive, but she and her computer companion were the sole occupants. The spacecraft was not sleek but was rather large from the cockpit to the stern where the massive engines provided the required thrust to move the ship across the galaxy. The flag of her country on the planet Habordiz was emblazoned across the side of the vessel in colorful stripes of red, blue, and white.

Entry into the ship could only be made through a hatch located toward the bottom of the craft. The cockpit, with its 360-degree view, was equipped with a shroud that slid into place when the craft was burning through the atmosphere of any planet she visited. A large section of its exterior could be slid aside to allow for the loading of large cargo. Inside was a suction hose and system for loading and unloading the salt she picked up from the planet Alpha2. The Pentemor was designed before the Drezil invasion of Habordiz and never intended to be utilized for any purpose other than transfer of cargo. For this reason, the Drezil had allowed it to remain functional, as it did not seem to present any danger as a weapon.

She had made this trip many times but felt her tenure as a pilot was about to end. The isolation, boredom, and constant lack of gravity had brought her to a point where she felt the need to face other challenges. As she gazed through the crystal clear windows which occupied the front of her craft, she could only see the immense expanse and barren void of the space which separated her from her home world. Her cargo was destined to help rebuild the sodium which had been stripped from her planet many years ago. The war had ended with very few resources left for the planet's remaining survivors.

Losing the conflict had extracted a heavy toll on the entire population. The process of rebuilding was closely monitored by the Drezil, who had to ensure their continued total control of Habordiz. They believed that their use of DNA tracking had spelled the end to any resistance by the inhabitants. Nothing could be further from the truth. So Atina knew her presence in this ship and her mission was only tolerated because of the Drezil's need to keep their prize as a viable alternative to their own planet.

The squawk of the proximity alarm split the silence of her cockpit with an intensity that could not be ignored. Atina began to desperately scan the space around her ship, trying to determine the source of the danger. Only black empty space was visible from her cockpit.

Her instruments continued to insist that another vessel was closing on her position with incredible speed. Knowing that a collision seemed imminent, the computer ordered the autopilot to implement evasive procedures by bringing the ship to a jarring stop.

Atina was slung to the rear of the cockpit and knocked unconscious by the force of the sudden decrease in the ship's speed. When she awoke, she was totally confused by what was happening. Her only thought was *What is going on? Is there really an emergency of some sort, or has my ship suddenly gone rogue?*

A sudden intense flash of light filled the viewing port and temporarily blinded her. As her vision slowly returned, she saw a glowing stream of plasma cross directly in front of her ship. It was decelerating at an unbelievable rate, not one that anyone could survive. The intruder slowed to a stop, and she noted its shape but could not classify it as anything she had seen or heard about.

The intruder was a round sphere, apparently made of some sort of metal with four ports which were glazed over as though they had been burnt or blasted by something. Moving her ship closer to inspect the craft, she saw what appeared to be waves of colorless gas surrounding the vessel which seemed to insulate it from its surroundings. *Finally,* she thought, *something out of the ordinary to break the boredom of this trip.*

The Pentemor was equipped with several loading devices which gave her the ability to carry any number of various cargos. One of the loading methods involved the use of a large conveyer belt in conjunction with a grappling arm. Anything found adrift in the void of space was a prime candidate for salvage and could bring a huge bonus for her after she returned to Habordiz. There did not appear to be any danger involved in snatching this craft, so she began to program her onboard computer loading process to bring the object into the storage hold of her vessel. As she initiated the sequence, the conveyer began to move from the now open hatch toward the sphere. The grappling arm attached itself to the object and placed it gently onto the belt. As the retrieval process began, the colorless gas surrounding the sphere dissipated. Atina continued the retrieval process until the vessel was safely deposited in her cargo hold. She now had to pressurize the cargo hold so she could examine her treasure.

Atina exercised extreme caution while approaching the ship. Although it was not large compared to her own ship, it appeared to be big enough to hold any number of creatures, depending on their own size. As the temperature of the cargo hold approach that of the inside of her ship, a large cloud of vapor began to surround the object. It was obvious that the temperature of the outer shell of the ship was well below that of its surroundings, causing it to condense the air around it. Atina resolved to wait until the ship warmed some before approaching it. Sensing no further dangers associated with the ship, she moved toward the object.

The skin of the object was cold, too cold to immediately touch. She would have to wait until more of the heat in the Pentemor's hold was absorbed by the object before she could attempt to find and utilize any method of opening it for her to investigate. All four of the windows were so opaque from the heat that they had experienced that she could barely make out the interior of the vessel.

How am I supposed to decide what to do with this thing if I can't tell what's inside? Peering more intently through the aperture, she could finally make out a figure seated inside the craft. To her amazement, it seemed to be a humanoid life-form. It was either unconscious or dead.

She examined the exterior of the sphere and found a circular hatch which could be opened from the outside. Waiting for the cargo hold heat to allow for her to touch the hatch was an excruciating experience. She wanted to get inside and see what she had captured.

After several hours of waiting, Atina was able to touch the exterior of the sphere and found the handle which was locking the entry. As she moved the handle counterclockwise, an audible hiss warned her that the atmosphere inside the vessel was much different from her own. Not knowing if the gas escaping from the hatch was poisonous, she quickly moved the handle back to its original position. *I think the time has come to begin approaching this thing with some concern for my own safety.*

Her ship contained instruments used to test for any unsafe cargo she might carry and could be used to test the environment inside the capsule. She carefully drilled a small hole into the interior of the sphere and inserted a sensing probe. The computer analysis which followed the sampling of the air inside indicated that not only was the gas inside the sphere nonpoisonous, it was also breathable and had approximately the same chemical makeup as her own air.

Flush with the success of this test, she again went to the entry handle and moved it back to the open position. The hiss that came from the hatch was much less intense than the first attempt she had made. As the pressure stabilized between the inner and outer atmosphere, she could feel the hatch begin to loosen. With only a small amount of force, she was able to open it enough to see inside the aperture.

The interior was very bare and had little instrumentation. She could see the back of the seat which appeared to contain the restrained form of a humanoid being. A gloved hand was wrapped around a handle which might have been used to control the craft. An almost imperceptible low moan could be detected coming from the bottom of the craft. No life support objects were anywhere in view.

Squeezing into the cramped interior of the craft, Atina moved to a spot in front of the life-form in the seat. Closely examining the being and feeling it for any sign of life, she found it to be warm and felt a heartbeat. She was astonished to discover that it was indeed alive.

Closer examination revealed that the occupant appeared to be humanoid. Assessing its vital signs as best as she could, she found

UNIVERSAL EXTINCTION

that many bones seemed to be broken, especially in the area which she assumed was the chest cavity.

In addition to the obvious injuries the humanoid form exhibited, it appeared to be extremely old, much older than anyone she had ever seen. It would be impossible, she thought, to move the human out of this craft without inflicting further injury. *Maybe if I can get some help, I may be able to help this life-form survive. I have already gone well beyond what I should do, but I cannot leave this person out here to die. I need to get back to Habordiz as soon as I can. Maybe my father and his associates can shed some light on my find.*

Atina approached Habordiz and moved to the ship's controls and turned the landing sequence over to the computer. She felt the final jolt which would indicate that she had landed and was secured to the launchpad.

As her father opened the hatch, she said, "I have discovered an alien craft which contains a humanoid life-form. Follow me to the cargo hold."

As they entered the hold, her father, Dlano, stopped in amazement. "Atina, what in the hell possessed you to bring this piece of junk back here? If the Drezil find that we have captured this object without their approval, we are all going to suffer the consequences. Let me see what you have found inside." What he saw was a humanoid form who appeared to be exactly like their own species. "You say this was found in space with no indication where it came from?"

Atina responded, "Father, all I can tell you is that the sphere suddenly exploded into my view, surrounded by a gas of some sort which I believe was protecting it. It came to a stop on its own, and I felt it was worth bringing home as additional cargo. I had no idea a life-form was inside. In my estimation, I think it is badly injured, and we need to try to help it."

Dlano, although very skeptical, had to agree. "Let's move it to my lab so I can determine if we can provide any life-saving measures. Do this as quietly as possible, or the Drezil will surely detect his DNA and come after us all."

With the help of her father and his associates, Atina carefully removed the humanoid from the capsule and placed it on an elevated table for transport to her father's laboratory. Following their arrival at Dlano's lab, they performed an extensive study of this humanoid. The subsequent diagnostics told a startling story. This was indeed a human, almost identical in structure and chemical makeup to their own species.

The only telling difference was in the DNA sequence that this human had coursing through its body. It was a male of average height and stature, but with what appeared to be a disease that made his bones fragile, his skin thin, and his overall makeup appear to be aged beyond anything they had ever seen. The damage which had been done to his internal organs and bones was significant, and their collective decision was to place him in the rejuvenation chamber that had been effective in restoring their own fighters who had sustained similar damage while fighting the Drezil.

Chapter 8

I slowly regained consciousness, totally unaware of what had occurred since I left Earth. Under normal circumstances, awaking from any sleep can be disconcerting. From a prolonged deep sleep, it can be extremely disorienting. But this awakening was something totally out of the ordinary. My vision was so clouded that I could not make out anything that was recognizable. Everything was a white blur, as though I was submerged in a milky bath of warm water.

I did not seem at all concerned by my circumstances but seemed to invite the sensations I was feeling to continue. I did not feel any of the aches and pains which had plagued me for many of my elderly years. I felt strength, insight, and vitality, which had long ago been lost as I aged. The many injuries I had experienced that resulted in back pain, leg pain, joint discomfort, and that overall tiredness were gone. I just wanted to stay where I was and experience this newfound contentment and freedom from the aging process. Although this was my desire, it was not to be. Then the thought formed in my head. *Where the hell am I?*

A sudden flash of brilliant light enveloped my entire body. I was forcefully extracted from my cozy new world into a cool white sterile room which was lined with numerous strange looking and sounding apparatus around all the walls and in the ceiling. Two human-looking forms were standing next to the platter which had slid beneath me as I was extracted from the tank that had held me in such a peaceful state.

Having been submerged in the fluid in the tank which had rejuvenated me, it was difficult for me to take a breath of the air in the room. Once I filled my lungs with the new atmosphere, I gagged and expelled what was left of the fluid from my lungs. After what seemed an eternity, I could breathe normally. The laboratory air was cool, damp, and the oxygen levels were such that I immediately became a bit drunk from the air's mixture. I was totally naked, but as my vision cleared, I noted that my body seemed to be quite different from when I had last viewed it following a warm shower.

"Holy shit!" I shouted. "This cannot be me. I haven't had this good a body for decades." My skin was thick and resilient. My body hair was no longer white but now appeared to be a deep shade of brown. My muscles were taut, large, and unmistakably powerful. As I started to take stock of what was occurring, I had to ask, "Am I dead?"

Without responding to my question, one of the individuals at my bedside placed an instrument against my chest, followed by a sharp sting as some type of fluid was injected into my body. The sense of peace again wrapped itself around me, and I faded into a pleasant sleep.

Slowly easing out of my unconscious state, I focused on my immediate surroundings. My vision was extremely clear, as though I had somehow been given a new set of eyes. Gazing to my left, I noted a woman who was tending to an apparatus which was connected by a series of luminescent cords to a cap that was attached to my head. She was manipulating a control panel which sent pulsating ribbons of light directly into the cap.

As she went about whatever sequence of actions she was programming into the machine, I began to see all sorts of colors, like patterns of waves that appeared to be liquid in nature. I heard a series of sounds which I interpreted to be a language of some sort. My investigative mind told me that something significant was happening to me, but the goal of the entire treatment escaped me as I weighed the possible actions they were taking.

My mind was clear, and my eyes seemed to have a newfound ability to focus clearly on all objects, both near and far. My joints and muscles were free from any pain, even though I distinctly remembered the horror of the sounds and the unspeakable pain which accompanied the acceleration forces that had pinned me to my seat and began to break my bones.

How was it possible that I had survived all that trauma? My caregivers seemed oblivious to my darting eyes, which were trying to decipher all my surroundings and my current physical state. Who were they? How had they saved me? What was I expected to do? When would I find any answers?

The scrambled sounds which had been unintelligible to me at my awakening seemed to be forming patterns which I was beginning to understand. As the woman continued to tend the system which was producing the kaleidoscope of color in my head, I began to decipher the words she was speaking. The sounds merged into an intelligible language which I was beginning to integrate into my thought processes. It was as though a translator of some sort was intercepting her sounds and converting them to the English I knew. The fact that this process was taking place in my brain did not seem to cause me any concern.

The other person in the room appeared to be about thirty-five years of age, but I got the sense that he was much older. He and the woman seemed to be partners in my care rather than leader and follower. He waved his hand as if gesturing for me to sit up. I complied and, with little effort, found myself sitting on the edge of the table. I felt strength, balance, and lacked any sort of pain which had plagued me for many years. Surveying my body, I found that my skin had a newly acquired resilience, which led me to think that I was looking at a much younger version of myself. *What the hell has happened to me?*

To my surprise, the female began to speak in a language I fully understood. "You were so badly injured in your flight that we had no other option but to put you into this rejuvenation chamber."

Maybe now I'll get some answers to all that has happened since I left the Earth, I thought. *Wait, did she just say rejuvenation?*

As if to answer my questions concerning my current status, the female continued, "Your body has been cured of its injuries, but in doing that, your aging process was reversed, and you are now barely out of your twentieth year. Hopefully, you are not overly upset with our methods, but life here is very precious, and we work hard to protect all of our race from the horrible degeneration which accompanies the aging process."

I now wanted to see myself in a mirror to verify what she had told me, but I saw none in this room. Dlano, the male in the room, had watched the entire conversation between the female and I. "Lay back and let the drug we have administered take effect. You will feel much better once you have rested from your ordeal." As I complied, I felt the warm curtain of sleep begin to cover me.

Chapter 9

The invaders of Habordiz had completed their takeover of the planet in one swift action, which had proven impossible for the planet's inhabitants to stop. Knowing very well what the consequences would be, the Drezil introduced some advances in technology to the Habordiz population which, at first, seemed to make life much easier for them. Technology for the use of fossil and carbon-based fuels brought about a leap in their knowledge of transportation and fuels for homes. It also led to the construction of the fleet of freighters which they utilized to prowl around their own solar system.

Not weighing the environmental damage from the poison they were pouring into their atmosphere, the inhabitants of Habordiz continued to pollute their planet with gas that only the Drezil found compatible with life. The stage had been set for the ultimate defeat of the Habordiz.

When the Drezil ships arrived and began to catalog every individual on the planet according to their unique DNA, it was too late to mount any kind of resistance. Those who tried were summarily erased by a single pulse of energy which targeted their specific signature. They would just drop to the ground and disintegrate. The Drezil annihilated well over 90 percent of the planet's population in their first action, leaving only a select group of caretakers to maintain the planet's viable resources. Compliance with the Drezil's commands was the only way the remaining population of the planet could survive. It never entered their minds that the fate of their species had been sealed.

The Drezil were only a few DNA strands away from their ancestral roots which were spawned from the reptilian world. They walked upright and had the same basic structure as humans, but their skin had a slight green hue. Their eyes sported two sets of coverings, one which was vertical and one which was horizontal. When they were calm, the horizontal set made them look very much like a human. However, when they became agitated in any way, the vertical set changed their entire appearance to more reptilian-like features, which could be extremely threatening to the Habordizites.

The Drezil all had extremely large hands and feet which were unlike their human counterparts. Although not webbed, they did not have what would be considered toes on their feet but rather narrow slits which could grab and hold objects. Their arms and hands were much larger than a human's, and the hands had seven fingers on each and a set of opposing thumbs. Their overall stature was much larger than a human, with the average Drezil height approaching seven feet. Any human would immediately be terrified by their outward appearance and never consider challenging any Drezil with only a physical attack.

If any weakness could be found in their sadistic makeup, it was their almost entire lack of any advanced intelligence. The technology they had available to them had been taken by force from other more intelligent species. Their ability to keep expanding their empire was due entirely to their willingness to destroy entire species and ravage their planets. It was their collective opinion that the ability to read and track the DNA of all the inhabitants of the worlds they had conquered could not be beaten. Given the proper set of conditions and commands, an individual's DNA could be altered sufficiently to cause their death. They now had the ability to selectively kill or spare any of the species whose DNA had been cataloged.

This part of their overall weapons cache was about to be tested. They may have made a fatal mistake in relying on a singular strategy to maintain control over their enslaved worlds. In thinking they were invincible, they were, of course, painfully wrong. As a sign to the conquered world's inhabitants of the Drezil's superiority, they would leave a single overlord in control of each of the worlds they occu-

UNIVERSAL EXTINCTION

pied. This overlord's charge was to monitor the planet and report any anomalies which occurred.

They had expanded so far and so fast that their numbers were divided across their empire to such an extent that few reserves were available for use as planet monitors. These overlords had the ability to cruise through the DNA sequences of all the inhabitants and check for adherence to the Drezil's demands. If any of the conquered planet's occupants were found to be planning any insurrection or not obeying the Drezil's mandates, they would be summarily eliminated. All the conquered world's inhabitants know of this threat, and it kept them from attempting any type of resistance. In their arrogance, the Drezil never considered that any one entity could escape their scrutiny.

Chapter 10

"I have never seen this DNA sequence in any of our population," the man said. His name was Dlano, and he was the father of the young woman who had saved me. His high position within the standing government of the planet gave him the ability to carry on his studies with relatively little interference. Had the invaders known the direction of his research, he would most likely have been tortured and forced to reveal all that he knew.

As one of the leaders of the resistance, he was committed to finding some method which could be used to break the Drezil's grip on not only his planet but also the other worlds which had been enslaved by their invasion. Dlano was a representative for another race called the Azdawns. His mandate was to steer all resistance activity in a direction which would benefit the Azdawns. It was forbidden for any of their species to become physically involved in any conflict, so they recruited other species to carry out any plan they had to become masters of the universe.

The Drezil's ability to read DNA and use it as a tracking, controlling, and death weapon was one of the major hurdles which would have to be overcome if any type of action against them were to be successful. They had no need to be physically present to control their prey. They only needed to scan each planet to ensure that their domain was secure.

The Drezil moved from world to world, conquering each in turn. Their goal was to terraform each planet so they could expand their empire while annihilating the total indigenous population of each world. Their methods included secretly introducing advanced technology into the targeted world which would seem, at first, to provide unbelievable benefits to the population. Energy, in the form of carbon-based fuels and nuclear fission, offered what appeared to be a limitless source of cheap power but was actually the catalyst for the terraforming process. As each world became more dependent on the use of these fuels, their atmosphere became more contaminated and began to evolve into a support system which was compatible with the Drezil's needs.

Future expansion to other galaxies was underway, with several worlds already being prepared for the invasion by the Drezil. The DNA mapping would soon begin, and each population would ultimately become part of their empire. Any species which resisted the mapping would be summarily destroyed as a potential threat to the Drezil's total domination of the entire universe. Although there had never been any resistance to the introduction of the Drezil's technology to the targeted worlds, it appeared that some individuals had seen through their guise. They were labeled as radical hand wringers and reactionaries. The alarms they were sounding fell mostly on deaf ears as the financial pressures from the elite of the populations formed a wall of indifference to the peril which was growing by the day. It was as though each conquered world had willingly given itself over to the Drezil's occupation.

As I learned of the Drezil's methodology from my caregivers, a very familiar scenario seemed to present itself. I thought, *Was global warming a signal that our time was running out? Could the Earth be next on their agenda?* It seemed that many of the problems which were currently presenting themselves on Earth were included in the Drezil's takeover scheme. If this were true, why had they not moved forward with their occupation as they had in other worlds?

Maybe it is a matter of timing, I thought. *It does not appear that the indigenous population of any of the conquered worlds could survive in the atmosphere which was prepared for the Drezil. If that is so, their only option would be to kill off the majority of the planet's inhabitants and leave only a few to keep the lights on.*

Dlano was becoming increasingly more curious about me—this person who had just entered their world. Where was he from? How had he made the trip to Habordiz without being detected by the

Drezil? These questions would eventually be answered by an authority well above Dlano's position. His secrets would be exposed eventually, but for now, he would continue to appear a dedicated father and leader.

Dlano

Dlano pondered, "How had the enormous damage been done to this visitor's body? Was he unable to overcome the effects which were associated with intergalactic flight? Had his DNA been changed so drastically by his journey that the Drezil could not detect him?"

All other questions were insignificant compared to this startling insight. Was this the missing piece of the puzzle which the resistance was seeking to begin to develop a counterattack on the Drezil?

Chapter 11

Atina was preparing to make her next run to Alpha2 for another load of salt when her attention was drawn to the plight of the young stranger she had rescued from deep space. Having discussed the entire situation with Dlano, she was at a loss of what she should do next. Her innermost being was drawn to her prize, and his future appeared to be in her hands. The vehicle he had arrived in was safely hidden in the belly of the ship Atina called home. The fact that he was on Habordiz seemed to have been missed by the Drezil, so she wondered if he had the ability to shield himself from their probes.

As her speculation grew, Dlano suggested, "Atina, why don't you consider taking our alien visitor on your trip to Alpha2? It might provide new insight into any number of questions concerning his origin, species, and answer our most important query. Can the Drezil detect him or read his DNA? However, it is your ship and your choice, so I will leave the decision to you."

Although the plan appeared to have many negative aspects, she found herself considering it. It was one sure way of testing his ability to remain undetected. As her mind wandered between the positive and the negative aspects of this move, she began to feel the need to investigate more thoroughly this person who had dropped into her life. She had already planted the language translator in his brain, so she felt now was the time to question him.

"Can you understand me?" she asked.

Not to her surprise, the reply was "I don't know how, but I can understand your words even though I know you are not speaking my native tongue."

"What are you called?" she asked.

Replying in a language he had never used nor understood, he replied, "My name is Durell."

"What a strange sound your name makes as I speak it. Maybe we'll have to give you a new more appropriate name sometime in the future."

"I am so confused by all that has occurred ever since I left my home planet that I am unable to think logically," he said. "Is there any possibility you might help me fill in the blanks of what has happened to me in the immediate past?"

Atina replied, "Until my father has had more time to study you and the events that precipitated your arrival in this system, I do not think it wise to burden you with all the particular minute events that you wish to explore. We are in uncharted waters here, and I would not want to jeopardize your physical or mental health by delving too deeply into these matters. Rest awhile, and I'll seek the guidance of my father before we move forward."

Dlano had moved to his small office just off the side of the main laboratory. Upon entering, he noted with satisfaction all the artifacts from the past projects he and Atina had completed. He was unsure about the situation his daughter had thrust upon him. In doing so, he assessed the past that had led them to this point. The Drezil had come suddenly, and with a vengeance. Their battleships had instantly overwhelmed the small defensive fleet which made up the entire body of Habordiz's armed forces. The instantaneous slavery of the population which remained after the reign of terror had reduced them to less than one-tenth of their original number, and it was done with no mercy.

Their DNA had been blueprinted much earlier, so the Drezil knew exactly who they were dealing with and how many had survived. There were enough numbers to maintain the planet's changing environment, but not enough to mount any kind of rebellion. The planet was now groomed for the Drezil's total takeover. When the proper time came and the Drezil needed to utilize Habordiz as a jump-off platform for further expansion of their empire, the remaining inhabitants would be wiped out, and the planet would become

UNIVERSAL EXTINCTION

another Drezil outpost. Dlano not only had suspicions of their intentions but had been given proof of their plan by a group of Drezil outsiders who had never agreed with the barbaric methods utilized for the colonization.

The resistance on Habordiz had contacted this Drezil group which had representatives on Alpha2. They were all waiting for the emergence of some sort of weapon they could utilize against their aggressors. Atina's freighter trips to Alpha2 were, in part, a guise to move valuable information between the two groups.

Although Dlano understood the danger her involvement put her in, he felt it necessary to sacrifice her safety for the overall good of the upcoming rebellion. He knew that there were other worlds which had been invaded by the Drezil that would gladly assist in their fight, if only a method could be found to communicate with them all.

A set of plans needed to be shared with all the other worlds to ensure that any movement to displace the Drezil would be a united effort and include all fronts threatened by their occupation. The inability of the Habordizites to travel the great distances between each of the enslaved planets was the major deterrent in the entire scheme. If a method could be found to quickly travel between the planets, a major offensive might be possible. The Drezil were not about to divulge their technology which gave them interstellar ability, without which they could never have built their empire.

Dlano knew that something historic was about to occur. Still sitting in his office adjacent to the lab, Dlano mused, *How had the stranger crossed the immense distance from the planet he states that he is from to Habordiz without being detected and without deadly consequences? Maybe there is more to this person than I first thought. Could this be the long-awaited answer which could lead to displacing and conquering the Drezil?*

Atina's thoughts moved along parallel lines. Her wish to know this man better and to determining the extent of his ability to help their cause was of paramount importance to her. She knew that the rejuvenation of his body and mind, which was necessary to save his life, had come as a complete surprise to him. She could see the confusion in his eyes as they began to discuss all the options that were open to them.

If only she could gain his trust, she might be able to discern how he had reached their galaxy, what his reasons were for the trip he had just taken, and how the resistance could benefit from his stewardship. It appeared that his DNA, while not a perfect match to theirs, was close enough to allow him to breath their air, eat their food, and accept the translation messages which had been implanted in his brain. She wondered what else they had in common. *If,* she thought, *his unique DNA could somehow be infused into mine, would I also be undetectable?*

It was well-known that whenever a new person was introduced into Habordiz's population that the Drezil would immediately know and investigate the origin of the new arrival, whether it was from a birth or any other source. Surprisingly, they had not yet detected his presence. This, of course, led to any number of possible examinations, including that his DNA was such that they just couldn't pick it up.

Atina thought, *If this were the case, I find that an entirely new spectrum of options are beginning to materialize. In addition to my own DNA alteration, is there some method that could be used to extract his DNA and immunize resistance members to hide them from the Drezil?*

*****

Atina directed me to a small cubicle which had a bed of sorts at one end. She followed me, and I began to feel the power and resolve that had once driven me to volunteer for military service and fight in two wars on my home planet. I was neither tired nor did I feel the need for any sort of rest. My mind began to assess my current situation and I was able to begin to focus on my problems. As I reviewed the different stimuli that were beating down on me, I felt the need to begin to categorize them and find some linear pattern that would help me deal with all that had occurred.

I thought about my travel from Earth, but I could only remember the instant that my cold fusion engine went into an uncontrol-

UNIVERSAL EXTINCTION

lable state. The crushing acceleration from the g-forces should have killed me, but something, or maybe somebody, had intervened. The sounds, colors, and feeling I last remembered had left a final thought in my head: *I'm dying.*

Awaking in this world was the very last thing I thought would occur. Finding my body rejuvenated to that of a twenty-year-old was a bit disconcerting, but I didn't seem to dwell on the how of it all, just the why. Having overheard a few of the conversations which passed between Atina and Dlano, I surmised that their planet had been overrun by a race called the Drezil, and my two rescuers were part of a group whose goal was to take their world back.

Could my presence be the work of a higher entity who wished to bring order back to the universe? What a thoroughly stupid thought. I could never be the stimulus behind anything as grand as an interstellar battle to save not only this planet but possibly my own.

*****

Still in his office with Atina, Dlano paced the floor as he tried to get his thoughts organized. Having spent some time studying their current predicament, Dlano began to consider some very radical options. "Atina, if this person's DNA is untraceable by the Drezil, is it possible that by injecting some of his blood into one of our species, they, too, might share his ability to become undetectable? If that were possible, we would have to come up with some rational explanation of where the injected person went. Whatever the case, our options are limited."

Drawing his hand across his throat, Dlano said to Atina, "This might be the result of mixing Durell's DNA with any of our species. However, it could possibly have the results we are looking for. The inability of the Drezil to track any of us who have had our DNA altered. Now you need to make the decision whether we will proceed or not."

Atina's face went ashen. She knew that any attempt to modify DNA could result in the death of the recipient. "As our DNA is so close to his, I can see some danger in injecting a blood sample from him into one of our species. Because that danger exists, I offer myself as the individual who would be injected."

Dlano seemed shocked by Atina's willingness to take such a chance. "You need to think this through carefully. We both know what might happen if we try to alter your DNA by using his."

Tossing her head in defiance, Atina said, "We would need to wait until I was completely out of their sensor range to perform the transfusion. That would make it unnecessary to explain anything to the Drezil. If we can develop some sort of plan which would allow us to carry out this test, I would volunteer to help in any way I could."

Dlano shook his head. "This is all coming too fast. We need to bring together all our best minds and develop a strategy which utilizes all the elements Durell has brought to us and apply them to defeating the Drezil. For now, let's just keep a low profile, keep all that has occurred secret, and begin to assess this situation in the new light that Durell has brought to us."

Chapter 12

A large screen was situated in the corner of Bordeth's control room. With it, he could monitor all the conquered worlds in his domain. A rotary dial at the bottom of the screen could be used to select the world to be studied. In addition, another dial allowed him to view a detailed map of all the worlds conquered so far and the worlds which were scheduled for the next attack. Bordeth gazed at the mammoth screen and laughed at the ease with which these inferior species had been taken.

The Drezil's home planet, Andop, was in the center of the galaxy which housed all the planets he had taken by force. As the leader of the entire Drezil empire, he was unchallenged in his quest for domination of every inhabitable planet his fleet discovered. He beamed with pride at his leadership successes and the carnage he had brought on each conquered world. "This is nothing. When we have gathered enough planets to satisfy my needs, the real slaughter will begin."

Of the twelve worlds which were now his, Bordeth had ordered the annihilation of the populations of only four. Speaking to his brother, Bordeth said, "Having the responsibility of caring for the needs of each of our new worlds is better left to the enslaved populations." He reached over to the monitor controls and switched it off. The large screen he had been monitoring went blank.

"If I need room for expansion or an additional homeland for our people, I will order you to eliminate all inhabitants on one of our conquered worlds. My sense is that the need is quickly growing to take total control of Habordiz. It would make an excellent jump-off point for the next phase of my plan, the assimilation of Earth into our empire. My fleet of starships is still assessing the universe for

65

additional worlds which might meet our needs, but I will be giving the attack order very soon."

The Drezil were a rather uneducated bunch of lizard-like creatures who were not inclined to put much thought into anything. Their scaly green-tinted skin was shiny and appeared to be wet. They were humanoid in structure as they had two appendages which served as arms and two legs which could be bent at the knees in either direction. What served as hands were webbed and had opposable thumbs. Their feet were also webbed, but there were no toes, just stubs where the webbing ended. They tended to hiss constantly, an ancestral habit which allowed their forked tongues to taste the air.

The Drezil's need was for an environment which was relatively hot, wet, and with an atmosphere heavy in carbon dioxide and methane and low on oxygen. Although oxygen was not toxic to them, it was uncomfortable for them to breathe for extended periods. Their focus was on conquering, enslaving, and killing all beings who were not of their species. They were ruthless and used their enslaved populations to provide them with the advanced technology that they needed to continue their rabid movement across the universe. Their entire society was formed around the main idea that force was required in all endeavors, including their social structure, if you could call it that, which was formed with the elite killers holding the higher offices while those who appeared weak were placed in the bottom of the hierarchy.

Unknown to Bordeth, a group of Drezil underlings who were considered unworthy of office, led by a large heavily muscled individual named Madille, were gaining ground as a force determined to put an end to the death and destruction the Drezil were spreading in the universe. They had made a few minor gestures toward some of the enslaved planets to see if common ground was available. Although no progress had been made, they were looking for a methodology to better communicate their desires to one world, Habordiz. Caution was required though, because if any information concerning their efforts were to be discovered by the Drezil leaders, it would bring their immediate death.

UNIVERSAL EXTINCTION

Quiet rumors were spreading about an impending invasion of another world, Earth. Before this occurred, the group wanted to find some way to derail Bordeth and his henchmen's unending quest for more blood. Some of their companions had taken refuge on the salt-bearing planet of Alpha2 and were in position to communicate directly with humanoids from the planet Habordiz. All that needed to be done was determine who they should confide in and when to make their move.

Madille called his companions together in the conference room of their workspace on Alpha2. The room was small but well-lit from a bank of lamps which circled the entire space, giving all those present a very pale cast to their skin. Madille, sitting at a round table, said to his seated companions, "We know that a ship from Habordiz will arrive soon to pick up a load of salt. If we can trust the crew of this ship, there is a chance we might be able to forge an alliance with the humans on Habordiz. If we do this, the first step will have been taken to stop Bordeth from any further advances in this universe."

The resistance movement, led by Dlano and his friend Lector, was keenly aware of the future that the Drezil had planned for their planet. Addressing a group of resistance members, Dlano said, "Thus far, we have directed most of our collective efforts at gaining an increasing number of our fellow surviving Habordizites to assist in the eventual battle we are planning, which might gain us our freedom. As the Drezil can detect the location of any of us who are involved, it was imperative that we meet only in small groups of four or five individuals to ensure that we were not detected."

Habordiz's overseer, Hawnl, was dim-witted and lazy but still extremely dangerous. As with all the Drezil-conquered worlds, four satellites were placed in orbit around each planet to act as instruments to catalog and store the DNA signatures of all the planet's inhabitants. These satellites had the capability to disrupt and destroy individuals whose DNA sequences fit the profiles which matched the planet's overseer's death list. Meeting with the small group of resistance leaders, Dlano's friend, Lector, raised his hand to get the attention of the group. "It will be one of our future tasks to disable these satellites so we can proceed with any plans we might have for

67

the uprising that may free us. Hawnl relies on his instruments to keep tabs on us all, but he has done little else to monitor our daily movements. It is this behavior that we believe is the weakness of our aggressors."

Walking to the rear of the room, Lector drew a circle with his hand. This entire galaxy is controlled by only a few overlords. Their grip is tight, and we have no offensive method to use against them. It was obvious that our lack of any type of advanced weapon is a major roadblock in any plan which we might implement to eject the invaders from our galaxy."

Dlano continued, "Habordiz is not the only world in danger of being overrun and whose population will be annihilated. There were many other worlds in danger as well. The problem was how to present a united force which could overwhelm the Drezil and push these green monsters back to their own territory." Taking the conversation further, Dlano added, "Secrecy is a paramount concern which must be addressed by all of us. It seems that any action planned in the past was counteracted by the Drezil, as though they had prior knowledge of the plot."

The entire group nodded in agreement. "It is not beyond all possibility that one or some of our group has made their own deal with the Drezil and are informing them of our plans. If there is a traitor in one of our groups, we are in serious jeopardy. Hopefully, I am mistaken, and the Drezil are just reacting to some behavioral changes which led them to discovering our plans."

Having brought to the forefront the possibility that there might be a traitor, Lector became very nervous and openly began to sweat. Had any of those present picked up on his discomfort, the future might have been much different. He felt the need to deflect any questions about his own activities so no suspicion was leveled at him.

Dlano knew that annihilating the Drezil species had never been discussed, nor would it be supported by any of the humanoid population or his own species. So it would not be the intent of any offensive attack to annihilate the entire Drezil species. It should be designed to simply force their submission so all the territory they had

UNIVERSAL EXTINCTION

added to their empire would fall back to the rightful inhabitants of each world.

Speaking to the gathered group, Dlano said, "Time is growing short. All indications are that the Drezil will make their move on our planet in the very near future, and we have no defense against their weapons. It's time to bring the entire resistance together and prepare for a battle which will decide the future of our entire species."

Atina attempted to access what was being discussed. She could not shake the sense of doom that fell over them all. "Is there nothing we can do to save ourselves?" she asked. "If we are all to die, the very least we can do is put up the best fight we can. Maybe that will encourage the other enslaved worlds to prepare better than we have."

Her mind kept wandering back to the stranger who had mysteriously appeared out of nowhere. She was physically drawn to him by the sense of impending doom. "I think Durell has the strength to not only understand our dilemma but to assist us in our search for offensive measures which might be used to dodge our expected fate. The technology which allowed him to travel between his galaxy and ours might hold the key to bringing all the enslaved worlds together. I feel it is imperative that we gain his trust and learn more about his interstellar travel and the engine that brought him here."

Chapter 13

Durell

I had waited, not patiently, in the building next to the launch site for Atina to return from her meeting with the resistance group and her father. Pacing the tiled floor, I would stop and peer out the only window in the room, hoping to see Atina returning. When she appeared, I could tell that something important had just happened.

I had already decided that the time had come when I would have to force Atina to tell me what was occurring in her world. Could the same thing be occurring on my own planet? I could only guess at what might possibly be in store for me.

Just as I was having these thoughts, Atina entered the room. It was evident by her rapid breathing and the tone of her voice that she was in distress. "I need to tell you something important, Durell. Our species is at risk of being annihilated by an enemy who overran this planet many years ago. We have formed a large resistance group but have nothing to use as a weapon against our aggressors."

I knew that something horrific was happening, but I had no idea it was as bad as this. Moving to her side, I put my arm around her to try to offer my support. "Atina," I said, "I will do anything I can do to assist you. However, you must trust me." I took a breath, waiting for a response. She said nothing, but I could feel her heart beating like a trip hammer. "I may not be able to give you all the information you need, but I will try. Who or what exactly are these creatures who have taken your planet?"

UNIVERSAL EXTINCTION

Atina pushed her fingers through her hair. "They are reptilian creatures, and although they are not terribly intelligent, their very numbers and the advanced weaponry allowed them to bring many worlds to their knees. Our hope is to band all the conquered worlds together so that our united force and weaponry might be enough to push the Drezil back to their own planet."

Even though she was aware that their lack of any type of offensive weapon might lead to their own destruction, she continued to have faith that I could somehow help, as though I had been sent specifically for this cause. And to be honest, I had wondered the same thing many times, but I quickly pushed those thoughts from my mind. Pointing in the direction of Hawnl's residence, Atina gave a gesture that I could only define as contempt.

"Many of our people want to kill all of them as they have killed so many of our planet's inhabitants, but some of us believe that this approach would make us no different from them. Your arrival seems to me to be prophetic."

"Really? What makes you think that?"

"The machine that got you here must have had some sort of propulsion unknown to us, and maybe even the Drezil."

I was stunned. I thought, I had no idea that my presence might help in turning the tide for these people. Not knowing how I managed to make the jump from Earth to Habordiz, I was hesitant to make any offer of assistance until I knew exactly where I stood with this group.

So much information bombarded me. I had little time to assess what was true and what was not. Although I was inclined to take Atina's word for all of this, I could not truly be sure who was enemy or friend. What if the Drezil were the non-aggressors and the Habordizites the conquering species? I needed a lot more information than these people were giving me.

"Atina," I said, stepping away from her. "I'll be very blunt with you. I have no idea who you are, or if you and your companions are trustworthy. You have told me very little about this planet, your people, or yourself. How do you expect me to react to all of this, and how can you prove without a doubt that you are friend, not enemy?

Is there any way you can think of to assure me of your sincerity?" I pointed to her ship on the launchpad. "Am I to assume that my ship is still in the belly of yours? If that is the case, I need to get aboard and assess the engine's condition before I can answer any further queries from you. If I am to partner with you, it will be on my terms, not yours."

Atina moved to the only chair in the room and sat. Her eyes dropped to the floor, and she clasped her hands, indicating that she was totally confused. In fact, she was surprised by my response. She had assumed that I would take her at her word and trust in what she was saying.

There seemed to be more to me than her initial analysis had revealed. Her lack of knowledge of my origin made her suspicious that I might not be what I seemed. I could be a Drezil spy, capable of exposing the entire resistance to their immediate death.

"Durell." She looked directly at me. Our eyes met. "I am not educated in dealing with males at any level other than professional. You seem to be honest, but I have no way, no machine to measure your sincerity."

She had a sense, however, that I was exactly what I appeared to be, a confused person who was totally unaware of the danger my very presence put them all in. How could she discern who or what she had standing before her? She could not make any judgments based on her attraction to me, even though she felt a quickening of her pulse every time we were close.

"No matter how we decide to deal with this trust issue, I am going to watch you very closely," Atina said. "If I get the slightest indication that you are not what you say you are, I will turn you over to those in our organization who will deal very harshly with you. On that basis, we can make plans for how to study the technology you have bought to us."

I began to sense her confusion. She was trying to portray a strong person, but I felt she was merely putting up a front to see how I would react. Was now the time to take the lead in this conversation?

"Atina," I said, "I am willing to share all that I know about my trip here, the engine that propelled my craft, and any other issues about which you might feel that I have specific knowledge. All that I wish is for you and your father to be truthful so I can accurately assess whether I can be of any help." I moved across the room to be close to her. "I know that you have been discussing how my DNA differs from yours, but I see little physical difference between us even though we are from totally different areas of the universe."

I raised my arms and flexed my muscled biceps and said, "I have noted that all the males I have met here have rather puny arms with very little muscle tone. So even though there seem to be some slight differences in our anatomy, they are only superficial. Let's put aside any speculation about our physical and mental differences and move forward with our investigation." I thought, *Good way to show Atina my rather impressive physique. I don't know why, but I seem to feel the need to impress this woman in any way that I can. Maybe I will find the opportunity to show her my six-pack.* Turning to face her directly, and having made an ass out of myself, I said, "Would you be open to a truce of sorts?"

My intense stare seemed to make Atina nervous. Her eyes darted from my face to her clasped hands.

Atina rubbed her forehead like she was trying desperately to concentrate on my question. She looked nervous, as though my presence so close to her was creating some sort of reaction. I felt like a teenager again, flattered by her obvious and perhaps romantic interest in me.

"I need to take this up with my father," she said quickly. "He is the one who will have to make the final determination. It will probably be necessary to take your proposal before the resistance leaders to get full approval. I personally am convinced that you have much to offer, and I think our technology might be of interest to you."

Moving back to the window for a better view of her ship, she gestured for me to join her. I observed, "Your ship is surrounded by technicians who appear to be making it ready for flight. Am I to assume that you are going to take my ship with you?"

"I am committed to another trip to Alpha2, so this might be an ideal time for us to test some of my suspicions about you and the Drezil's inability to detect your presence. If we can find a method of using your DNA to our benefit, I think it would make our ultimate mission much more attainable."

Shaking my head, I said, "I have no idea how I actually made the jump from my planet to yours. I will need your help in studying my engine. You must understand that my focus will always be finding some method of returning to my own people. Although I am not focused one hundred percent on my return home, it will always be on my mind." I sucked in a deep breath and blew it out my nose like a bull. "I will never let my personal needs override any agreement we happen to forge, but if we cannot come to some common ground, I will do everything in my power to focus solely on my return home."

It appeared that now was the time for the future of all the planets and people who had been enslaved by the Drezil to be decided. The decision which her father and the other resistance leaders would make will ultimately determine the future of the known universe.

Chapter 14

Lector was busy with his duties as governor of the small state of Nepapile. The call came in late in the evening for a meeting of the leaders of the resistance. As gatherings of large numbers of people were prohibited by the Drezil, it was important that each faction of the group's membership be represented by a single individual to keep the secrecy of their actions intact. Little had been done by this group except to consider options which were far-fetched and clearly running out. They had not found a single method which could conceivably wrench their species from the Drezil's grasp. It was with little enthusiasm that he went to the meeting place to hear what information Dlano was about to share.

Earlier in the day, Atina had shared my proposal with Dlano. He had spent many hours assessing the entire situation and concluded that if no evidence could be found that I was anything other than what I professed, he would support Atina's request to immediately begin to study the engine and craft in which I had arrived.

Having called the leaders of each resistance cell together at his laboratory, Dlano sat in the large chair facing the group and pointed directly at each of them. "You and you and you," he said as he singled out each of them in turn, "will need to be extremely vigilant and report any situation that you think may lead to Hawnl discovering our new plans. Please listen closely to Atina because she has some insight into our plan."

Dlano stepped to the rear of the lab, allowing the group to focus solely on Atina. She took her place in front of the group. "We have not found a single way to force the Drezil from our planet. They will soon begin to destroy us so they can complete terraforming this

75

planet for their own purposes. A visitor has arrived from another galaxy who may hold the answer to our salvation. We have his ship and the engine which brought him here. He was badly injured during his transit, but we have cured him of all his ailments.

Aballm, the leader of the group from the southernmost province, interrupted Atina. "We have all heard about this traveler, but we have no way of telling if he can assist us in this conflict. It is my opinion that we should take his vessel and study it ourselves. He should be imprisoned until we know for sure that he really is on our side."

Atina waved her hand to quiet Aballm. Without giving him the satisfaction of disrupting the meeting, she continued, "He is willing to share all that he knows with us in exchange for our promise to help him return to his own world. We already know that the Drezil cannot read his DNA, and therefore have no knowledge of his arrival. If we can use his technology to power our own ships, we may be able to connect with other worlds the Drezil have conquered and forge an alliance with them to fight the Drezil and take back our planets."

From the back of the room, Dlano said, "One other possibility has arisen. If we can find a method of harvesting his DNA, we might be able to change our own to become undetectable. Our time is running out, so we need to formulate a feasible plan for our own survival. I am open to any other proposals you might have but would like to have this body weigh in on the plans we are proposing."

Following a long silence, two members of the group stood and, making an obscene gesture with their hands, abruptly left the room, slamming the door behind them. All those who remained had stunned looks on their faces.

Dlano said, "Without the support of our entire group, we have little chance of being victorious in any fight with the Drezil. In addition, we have no way of knowing if someone from within one of these two nonconsenting groups is responsible for leaking our plans to Hawnl. I will consult with Atina and our visitor to determine where we should go from here. Please return to your own provinces and await our contact."

UNIVERSAL EXTINCTION

Having failed to get support from the entire resistance, the remainder of the group dispersed. It seemed impossible that their species could possibly be eradicated, but each member knew in his own way that the time to fight back was quickly approaching.

Lector said to Dlano, "It is abundantly clear that we are totally out of options, with the singular exception of this person who has suddenly appeared. If I were a believer in fate, I would suspect that he was thrown into this world to become a partner in our battle."

Dlano was beginning to become very uneasy about Lector's association with Hawnl.

Lector continued, "I have learned from Hawnl that this visitor's own planet Earth is currently being groomed for an invasion by the Drezil, so his assistance could have a far-reaching impact on his own survival and that of his species. I cannot see any choice we have other than to ask him to share anything he can with us for the benefit of us all. I will support your request to bring the stranger into our struggle."

Dlano noted that for no discernable reason, Lector seemed determined to get any information he could from the visitor. Looking directly at him, Dlano noted that Lector's eyes seemed to be avoiding his gaze. Could it be that Lector was not what he seemed to be?

It became apparent to all that this was indeed the crisis which they had all been awaiting. Their time had run out, and the Drezil were close to the final act which would result in their species' demise.

Standing again, Dlano said, "We have noted that many of us who survived the first onslaught are beginning to die at an accelerated rate. All signs point to the beginning of the final solution that we have been expecting. If we are to do anything to derail this annihilation, we had better act very soon."

Atina had been standing in a corner in the room where the meeting had taken place. She moved to her father's side and took his hand in hers. Looking into his eyes, she said, "Father, I do not trust in the resistance group. I think it would be very easy for someone to convince them that taking the visitor's technology by violence would be the best thing to do. You were not successful in gaining total approval from the resistance, so I intend to take a new direction."

MICHAEL BRADLEY

Atina felt Dlano squeeze her hand very hard. She knew he was trying to tell her to keep her thoughts to herself because those present were beginning to take sides.

"I have already formulated my own plan concerning Durell's involvement in the upcoming battle. My intention is to be totally honest with him and attempt to gain his trust."

*****

Not knowing what had been discussed at the meeting of the resistance group, I could only speculate about the outcome. I could not decide how I should react to any proposal that either Atina or her father made. Neither trust nor any kind of kinship had been established between us all, and I could only follow my instinct, which told me that these were people I could rely on. My previous decision to trust them would have to be followed if any type of resolution were to be made concerning my return to Earth and the impending total takeover by the Drezil.

Following her hasty withdrawal from the resistance group's meeting, Atina came to the building where I was seated, gazing at the ship. She took my hand and sat next to me.

"Durell," she said, "our meeting with the resistance group did not go well. There are those who wish to take your ship and its technology and attempt to decode all its secrets. Neither myself nor my father will allow this to occur, so it is imperative that we leave here as soon as possible. My father has encouraged me to take you out to the hangar that contains my ferry ship. It is his hope that you might be convinced to show me the secrets behind the propulsion system that had brought you to our planet."

"Atina," I said, "I am willing to try to assist you in learning how my system functions, but I need your personal promise that any secrets we discover will remain between you and me until I decide differently. Based on the failure of your meeting, I am now convinced that you may have a traitor in your group. For now, let's move ahead as if nothing was amiss."

78

UNIVERSAL EXTINCTION

Atina pulled me by the hand outside and toward her ship. It was massive. It had a huge belly that was used for the payload Atina was ferrying between the planets. On the very top of the ship was a cabin which had a 360-degree view of the area surrounding the ship. A hatch was visible on the side of the vessel. Atina pointed to it, indicating to me that this was the entry point. Keying in the entry code, the hatch moved silently to the left, revealing the dark interior of the ship. A set of steps began to protrude from beneath the hatch.

"This will be our entry port. I will give you the proper code to open the door, but do not attempt to enter without it, or you will be severely burned by the gas which would be released."

Having issued the warning, Atina proceeded to climb the steps to the open hatch. I was at first hesitant to follow her, but with her encouragement, I set foot on the steps. I could feel a slight tingling in my feet as I ascended the stairs toward the hatch.

I don't think I'm gonna like what I find in there, I thought. Atina gestured for me to enter. Taking a deep breath to build my courage, I slowly entered the ship.

Chapter 15

I thought my small craft was barren. In contrast, there was nothing in Atina's ship but bare metallic walls, rounded and extremely shiny. I saw no interfaces of any kind. The platform on which we were standing seemed to vibrate and move slightly under my feet. Atina passed her hand over a small section of the curved surface, and the platform began to move upward.

"You will be temporarily disoriented as the atmosphere of my ship begins to prepare us for our journey. If you begin to feel nauseous, let me know, and I'll slow the process a bit. It will take some time for your body to acclimatize to this new environment. Without this preparation, we would be crushed by the acceleration of this craft."

As the platform rose farther into the ship, I noticed some large openings in the side through which I could see some extremely large empty storage areas.

"Your ship is in the container next to the top of our cockpit entry point," Atina said. "It is the only space that the Drezil cannot scan due to the thickness of the container's walls. As soon as I feel it is safe, we'll go to your craft and see what it contains."

I had much more curiosity about Atina's ship than of my own. I could only nod to indicate my approval of her plan. The only concern I had was her reference to finding a safe time or place to proceed to my craft.

I said, "I am willing to share any of my technology with you, if you will do likewise for me." I scanned the control room and tried to decipher the meaning of each control. I knew I could never fly this thing but knew I would try if I were given the chance. Moving

80

from control to control, I found it difficult to restrain myself from touching them.

"Your ship is beyond anything I have ever seen, and the technology you have at your fingertips is unbelievable. Could we possibly be in a position to combine our assets and find a mechanism to not only return me to my home but to assist in ridding you of your oppressors?"

"That is our only hope of getting our independence back," Atina said. "From all we can determine, the Drezil are about ready to exterminate all life on our planet, and if we do not act very soon, no further action on our part will make any difference."

"I think we have a common enemy, so I suggest we partner to find some way to stop these barbarians," I said. "If the Drezil have the ability to kill an entire species, no planet is safe from their attack. Let me try to recall all the steps I and my assistant, Rachell, took to develop the technology that led to the construction of my engine."

When the lift reached the top, I could see my ship resting in the upper hold of her vessel. It was strange to see the craft I had built. The capsule was smeared with long black trails of what could only be described as soot. I could not keep my mind from returning to the point in my trip that rendered me unconscious. The sound and pain associated with the breaking of my bones was vivid, and I still could not believe that I had survived. It seemed that ages had passed since I first felt the acceleration caused by my fusion engine.

My craft appeared extremely crude when compared to Atina's ship. The portal I had used to enter my sphere was open, and I could still see the glow from the fusion engine. Atina asked, "Is your machine still functioning? I hear something that has never been part of my ship's noises and can only assume that it is coming from your ship."

I could now detect a low hum which was coming from the area which held my ship. I was acutely aware of the massive power I had discovered but had no real idea how it operated. I felt there was a need for me to offer a truthful explanation of what had occurred during my transit to this galaxy.

I said, "The reason I was injured so badly during my transit between our worlds was that I had no way of controlling the engine's power. Even with no input from me, it had powered me across the cosmos with little effort. I was not conscious during my travel between our galaxies, so I am not too sure what I could tell you concerning how to implement this technology in our fight with the Drezil."

Knowing how difficult it was for me to offer this explanation, Atina took me by the hand and led me into the main living quarters of her ship. Although it was sparsely furnished, it seemed enough for our needs. The area that served as a galley held some rather unique-looking devices which I could only assume were food preparation stations. In the one corner was a bed that was unmade and appeared to have been so for some time. In the opposite corner was another bed which did not appear to have ever been used. Atina went about explaining the operation of all the equipment but made little mention of the beds. It was possible that she had never had another crew member on this ship and would find it hard to share these sleeping spaces. I couldn't help but notice Atina's attempt to distract my attention from the beds, so I assumed that she was very nervous about the two of us being so close together.

Chapter 16

The loading process had begun for Atina's return trip to Alpha2. I peered out the cockpit windows and observed a large crane-like arm moving between each of the tubes which led to the separate cargo holds.

"Atina," I asked, "what is the material being loaded aboard your ship? It looks like salt, but you said that is what we would pick up on Alpha2. I don't really understand what is happening."

Atina went to a passageway leading to the cargo areas. "The stuff you see being loaded is actually potash. It is not safe to breathe, so we won't spend too much time down here." Moving back to the cockpit area, I felt a slight tingling in my nose. "I bring salt from Alpha2 to replenish the pure salt that the Drezil have harvested from our planet. The potash being loaded now will be used to fill the voids left by our salt harvest on Alpha2. We are trying to keep some balance between our two worlds to ensure that no undesirable effects result from the transfer of so much material."

The potash was cycled between the separate holds and made a whispering sound as it moved through the internal piping of her vessel. Normally, Atina could relax until her craft was filled, but this time was different. She gestured for me to follow her down a winding staircase to the deck below where my craft was interned. Reaching the lower level, I felt a tingling sensation throughout my body. Atina was busy explaining the internal structure of her ship when she stopped suddenly and seemed frozen in midsentence. She did not respond to my attempts to gain her attention, and I noted that her eyes had gone totally blank. The tingling I felt grew much more intense. I was not able to focus my attention on any of the space around me. Atina

83

seemed totally unaware of either my plight or her own. Suddenly, the tingling dissipated. Atina moved again toward her destination and picked up her conversation as though nothing had occurred.

What was that? I wondered. *Had some feature of this ship taken control of Atina for that short span of time?* As we approached my craft, I stopped Atina to ask, "What just happened back there?"

She looked at me with a furrowed brow, indicating that I had just asked a question that she could not answer.

"Please explain to me what you are talking about," she said. She grabbed my arm and spun me around. We stood face-to-face. The passageway between the cockpit and the cargo area was too narrow to allow us to stand side by side. I saw something in her eyes that made me acutely aware of her concern. She continued, "I have no idea what you are referring to. If you are picking up some strange feelings, I need to know exactly what occurred. You have to describe it. What did we just experience?"

Atina looked agitated, so I felt obliged to grant her request. "I suddenly felt a slight tingling all over my body. When I turned to you to ask what was causing it, you were in a trance of sorts. You could neither talk nor move, and your eyes were totally black, as though you were dead. The tingling I was feeling had intensified but then suddenly left me. At the same time, you picked up our previous conversation as though nothing had happened."

She gave me a knowing glance that communicated that she knew exactly what had happened. "Durell," she said. "Although I have a good idea of what caused this, I do not want to burden you with all the consequences of the Drezil's ability to read our DNA. I assure you that when I feel the time is right, I will explain in detail what happens when they scan us."

Entering the space that held my craft, I felt the first pangs of fear enter my psyche. I had barely survived the last journey I had taken in this sphere. I remembered Rachell. I'm certain my disappearance affected her greatly. I had become quite close to her and hoped she had not taken any responsibility for what had occurred. We had created this ship together, but I could not envision taking another trip in our insane creation.

I thought, *Had it not been for the intervention by Atina and her father, I would certainly have perished from this experience. The entire affair had an impact on me that was yet unmeasured. Would I be able to overcome my fear?* I was tempted to tell Atina of my concerns but opted to try and push through any negative feelings I might have.

The craft was well-preserved after its trip across the cosmos. Nothing seemed out of place to me, and the personal belongings I had taken from home were still in the box I had installed in the floor. Although there were no items that would cause anyone concern, I opted to keep the location of my personal items a secret for now. I did, however, take a long swig of my favorite beverage.

I noted Atina's darting eyes as she scanned the interior of my ship. She had a puzzled expression, most likely wondering how in the hell I had survived the trip from Earth to Habordiz. *Oops,* I thought. *I think the cat is out of the bag. My ship is so crude by her standards that she is starting to question my ability to help in this fight.*

This was not the leap in technology Atina had expected to find. Although she had been inside my capsule when I initially arrived, she had taken little time to study the interior. Now she felt a rush of depression as the prospects of a joint venture between us seemed far-fetched. How could this alien possibly provide technology that would enhance their own when my craft was, without a doubt, inferior to anything that her species had developed?

Sensing her thoughts, I said, "If you are concerned about what I might be able to provide to assist your cause, let me ask you how many times any of your species has made a trip across the galaxy? You do not possess the technology to support such a trip, but as evidenced by my very presence, I do."

I knew that I needed to take control of this discussion if I were to have any chance of making my demands known. I had finally convinced myself that I had much to offer but needed to leverage my knowledge of my engine's design to get what I needed.

"This will not be a one-sided effort where you benefit from my resources and I get nothing from you. I expect you to teach me about all your advances in medicine that led to saving my life and resetting my biological clock. This will be a two-way collaboration, or we will go no further."

Atina gazed around the cabin, noting the low glow coming from a grilled screen in the floor of the craft. "If you can provide any insight into how your engine works, I will open our entire book of technology to you. We desperately need a way to communicate directly with other worlds which the Drezil have enslaved. If we are to forge a lasting bond, we need to be completely open and honest with each other."

I had been in similar situations in the past. Turning to Atina, I said, "When I partnered with someone on a Salt Flats race car, I had to take a leap of faith in trusting him. Although we planned and built our car as a team, it ended there. Eventually, I was forced out of the partnership and built my own car."

My life experiences had a dramatic effect on how I viewed the world and the people in it. I was difficult to get to know, and I did not offer my trust easily. So the situation I found myself in could play out in several ways.

"I am hesitant to offer my complete trust to you but, knowing the stakes, I suggest we get started. I am agreeable to take the first step with you, but with you only. As we build our trust, I will expect access to all that you have promised. My overriding goal is to get back to my home, so I will assist you in any way that I can if you do likewise. Now let me show you my engine."

Moving to a position above the container which held my engine, I grabbed the two handles which protruded from the side and pulled up forcibly. The container lid began to slide upward, exposing its contents for us both to see. As soon the protective cover cleared the top of the engine, Atina gazed with utter astonishment at the size of this device. I'm sure she was thinking, *There is no way that this device can develop the massive amount of energy needed to jump across the cosmos. It is just too small.*

The engine emitted a subtle but visible glow. How it developed any power was beyond Atina's comprehension. She had to admit, however, that it apparently did work and might provide a solution to our current problem. I showed Atina the controls that had initiated

UNIVERSAL EXTINCTION

my trip across the cosmos. The control stick was very primitive, and Atina was tempted to see if the craft would still react to its inputs. I blocked her access to the stick as my own experience told me how dangerous the power of this engine could be. Without some additional safeguards, I was not going to tempt fate by trying it again.

Although scheduled to leave Habordiz for our trip to Alpha2, Atina was hesitant to depart without contacting her father for help in assessing this new source of power. "How can we use this technology to our advantage if we are unable to control it?" she asked.

I was aware of the issues which we faced. I had received her assurance that she would not divulge any of my secrets with anyone. "I think we are both in need of your father's advice, but I would not feel safe by including any of his associates in the planning and execution of this project. It is imperative that we keep secret any actions we take in moving forward with any infusion of my technology into yours," I said. "Is it going to be possible for me to take my machine to a safe place and work with your father to formulate a plan for our survival?"

The glow from the engine seemed to hold her attention, even though she was doing her best to offer some insight. Her eyes began to take on a lavender hue, which seemed to get more intense the longer she was exposed to the engine.

"Durell," she said. "Any further speculation concerning how or who is to be involved in the development of the fusion engine is useless. I have to make the trip to Alpha2, or the Drezil will immediately know that we are plotting something. It seems that our only option is to move the craft to a secure place and hope the Drezil are not aware of our plans."

Not waiting for any response from me, she walked to the ship's control panel and continued, "I'm going to contact my father, and we'll proceed in moving your capsule out of my ship." It was now apparent that they needed all the help they could muster to move my ship anywhere. I, however, was totally opposed to any such plan because it would undoubtedly expose us to unwanted scrutiny by the Drezil. The danger, of course, was that the Drezil would gain knowledge of our plan and annihilate us all.

87

Chapter 17

The Drezil

Hawnl was a lazy and stupid henchman of the Drezil elite. His assignment was to monitor all that occurred on Habordiz and report any irregularities to Bordeth. The slow pace of life on this planet had lulled him into an apathetic state where he didn't respect the population or feel they had any chance of mounting any type of resistance. The trips that were taken to Alpha2 to move salt to Habordiz were concerning at first but had become increasingly normal and not considered out of the ordinary. His reports to Bordeth had ceased to include any mention of these trips.

He still scanned the planet on a regular basis but had reduced his scrutiny tenfold since he was given jurisdiction over these people. Each time he initiated a scan, the inhabitants went into a palsy state where they could not function. Although I had no firsthand knowledge of the effect these scans had on the Habordiz people, I had seen the results when Atina froze when we were aboard her ship. This palsy state reduced their ability to provide the labor which the Drezil required for their terraforming.

So it was not surprising that he was unaware of the mounting resistance and the planning which was going to spearhead a rebellion that could lead to the end of the Drezil's occupation across the universe. He had become fatter and more sluggish looking than his reptilian counterparts. His only focus was on his own comfort and the native women he had enslaved to meet his own perverted needs. His lack of commitment to his assigned tasks was becoming key to

88

UNIVERSAL EXTINCTION

overthrowing the Drezil. No alarms had been triggered by any of the planet's inhabitants other than a passing reference to a sudden low-level flash of light which had occurred several days before completion of the last freighter's arrival from Alpha2.

Lector arrived at Hawnl's home early in the afternoon. Hawnl considered him to be his friend and confidant, so he felt safe in discussing his job responsibilities with him. "Lector," he said, "I am putting together my communication to Bordeth but have little to report. The only thing that has occurred that is a bit out of the ordinary is the bright flash of light that occurred in deep space some days ago."

Lector had no knowledge of the event which Hawnl was referring but assumed it had something to do with the arrival of the stranger who had appeared recently. Without direct confirmation about the bright flash, he could only nod in agreement when Hawnl told him of his decision to withhold the sighting from Bordeth.

"Nothing has occurred since that event," Hawnl said. "So I do not consider it important enough to include any reference to it in my report to Bordeth. I have not mounted any type of inquiry into what had caused it, so I have nothing to report."

"Hawnl," Lector said, "you would be wise to keep this to yourself. Bordeth might punish you for not following through with the investigation. So best to just forget it. By the way, is there anything or anyone I can get for you that will ease your stay with us?"

Hawnl slouched back into his seat, exposing more of his protruding scaly midriff. Fat as he was, he still insisted on gorging himself on the delicacies Lector provided. "Having you as my information source, I will feel safe not including all that is occurring here on Habordiz. Keep up the good work, Lector."

*****

This would be the first of many errors which Hawnl would make in the next few days. The stage had been set for revolutionaries to make their move.

Dlano had encouraged all the leaders in the resistance to band together and form a united front. This would allow them to support the use of the technology which had fallen into their hands as a springboard to bring about the eventual defeat of the Drezil. The subtle push by Dlano to support the plans currently under consideration did not seem out of the ordinary for anyone involved, but they should have taken note of his insistence to move forward with their plans immediately. Had anyone questioned his motives, he would most likely been exposed as the fraud that he was.

The resistance leaders were again gathered in Dlano's laboratory. Their mandate was to plot a course for their future activities. "The power of the spacecraft engine that Durell has brought into our midst could, conceivably, foster the development of many additional devices that would be useful to our cause." Rushing to the window of his laboratory, Dlano gestured to Atina's ship standing in the launch tower. "I assume that the ship which brought Durell to this galaxy is still securely lodged in the hold of the Pentemor. Once we have taken it to a safe place, it can be studied at leisure by the intellectual elite of our group."

His assumption almost led to a disaster in which the Drezil learned about their plans for revolution. "All our previous attempts to keep our activities from falling into Hawnl's hands have been unsuccessful. We have no idea how the Drezil have been able to track our activities, but we must assume that there is a traitor in our group."

Dlano's posture became rather threatening as he stated, "When we identify the perpetrator, it will not go well for them. Our planning in the past has been lacking in any real threats to Hawnl, but that is about to change. I am convinced that the removal of the sphere from the Pentemor is essential to learning how to infuse the technology it contains into our own offensive plans. Hopefully, you all agree with this plan."

They settled on a plan to leave the sphere in the hold of the Pentemor for a short time where, for some unknown reason, it had not yet been detected. Dlano reminded those present, "Atina was not included in our planning process for the study of the craft. She is not going be too thrilled about losing control of the technology it contains."

UNIVERSAL EXTINCTION

Dlano knew he was drastically understating how Atina would react to this plan. He dropped his voice to a whisper to keep anyone outside the group from hearing him. "Now is not the time to splinter our group, so I have decided to take the alien spacecraft off shortly before her launch time. If she does not launch on time, she will immediately come under the scrutiny of Hawnl."

Although Atina had discussed and agreed with Durell that his craft would be moved before she left for Alpha2, she thought that the part she would play in its relocation would be one of total control over the craft and its extraction. Dlano boarded the Pentemor and moved to the cockpit where Atina was found seated in the captain's chair.

"Atina," he said, "it has been decided that you and Durell will not play any part in the relocation of his ship. The only part you would play is to allow the extraction group access to this ship's hold."

That, she thought, *is not going to happen.* She abruptly turning her back on Dlano, exited the ship, and made her way to the small building next to the launch tower. She pulled on the door, which refused to open. *This damn door always sticks. You would think someone would fix it.* She forcibly yanked on the handle, and the door flew open with a loud bang. Her irritation about being left out of the entire planning process was quite evident. She rushed into the room to find Durell staring at her with a concerned look on his face. His brow was furrowed, and his eyes were half closed. She grasped his arm and led him to the viewing window. Her voice dropped to a low growl, showing her displeasure with Dlano and his associates' plan for moving Durell's ship.

"You and I have been banned from any further input concerning your ship. I have some serious questions about the plan my father and his colleagues have designed for the removal and subsequent study of your ship. I am beginning to question my faith in my father's leadership. I think you and I need to reassess this entire strategy. Be prepared to protect your ship, even if it means a physical response."

*****

Atina moved to the chair closest to the window and sat with her head in her hands. I could tell that any decision we were about to make would weigh heavily on her. I thought, *Now would be an excellent time for me to take control of this entire situation. Atina has way too much on her mind to shoulder all the decision-making on her own.*

I was beginning to sense that the group who appeared to be most interested in my craft were about to act on their own in determining the future direction I would be required to follow. I felt that any leverage I might have in determining my place in the resistance was waning. My past had been one in which I typically took control of most situations and was the decision maker.

"Atina," I said, "if any altercation develops when your father's group tries to move my craft, I will forcibly eject them from your ship. I do not think any of those wimps will try to challenge me. If they do, I will find out the color of their blood. Any other position is one I would not tolerate, especially when it includes my own property."

Atina was shocked by my strength. I now seemed capable of spearheading their personal rebellion against her father and his henchman.

"Let's formulate a plan of our own that will give us the control over the use of my ship," I said. "We really don't need any assistance in studying my craft because you and I can very easily do that on our own."

Shaking, Atina said, "I had agreed with father that the relocation was necessary, but now I can see no advantage in moving it. I think you are right, and the two of us need to study your engine and see if any method can be found to use it. If you agree, let's go back to my ship and seal the storage section which contains your ship so no one can enter."

I moved ahead of Atina and opened the door with one powerful jerk. Holding it open as I would for a woman on Earth, I said, "Let's get aboard your ship so we can protect my capsule. It now makes no sense to move it at all. It would be extremely vulnerable to detection by the Drezil if we attempted to move it out of your ship. The most prudent course of action would be for me to accompany you on this

UNIVERSAL EXTINCTION

trip to Alpha2, which would allow us to study my engine and determine if there is any way we could infuse its technology with yours."

Atina thought for a few seconds and replied, "I have never fallen under their scrutiny on any previous trip, so I can't see why we would this time. It would give us the time to assess your engine and determine if there is any way we could safely utilize it to power an interstellar craft of some kind. I agree that we should launch with it in our hold and prevent any other group from taking it from us."

Atina, followed closely by me, climbed the ladder and entered the belly of her ship. Once we were safely inside, she thought, *How had Durell suddenly taken control of this situation? As I suspected, he is going to become a major player in this entire war.*

As our collective thoughts took shape, it was evident to us both that we needed to inform Dlano of our decision to keep my craft on board. I still did not trust Dlano, so I vowed to watch him very carefully once we informed him of what we were about to do. Not knowing that he had already made his own decision with the collaboration of the others in his group, we were unaware that our decision would start an internal battle for the ship.

Atina sensed some dissention between her father's cohorts, but she never thought they would betray his confidence and try to take Durell's ship. A new sense of urgency began to creep into our planning for the launch, but early departure would not be an option if we were to run undetected by the Drezil.

"Durell," Atina said, "you will need to move freely around my ship. Please restrict your activities to the maintenance and movement of your ship." Having given me the approval to wander around her ship, Atina left to tell Dlano of their plans. I went down to the hold to secure my ship and remove the engine. It felt that things were about to get very heated.

Dlano and his group had assembled near the bottom of Atina's ship to begin the extraction process of the craft from the Pentemor. The small group was made up of the various resistance leaders who represented several of the participating countries. Dlano was saying, "When we get into the cargo space where the capsule is stored, we will—" He stopped speaking when he saw Atina approaching.

93

She was greeted with a deafening silence. The atmosphere within the group she was facing was very tense, leading her to think that she had interrupted a serious discussion to which she was not invited.

"Father," she began. "I have made a decision concerning Durell's craft, and he agrees that we should leave it where it is for the time being. I am beginning to feel that this group has other plans, and I know that Durell will not agree to losing control over his ship. So we will take the craft with us to Alpha2 on this run and study its possible usage."

The group let out a collective groan. It was obvious by their threatening postures that they had no intention of allowing Atina and I to dictate any terms concerning the capsule. I viewed their reaction to this news as an empty bit of posing which was supposed to intimidate us.

I said, "Your attempt to push ahead with your plan to take my ship will only end in a physical altercation, which you will lose. Now listen to Atina and make no further threats that you are not willing to back up with action."

Speaking again directly to the group, Atina said, "If you have any one person who could help with our investigation, we could probably inform the Drezil that they are on board to help with some repairs." She glanced at me. "Durell has stated that there will be no further discussion concerning his vessel and that any plans you have made need to take into consideration his ability to not only build the engine that powered him to our galaxy but that he holds the secret to modifying it to use in our upcoming conflict."

Dlano's group began to mutter among themselves, and I heard the shuffling of their feet as they mingled around, trying to decide what to do. I said, "If you are hesitant about what you should do, why don't we just have at it? I have been spoiling for a fight since you all decided to leave Atina and I out of your discussions." Flexing my large toned muscles, I tried to impress the group with the physical power I could bring to any fight that developed.

To emphasize my determination to control this situation, I said, "I have not had a body powerful enough for many years to challenge

UNIVERSAL EXTINCTION

anyone to a good brawl. I will leave it at that, but let me warn you again, do not attempt to take my craft by force. In addition to getting some of you hurt, it will doom any chance we might have of ridding our galaxy of the Drezil."

I saw a shiver course through Atina's body. Strange, this effect I was having on her. But secretly, I delighted in it.

Atina moved in front of the group as if to block their way to the ship's entry port. Now, speaking to her father, she said, "I will launch at the prescribed time and expect no further interference from this group."

Dlano was taken back by this sudden turn of events. He had never thought that his daughter had the strength and willpower to oppose his group and his decision. It was obvious that the influence I had over her was growing and that she was preparing to partner with me in the planning and execution of the alteration of the engine for their own use as an interstellar power plant. Was it possible that she would replace her father as the leader of the revolution?

"Atina," Dlano said, "we never had the intention to isolate you and Durell from our planning process. We just thought that you were focused on the flight to Alpha2 and would have nothing to offer in the study of the engine. Our hope was to keep Durell here to assist in that operation after we had hidden his craft from the Drezil. If you and he have come up with a better solution, we are willing to listen."

Atina and I glanced knowingly at each other. The thought *We have them now* was shared between us. Both Atina and I took a step backward in response to the mental thought that we recognized as telepathy. *Did I originate that thought, or did it come from Atina? Very strange.*

"Father," Atina said. "Evidently, you have not yet processed what I have said, so all I can do is proceed with our launch and take the craft with us. If you need to hear this from Durell, I'm sure he would be glad to repeat all that I have said in his own special communication manner. Do not forget, however, that he is able to determine the future of our entire species and has the capability to launch his craft out of our galaxy at any time he wishes." She took me by the arm and guided me toward the ship's entry port.

MICHAEL BRADLEY

"The injuries he suffered from his last trip are healed, and he feels he can modify the controls in his ship to reduce or eliminate the physical damage he experienced the last time he flew his craft. So this discussion is at an end. We will proceed with our plan, and any addition to our crew that you might think would assist our efforts needs to be done immediately. The decisions are now yours. Choose wisely."

With a wave of her hand, she dismissed the entire group as though they were children. Although not pompous, she had an air about her that demanded their respect and obedience.

As Atina left the gathering, her father could not help but admire her resolve. Did her new companion have such an impact on her that she was ready to oppose not only him but the resistance leadership?

Addressing all those gathered, Dlano said, "It appears there is little to be gained from further discussion or action about moving the ship. I am ordering you all to cease any activities associated with our intended abduction of the craft in the Pentemor's hold."

It was no surprise that his suggestion met with much opposition. Lector said, "The consensus of this group is that we go to the Pentemor and forcefully remove the craft and take it to the safety of your laboratory."

The discussion became more heated, so Dlano excused himself from the gathering and made his way alone to Atina's ship. He approached and noted that all the external hatches were secure, and it appeared that the ship was preparing for liftoff. His attempt to enter the main hatch was met with little success as all the entry codes seemed to have been modified. In frustration, he began pounding on the entry port to get Atina's attention. Finally, the hatch was opened from the inside, and he was greeted by Atina with little enthusiasm. Dlano entered the hatch, only to see me standing at the top of the entry, looking menacingly down at him.

"What is the purpose of your visit, Dlano?" I asked. "We have given you and your group our ultimatum and wish only to begin our journey. If you have chosen a qualified scientist from your group to accompany us, please have him or her come to this port as soon as possible. We have received clearance to leave within the hour, so you need to move quickly if you are to assist in our plan." Dlano reached the top of the entry way and slouched against the bulkhead. I turned my back to him and went into the control room.

He followed me and, shrugging his shoulders in defeat, said, "Although the group was hesitant to agree with your plans, I am not. Their intention is to take your ship by force if necessary and move it to what they consider is a safer location."

Looking out through the cockpit windows, I could see the group moving toward the sealed entry. "I have decided that the scientist from our group who will accompany you will be myself. If you have any objections to this, you had better express them right now because the group is approaching in force, and we need to depart immediately."

Just as Dlano finished speaking, the large group of individuals approaching the ship reached the entry. Their intentions were instantly obvious. Atina ushered her father to his seat and prepared for the launch. In the meantime, using the exterior communication device set in the wall above the throttles, I warned the approaching group to stay away from the ship.

"We have no intention of delaying our departure, so you all had better get as far away from the ship's nozzles as you can. The force of the launch will kill anyone who is within the exhaust zone." Several of the group now hesitated and began to retreat. "If your intention is to force your way into this ship, you will be unsuccessful. I have control of the power which resides in my engine and will sling the Pentemor into space if you attempt to board." *Okay, so I lied a bit.* "Your best option is to let us proceed with our journey to Alpha2 and find a method for infusing my technology with yours. You will have no input in this decision, but we will rely on you all to keep any reference of our plans from Hawnl. If they catch wind of our intentions, all of us, including you, will pay a horrific price, most likely with our lives. Support us or pay the consequences." With that, I cut off the external communications and descended to the hatch, which I sealed. The group began to disperse, moving to a safe distance from Atina's ship. Their interference would not stop the chain of events which was about to unfold.

Chapter 18

The blast from Pentemor's engines threw a halo of fire and smoke hundreds of feet from the base of the ship. The shuddering from the engine's violent explosion shook the entire ship and produced a deafening roar that could be heard and felt for miles. The ship slowly began to rise off its launch platform and arch upward on a tail of fire. Atina's delicate touch on the controls negated any need for the computerized functions that were built into the ship. She had always taken positive control of her ship from takeoff to landing. Her only concession to the computers was to rely on the autopilot to perform the mundane functions required during the boring transit from Habordiz to Alpha2.

The ship rose, and the tail of fire became longer and less intense, changing to a narrow white sliver of vapor as it gained altitude. The thrust of the engines produced a force on our bodies which increased exponentially as we ascended. I had a flashing memory of the first time I felt this amount of gravity impact me. I hoped I wouldn't react the same way as before, because losing consciousness from the effects of the force would make me seem weak and not prepared for this journey.

The screen which Atina monitored was split to reveal not only the black space in front of them but also the receding mass of the planet Habordiz. It was evident that our speed was increasing with each passing second, and the force on our bodies was approaching a level that would leave us unconscious. As the planet shrunk in the tail screen, the force on our bodies began to recede, and I could feel the relief which came with my ability to withstand the violent launch.

98

UNIVERSAL EXTINCTION

No wimp here, I thought. Despite all the roadblocks we had encountered, we were now in transit to Alpha2 with the engine that might provide our only avenue to defeat the Drezil.

Hawnl had monitored the launch of the Pentemor with little interest. He noted that the DNA scan had revealed that Atina was not alone in the ship, but he quickly discarded any concern as the additional DNA belonged to the father, Dlano. Although it was out of the ordinary for him to accompany her on her trip to Alpha2, it just seemed too taxing on his part to launch any kind of follow-up investigation to determine why Dlano was aboard the ship. His laziness was true to character as his main interest was to do as little as it took to stay in Bordeth's favor.

He surrounded himself with the spoils of the occupation of Habordiz which the leadership had left in his hands. His appetite for the finer things this planet had to offer had no bounds. The females of this species provided many hours of entertainment and physical fulfillment for a reptilian who devoured all that he could for his own amusement. His temperament mirrored that of his entire race, and it did not take much imagination to tell what was going to occur once the Drezil decided to move on with their assimilation of Habordiz into their empire. He almost pitied this species when he thought of the future they did not have.

He had discussed all of this with his brother Madille, who had a decidedly different mindset when it came to the forced occupation of planets which were the homes of other species. Madille had recently been assigned to monitor the salt mining on Alpha2 and was in position to speak directly to any humanoid who happened to visit this planet. He had established a direct communication link with Hawnl on Habordiz and used it often to try to persuade him to join in the attempt to stop the Drezil from expanding any further.

Where Hawnl's needs were satisfied by physical contact, Madille was more concerned with the treatment of the other races who were assimilated as the Drezil expanded their empire. "Hawnl," he said, "you are a disgrace to our species. Your appetite for liquor and females seems to have no bounds. I think we would be better off to bring a peaceful end to our occupation than to continue this senseless slaughter of these humanoids. I am sure that a day of reckoning will be upon us soon. What will you do when that day comes?"

"Madille, you are a traitor," Hawnl said. "Your attempts to undermine our cause has not gone unnoticed. As far as I am concerned, you are no longer my brother, and I will treat you like any other criminal. Do not contact me again, or I will contact Bordeth and have you arrested."

Madille was working diligently to sway other members of his species to try to either contain the outward expansion or target only uninhabited worlds for inclusion in their empire. He was aware that a group on Habordiz, led by a scientist named Dlano, had been formed to try to eject the Drezil from their planet. The group's leader had a daughter who was a well-known ferry pilot. She was currently on her way to Alpha2 to load a cargo of salt. He had also been informed that on this trip, her father, Dlano, had accompanied her for some unknown reason. Although not unusual, his presence might give Madille the opportunity to communicate with Dlano and inform him that they were not alone in their struggles. An unusual alliance it might be indeed, but the seeds of revolution make for some strange bedfellows.

Chapter 19

As the Pentemor made its way toward Alpha2, Atina, Dlano, and I climbed down to the hold in which the sphere resided. "Okay, you guys," I said. "Before I open this hatch, I want to warn you that many of the people who have attempted to approach this engine have suffered some strange physical reactions. If you begin to experience anything out of the ordinary, please let me know immediately."

I opened the hatch and entered the engine room. When I heard a faint mumble, I turned and noticed Dlano start to sway a little. "Durell," he said, "I am not only experiencing a sense of overwhelming disorientation, but the entire room seems to be rotating around me. I am unable to move any of my limbs, and my vision is beginning to narrow as though I am entering a tunnel. The tunnel is now beginning to narrow, and the light is waning."

Now that Dlano had told me what was happening to him, I knew that whatever I had brought to them was not only extremely dangerous but so powerful that any attempt to contain its power would be futile. In addition, my observation was that of the three of us, only he seemed to be affected by this force.

Neither Atina nor I were showing any kind of distress. How could this be? Had Atina and I found some way to remain active when exposed to the device? Was our very makeup so in tune with one another that we each one took on the attributes of the other? Something had occurred since we had met that gave us each the DNA sequences of the other.

Dlano dropped to the metallic floor. Atina dashed to his aid. "Father," she said, "what is happening? Please speak to me." Not knowing what was causing his distress, she turned to me. "Would you please assist me in moving my father back up to the cockpit?"

We picked him up, and as we moved him away from the sphere, I noted a slight purple glow emanating from Dlano's midsection.

"Atina," I said. "Do you see the lavender glow coming from your father's clothes? It is unmistakably the same as the glow which is surrounding the engine."

"Let's strap him in his seat until we see some sign that he is recovering from whatever has affected him." Almost as soon as he was secured in his seat, he opened his eyes.

"Atina!" I shouted. "I just saw a sudden flash of purple light coming from your father's eyes, but now it's gone."

I began to speculate, *Was the engine queued into some part of the DNA which Habordizites shared? Could this weird behavior be a warning? If so, how am I supposed to respond?*

It only took a few minutes for Dlano to recover from the strange malady which had momentarily incapacitated him. He wanted to return to the sphere. "I know that I have experienced some type of external stimulus I felt the moment I came close to the engine. For whatever reason, I think I can now approach it without the reaction I had previously." Dlano began to rise from his seat, and Atina rushed to his side, steadying him by grabbing his arm. Dlano brushed her hand off his arm. "I do not need any help right now. I feel well and wish only to revisit Durell's engine." He got to his feet and steadied himself. "We must assess its power and adaptability for our own uses. Let me lead the way into the craft, and if I begin to act strangely, you can get me away from it quickly."

With that, he proceeded to the ladder that led to the hold. When he reached the hatch, I opened it again and stepped back to observe his reaction. After standing in the hatchway, he entered and moved toward the engine.

"I feel a strange tingling in my chest," he said. "I do not, however, feel the intense physical reaction that had occurred the last time I entered."

UNIVERSAL EXTINCTION

I wondered, *How in the world is this possible? Could it be that the artifact that powers the engine has somehow altered Dlano to the point where he can now approach it without any distress?*

After I removed the containment cover from the engine, Atina was finally able to view its internal elements. "This seems so simple," Atina said. "What I see is only a single glowing substance which is emitting a lavender plasma. There is a nozzle which is aimed directly at a piece of rocky material that is anchored to the bottom of the vessel. The nozzle, however, is not emitting any type of solution or gas." Trying to study the contents of the engine compartment, Atina could only say to her father, "I see a low-level emission which is a purple glow that appears to be the only active element within the confines of the engine case."

"Atina," I said. "That purple glow. It's coming from you now." Atina looked at her chest and then back at me. I was totally unaffected by the presence of the engine.

I moved to the device and removed the glowing rock from its container. As soon as the object was several inches away from its enclosure, it ceased emitting the purple glow. At the same time, the glow which had shown from both Atina and Dlano's chests was no longer visible. "There can now be no doubt that this rocky substance has some properties which are totally unknown to us. The fact that both of you responded the same to its influence while I did not is a puzzle which we need to solve."

As I finished my assessment, Dlano began to struggle for breath, reeling back toward the open hatch. "Durell" he whispered, "I feel as though some part of my very life source is leaving me. My vision is beginning to fade, and I know I am about to lose consciousness."

He pointed to the rock, which was no longer glowing, and gestured to the engine. Reading his intent, I quickly replaced the artifact back into the engine, where it again began to emit the purple glow. Immediately, Dlano recovered from the physical and mental distress that had assaulted his body.

"I guess I've asked this before," I said, "but what the hell just happened?"

"It is apparent to me that we had not even scratched the surface in our study of this most unique engine. My only guess is that Dlano's DNA has either been permanently altered by exposure to the device or he has experienced some type of mental collapse."

Atina's eyes grew wide at the statement. I moved closer to Dlano and said, "Given that this had all occurred after your first exposure, I think we can discard the latter reason. The device is having a profound effect on you, and unless you have some secret heredity that you have not told us about, we have to assume that the same would be true for most of the Habordizites."

We were delving into some extremely dangerous waters. I would have to find a method which would negate the effects the engine had on Dlano. Obviously, both my own and Atina's bodies had formed an immunity to the adverse effects of the device, which allowed us to experiment with different strategies for control without suffering any side effects. It appeared that Dlano's DNA was not truly identical to ours and had been altered so severely that he could not survive if the stone was removed from the engine.

I was now getting very suspicious about Dlano's agenda. Could he be something other than he claimed? I began to wonder, *Was this device a two-edged sword offering both a possible solution to interstellar travel, but at the expense of many of the planet's population?*

"I want to try something that may help Dlano escape the influence of the engine," I said. The ship was equipped with medical supplies that included many of the items which a doctor might utilize to treat an injured patient. I located a scalpel inside the medical bag, and without saying a word, I pierced my finger with the knife. As a small trickle of blood began to ooze out of the wound, I placed my hand up to Dlano's mouth and smeared my blood on his lips.

Dlano immediately pushed my hand away and tried to wipe the blood from his lips. Atina was shocked by the suddenness of my action and said, "Durell, you have no right to attempt to infuse your DNA into my father. I will hold you completely at fault if something bad happens."

"I know you're upset, Atina," I said, "but I saw no other recourse. It is my hope that that the DNA in my blood will be recognized by the engine and give your father immunity to any more ill effects."

Atina nodded toward her father. It was an odd moment of understanding between father and daughter.

"I will now remove the stone from the engine to see how you react to it. If you no longer feel any ill effects, we may be able to get better control of its influence on you." Having set the conditions for this experiment, I removed the stone from the engine.

Atina and I watched Dlano, not knowing what to expect. "I feel totally normal right now," he said. "Let me try to go to the cockpit and see what happens." With that, Dlano climbed the stairs leading to the cockpit.

"Dlano," I said, "I am now going to remove this covering, and you can place the stone back into the chamber. Then I am going to reenergize the engine. But please, let me know if you feel anything unusual."

Atina and I brought the interstellar engine back online. None of us felt anything that caused the slightest discomfort.

"All right," I said with a sigh of relief. "You seem to be immune to the effects. I, however, have become concerned about the proximity of the interstellar engine to the instrumentation in the cockpit. I suggest that we move it more toward the other end of the vessel to remove any chance of possible interference. If you agree, let's get it slung so we can move it to a hold further from the cockpit."

Atina said, "I can use the overhead crane to attach this webbed chute to the engine. Once it is cradled in the web mesh, I will swing it out of the hold onto the salt conveyer. That way, I can transport the engine to the salt chamber just above my ship's engine room."

As the engine was placed in a cradle we had fashioned, a sudden surge was felt in the forward motion of the Pentemor.

We all rushed back to the cockpit. The instrumentation indicated that the ship had indeed begun to slowly, almost imperceptibly, gain speed.

"I have absolutely no idea what is happening," Atina said. "So all I can think to do is begin a full diagnostic on the ship's condition."

"Yes, good idea," I said. "The main engines were shut down hours ago, and there still doesn't appear to be any planets close enough to us to impose a gravity force on the ship. The only possibility is some type of influence that Durell's engine might be having on the ship's own engine."

Had we accidently found a way to interface the new engine with Pentemor's own engine? If the current level of acceleration were maintained for any length of time at all, we would be traveling faster than any ship in the fleet had ever traveled. The consequences of this last fact hit home like a bombshell. If we did not stop the uncontrolled engine thrust, we would soon overshoot Alpha2, which would alert the Drezil of our latest discovery. Thankfully, the increased speed and acceleration was small enough to go unnoticed for at least the next hour or so. We needed to get control back before that clock ran down.

"I have no doubt that the initiator of the change in speed was the influence my own engine was having on the Pentemor's systems," I said. "Moving it back away from the engine room might reduce the interaction which was causing the problem."

Both Atina and Dlano looked at me as though I was insane. "You don't actually believe that we have some amount of control over your engine that is as simple as this," Dlano said.

I pushed my hand through my hair. "We may have just stumbled on a mechanism for controlling the degree of acceleration which my engine produces. As simplistic as it is, the solution appears to be the issue of distance between the two engines equating to the amount of increase in speed that we will experience."

I directed Atina to return to the cockpit and monitor the accelerometer while Dlano and I carefully moved the engine back away from the ship's main engine room. As we did so, Atina reported that the accelerometer dropped back to zero. *Had we just solved the problem which almost led to my death?*

As our journey toward Alpha2 continued, we all were trying to absorb the enormity of what had just occurred. Whatever force the engine had developed was now responsible for altering Dlano's DNA and interacting with the Pentemor's engines to produce more thrust.

UNIVERSAL EXTINCTION

It was going to be a mystery for a long time to come, but I sensed that there were more hands in this game than I had originally thought.

I began to wonder if the substance I found so many years ago in the wilds of Africa have been placed there for me to find? Was it beyond all speculation that another entity or species was giving me the mechanisms to free the universe from the Drezil's tyranny? The string of events that led to our current ability to mount an offensive were tied too closely together to be coincidence.

Knowing that the assistance we had been granted was very finite, I was determined to take control of this entire situation and bring to bear this new source of power that had fallen into my hands. The ability to provide interstellar travel was within our reach and would play a definitive role in the conquest that was about to begin.

Chapter 20

Alpha2 began to loom larger in the blackness of space. It was a crystal white planet that seemed to radiate a lavender glow that appeared as an aurora surrounding it. Atina had already programmed the ship for its arrival and subsequent positioning for loading its cargo of salt. "I will be manually landing the ship," she said. "I hope all interference from the interstellar engine has ceased because this landing is very difficult."

The landing site was a stone's throw from the salt extraction site, and a huge cache of salt bordered the touchdown area. She deftly maneuvered the ship to bring the planet around to the stern so she could utilize the engines to slow her craft in preparation for the landing. To her surprise, the ship had gained so much speed during the short acceleration period caused by my engine that she could not get her speed down low enough for a landing.

As the planet continued to grow on her screen, she opted to abort this landing and circle the planet until the craft's speed could be safely reduced. Rounding the far side of Alpha2, she noted a structure on the surface which she had never seen before.

"What is that?" she said. "It doesn't appear on any of my charts and seems to have mysteriously appeared since my last trip to Alpha2."

I looked at the instrument panel. "I have no idea what that is. But we haven't time to study it now."

"Right," she said. "I need to prepare the ship for landing. But I will investigate this further at some time."

As the ship slowed to a suitable speed for the transition, she rotated it so her braking engines faced the landing space. She moved the throttle from its low setting toward the maximum thrust posi-

UNIVERSAL EXTINCTION

tion, causing the ship to shake violently, forcefully slamming us into the back of our seats. She continued to increase the thrust until the ship thundered to a stop just meters from the ground. Easing the thrust allowed the ship to settle gently onto its landing pad where the metal restraints deployed, capturing the ship. The landing sequence had taken only a few minutes, but the additional trip around the planet was totally out of the ordinary for the Pentemor and caught the attention of the Drezil overlord. Atina knew she would have to explain this departure from the norm and was ready with a plausible story.

"Father," she said, "we need for you to stay with the ship and monitor the salt loading process. I need to be sure that the loading process is completed without any interference."

Dlano knew he had been given a job that was designed purely to keep him from joining Atina and I on whatever journey we were about to take. "Atina," he said, "I see no real need for my expertise during this loading process, but I will do as you ask."

The Drezil were not all that informed about the mechanical operation of her ship and did not trust the technology it contained. Keying her communication device, she said, "This is the starship Pentemor. We have experienced a failure in our thrust controller. We were forced to circle the planet to scrub off excessive speed. Please note our time of arrival was extended due to the malfunction."

The planet overlord, Stuaaf, responded, "I have noted your explanation and will forward it to Hawnl on Habordiz."

It seemed that Stuaaf had accepted Atina's explanation without questioning her. We both knew that any of these deviations from the normal routine could be cause for suspicion concerning plans for a rebellion.

Having safely landed her craft, Atina rose from the pilot's seat and turned to Dlano and I. "We are going to have to split up so that the overlord does not become suspicious of our activities. Father, you know what you are to do, but Durell and I have another activity in mind. Let's get to our respective jobs so we can load this ship and head home."

109

Dlano paused on the ladder leading to the outside of the ship. Speaking to Atina and I, Dlano expressed his thoughts concerning the present danger. "If we try to do this on our own, we will be discovered, and our species would be wiped out. If any action is taken and discovered by the Drezil, not only will we doom our own planet, but most likely many of the other occupied worlds." Dlano continued down the ladder, one slow step at a time. "It is imperative that whatever we do is a calculated event which must include as many of the occupied worlds as possible," he said.

I could not shake the feeling that Dlano was trying to put us all into a position where we would be the aggressors against the Drezil. He had given no suggestions on how this was all to occur but seemed to be pushing for us to make all the decisions based on his input.

"The only way this can happen is with direct communication with each of the resistance movements on the other occupied planets. I am assuming that your hatred for the Drezil is emulated by the inhabitants of all these other planets."

Atina opened the ship's access hatches in preparation for accepting the tons of salt she would be ferrying to Habordiz. Atina said, "We will be exiting the ship for some relaxation, so if you have any questions for me, now would be an excellent time to ask."

"No questions," I said.

Turning to face me, Atina said, "I think we have enough time to investigate the structure I saw when we passed by the other side of this planet. The loading time for my ship will stretch over many hours, so I want to try and commandeer a flyer to study the site we saw more carefully."

Following her superb landing on the planet, I rose from my untethered chair and walked up behind Atina. Not knowing why, I placed my hands on her shoulders, trying to make some physical connection.

"I guess now would be a great time for me to show off my piloting abilities," I said. "In my colored past, I have been known to borrow vehicles for my own personal use. The Drezil do not seem to be able to detect me, so I am free to move about without their knowledge."

UNIVERSAL EXTINCTION

Dlano had just completed his meeting with the team who were about to load the salt cargo into the Pentemor. He was concerned that Atina had chosen to separate him from the activity that she and I were going to pursue.

Do they suspect what my true goal might be? Dlano thought. *I need to be careful to not reveal anything about any of my activities.*

With her ship tethered to the unloading platform, we prepared to exit the craft. Atina pointed to the storage compartments lashed to the side of the walls. Opening two of the compartments, she said, "We are going to have to don these pressure suits to withstand the environment here on Alpha2. It does not contain any of the gasses we need for survival. Make sure you have sealed your helmet before we exit this ship."

Peering out of the cockpit window, I noted a small craft which appeared to hover several feet above the ground before it landed. *This,* I thought, *reminds me of the helicopters I flew back home. It might provide us with our transportation. All I had to do was borrow it for a short time.*

"Atina," I said, "I am going to borrow one of those hover machines down there so we can go around to the other side of this planet and investigate the structure you spotted."

Atina wholeheartedly agreed with my plan. She moved to the hatch which led to the outside and motioned for me to accompany her. Dlano had attached a cabled carriage to the side of the Pentemor to allow for a quick transit from the ship to the ground. Riding the carriage to the ground beneath the ship, we got a panoramic view of the landing site which included not only one of the hover machines but an additional group of twelve of these machines which were positioned off to one side of the Pentemor.

I walked to the row of aircraft and, after inspecting each, decided to enter the smallest one. My inability to read any of the control functions did not cause me any concern as it was relatively easy to discern the function of each. Peering around for anyone who might notice my actions, I saw nothing that aroused my concern. Atina boarded the machine, and I found the appropriate switches and lit the engine. Once it came to life, I tested each control to determine

111

its function. Having convinced myself that I could fly this machine, I pushed the throttle lever up and eased another control foreword. The craft left the ground with a lurch and began to climb at a steep angle. I moved another handle forward, and the craft shot ahead as it rapidly gained altitude. This all scared the hell out of Atina. She was an accomplished spacecraft pilot but found my piloting skill to be reckless.

I smiled at her and said, "I was a great pilot on Earth, so trust me, I'll get used to this thing if it kills us."

Alpha2 was not a huge planet even by Earth standards. It was once considered a barren rock that was of no possible use to anyone. After the discovery of the huge salt formations, mining it had become a priority for the Habordiz. As the Drezil depleted Habordiz of this valuable resource, it was necessary to try to replenish the salt supply even though this salt was nowhere near as pure as that on Habordiz. The Drezil did not even consider mining the salt themselves because that would have taken time and effort and would require the assignment of many of their own workers to extract the substance.

It was much easier for a lazy species to steal it after it had already been processed by the Habordizites. This small insignificant planetoid had become the source which supplied the valuable substance to this sector of the system. Its value to all carbon-based life was incalculable. Without sodium, life would cease to exist in many of their worlds. It was necessary, however, to wear their cumbersome space suits because there was no atmosphere on Alpha2. The sky was black as space, and any attempt to move around without wearing their protective suits would spell immediate death. The only native light seemed to be a purple glow that came from the opposite side of the planet from where the salt loading station was located.

The craft we had procured was extremely fast, and as our speed increased, a set of wings deployed from the main body of the craft. Each wing had an additional engine which pushed the machine to speeds which I had never experienced in any helicopter. We shot upward, and our view of the planet provided an increasingly wider panorama of the landscape.

UNIVERSAL EXTINCTION

At this speed, I thought, *we will be over the area Atina saw shortly. All I must do is figure out how to land this thing. I guess now is not the time to bother Atina with these small details.*

For her part, Atina had already considered my lack of experience with this craft and was looking around for a suitable escape route or some other life-saving device. "Durell," she said. "Maybe it would be best if you left the piloting up to me. With no parachutes aboard, I envision myself being just a red spot on the white salt below if I continue to rely on your skills."

I guess that since I had been associated with Atina, I must have developed a thicker skin because I just ignored her concerns and prepared myself to land this machine.

The structure came into view, so I began to bring the controls back toward the position they had been when I first started the engine. Doing so caused the craft to slow and begin a gentle drop in altitude. *Piece of cake*, I thought. *I am really going to impress Atina with this landing.* In the back of my mind, however, was a nagging thought: *Why am I trying to impress her? I think I'd better get control of my hormones, or this could turn into a very sticky situation.*

The craft came to a stop over the structure, so I picked out a flat area and brought the machine down to a gentle landing. Now I even impressed myself. *I could never have done this at home, so what in the world has given me the ability to fly this foreign machine?* Atina was relieved to be on the ground after that harrowing flight, so she had to admit that I exhibited superior skill as a pilot. She was convinced that had any other person tried that, they would have come down in a fireball.

"Nice job, Durell," Atina said. "Maybe I have drastically underestimated you."

Exiting our borrowed craft, we noted what appeared to be a hatch or door in the exterior of the structure in front of us. In addition, we could hear an audible hum coming from inside. I moved to the hatch and was about to feel for a handle or button to open it when, without any action on my part, it opened.

"Now that scared the hell out of me," I said.

113

Atina shrank back from the opening, saying, "If you think for one minute that I am going in there, you are totally out of your Earthling mind." She then sat down next to the open door and seemed to hang her lower lip out as though she was pouting.

I was more than a bit amused. Laughing, I said, "Atina, quit acting like a child. I'll protect you from the boogeymen inside."

Fire flashed from her eyes as she digested what I had just said. "You dumb ass," she said. "It will be a warm day on Alpha2 before I concede any leadership or hero worship of you. Just get your butt in there, and don't worry about me following you. If need be, I will lead."

Wow, I thought. *I guess I really stirred up a hornet's nest. She seems to have a temper she has kept well-hidden until now. I think I like that.*

Following our little spat, we were again prompted to enter. Without hesitation or thought, I stepped into the structure, followed closely by the angry Atina. As soon as we cleared the hatch, it abruptly slammed shut, leaving us in total darkness. We both heard a whisper, which seemed to direct us to remove our helmets. Without the slightest hesitation, we removed our helmets and were met by a breathable cool air with a mist of water vapor.

Chapter 21

The darkness was pierced by a bright light emitting from another door which had slid to the side to reveal a corridor lined with small openings. I moved down the corridor to a spot which seemed to be a junction for several tunnels that were identical to the one I currently occupied.

I moved forward, and a full section of the wall disappeared. *This is all so cool. I kinda think I might be in a science fiction movie.*

We were met by a male humanoid figure. He was not too unlike the other humanoids I had seen, but there was something truly strange about him, even sinister. I decided to keep my guard up with this guy.

"Although we have not allowed you to know why or how you related to our species, you have been selected as emissaries to bring our message and assistance to the humanoids on Habordiz. We have total confidence in you both because we share a common DNA. Durell, your success in hiding your true identity from everyone on Habordiz has given us a great advantage in shaping the future of this universe. You hold the key to our survival."

"You know," Atina said, "I will believe just about anything, but this guy is really pushing my gullibility meter. Any more of this mutual admiration shit and I'm going to gag. Who the hell is he?"

Not knowing what surrounded us or if it was safe to move, fear began to creep into us both. As sudden as the outside hatch had closed, another door slid to the side to reveal a corridor which was lined with small openings that were alternately opening and closing like a breathing creature. We moved down the corridor to a spot which seemed to be a junction for several tunnels that were identical to the one we currently occupied.

Atina asked, "Now what are we supposed to do?"

A panel previously unseen by either of us slid open, and I saw a large silver control. Without thinking, Atina reached in and pulled the handle forward. As she did, a full section of the wall disappeared, and we were confronted by a male humanoid figure who was looking at us very inquisitively. Without moving his lips or uttering a single word, we both heard him in our minds.

"My name is Rotan, and I represent the Azdawn species which has been displaced by the same alien entity that you are fighting. We have been waiting for you to arrive."

"O-o-o-o-o-okay," I stammered. "What in the hell is happening? This person is not talking as we do but seems to be injecting his thoughts directly into my mind. Atina, are you experiencing the same thing as I?"

"I am getting the same message as you. Let me try something." Atina closed her eyes for a moment and seemed to be concentrating very hard. And then, like magic I heard it—not in audible words, but I could hear her thoughts. *If I can communicate by just thinking about something, it would sure ease our communication process.*

I was astonished. *My turn,* I thought.

Atina immediately said, "Okay, this is really weird. I can hear your thoughts, so something here must be giving us this ability. Let's let this alien continue to tell us what is going on."

Rotan continued, "We allowed you to see our facility in the hope that you would be curious enough to seek us out. We are not native to this planet but share a common heritage with both of your home worlds. Your future is our past, and based on our knowledge of your plight, we can assist you in formulating and implementing a plan to save your species from annihilation by the Drezil."

Atina and I were both overwhelmed by the very presence of this alien being. This entire experience was foreign to us both, and the feel and texture of our surroundings was not only strange but a bit frightening. New feelings began to course through our bodies, and any hesitation we might have felt was now gone.

UNIVERSAL EXTINCTION

"We have been sequestered here to assist in stabilizing the universe, your universe, and that of many other conquered systems," Rotan said. "Although our numbers are few, we are dedicated to finding another species who can use our technology to defeat the Drezil and drive them back to their home planet."

Turning to me, Atina threw her arms in the air, indicating that she was becoming very exasperated with what was going on. "Durell," she said, "what is this alien talking about? Who is he, and how does he fit into what is going on between the Drezil and our species? All my senses tell me that we could be in extreme danger if we follow him."

Rotan could hear and understand Atina's thoughts but continued, "The current state of this quadrant has concerned us for centuries, but our reduced numbers have never allowed us to formulate a plan for confronting them. We are not here to render any kind of forceful assistance but might be able to point you in a direction which would be in all our interests. Durell, do not think that your planet is any more immune to being conquered than these others. The takeover has already begun. The history of the Drezil's empire expansion is one which has been repeated many times."

I was peering around the room and noticed some strange slits in the walls. I could hear a sound that seemed to come from the slits. It was like someone breathing. It was like this structure had a life of its own. An odor not unlike a citrus fruit accompanied each wave of breath that was emitted from the walls.

Man, I thought, *I could sure use an orange right now.* I noticed immediately that an orange had suddenly appeared on the floor next to me.

Rotan continued, "Being a peaceful species, we approached the Drezil many years ago with the intention of becoming allies and neighbors. We did not expect that they would turn on us, steal our technologies, and attempt to wipe out our entire species."

Atina was overwhelmed by this new insight. She now knew that her species was not the only one which had been targeted for extinction. Turning to me, she said, "Durell, this is what your planet and its inhabitants can expect when the Drezil invade. I cannot stress enough the need for haste."

As nervous as I was about being in this invisible habitat, I could only marvel at where we were. Could this all be an opportunity to take this conflict straight to the Drezil?

Atina faced Rotan, and her facial expression showed her disdain for this individual. "It seems to me that you and your society are willing to stand by and let the Drezil run rampant throughout the universe even though you could stop them. Your inability to aid in the defeat of these aggressors sounds more like you are all a bunch of cowards. Even though we do not have a credible offensive weapon, we still intend to fight them."

I was overwhelmed by Atina's verbal attack on Rotan. *I have definitely underestimated her, and my admiration for her is growing by the minute.*

Rotan acted as if he had not heard one word that Atina had said. "A small group of us escaped death, and we have worked for many centuries to bring their reign to an end," Rotan said. "By placing artifacts on many of their intended targets, we hoped that a coalition might be formed to intervene in their domination."

Moving into the light, Rotan revealed his physical appearance. It was not unlike any other humanoid which Atina and I had seen. We did not know that his species had the ability to shape-shift into any appearance they wished. Other than a slight lavender glow which surrounded his body, he appeared to be quite human.

"Durell," he said. "Your travel across the expanse of the universe is the first sign we have seen that the movement toward a viable retaliatory force has begun. Your world is the next in a series of worlds that the Drezil need to continue stepping further into this universe."

What? I thought. *Earth is on these asshole's hit list? Maybe the global warming was a prelude to our planet's demise. Damn, maybe the handwringers were right. Atina, I think we have just been joined in a fight to the end for our own species.*

Without pausing for us to let this all sink in, Rotan said, "Although we could stop them, our species is not allowed to perform any action that would be violent in nature. In any case, any action against the Drezil could require the annihilation of their entire species. We find that to be adherent, especially considering that their destruction could not be accomplished without much collateral damage to your own worlds. So we have left you with the tools which might be employed to defeat the Drezil if you can determine how to use them."

Sharing our thoughts, I said, *Hopefully, the tools this guy is giving us are better than what we have received before. I have a feeling that the artifact I found in Africa may be something they left for me. I can't really figure out how to use that, so maybe he will include some instructions with the next gift.*

"Your ship's engine has been modified to allow for interstellar travel through interdimensional conduits which will allow you to jump between galaxies almost instantaneously."

"Holy crap," I said. "This is looking better all the time. Atina, you are about to become the proud owner of a trans-dimensional vehicle. Maybe I could talk you into running me home. I would be eternally grateful."

"Not a chance!" Atina said. We were standing in the center of the room and clutching each other's hands when a shimmer of light started to envelop us. I could feel a tingling course through my body and knew that Atina was feeling the same thing by the increased pressure from her hand. Had we just been given another tool to use against the Drezil?

Rotan said, "One last thing we have for you is a tool which will allow you to travel without the Drezil detecting your ship." With that, he produced a device which looked like a chain mail cloth about three feet in diameter. It emitted the same pale lavender glow as the artifact I had found in Africa.

"Atina, when exposed to the artifact I used to power my ship, it will provide you with stealth capability for your own ship. This same technology was used to camouflage this site so that we can remain undetected by the Drezil. Although our assistance is not meant to be self-serving, we are anxious to return to our own homes, and we will be able to do so if you are successful in your quest."

Atina took the tool offered by Rotan and placed it over her left shoulder. "I can feel a strange vibration coming from this device," she said. "Is that an indication that this is working?"

Walking around to Atina's back, Rotan adjusted the device to cover from her waist to her neck. "Now," he said, "whoever or whatever is covered like this will be entirely undetectable by the Drezil."

In what appeared as a dismissal of the meeting, Rotan said, "Let there be no doubt, however, the Drezil are formidable enemies, and you need to do your utmost to remain secretive about your plans. One slip and you will doom your future. Now take this and go back to your ship. We will continue to monitor you and your worlds."

We made our way back to the hatch. It was now open, and we passed through without any problem. We cleared the hatch, and it slammed shut. The entire structure now began to turn transparent. It was no wonder that no one had found this place. It was totally invisible by the time we reached our transport.

"Atina, do you think we have just been handed the tools and knowledge which will allow us to defeat the Drezil? If so, we need to design a plan for using this technology to run them out of this galaxy and mine. I am not, however, convinced that the entity we encountered was being totally honest with us."

Atina and I had donned our pressure suits before exiting the structure, so we were prepared for the vacuum outside. Looking back to where the structure first appeared, she said, "Why are the Azdawns on this planet? There must be more to their presence than was shared with us."

Although the structure had now completely disappeared, a soft lavender glow remained in its place. My mind seemed incapable of putting all the pieces of this puzzle together. *Purple glows everywhere. What is the significance of this?*

Standing on the surface outside where the building once stood, we both recognized that something very unusual had just occurred.

Atina turned to me. "They appear to be guarding something, but what? We need to be very careful and not just assume everything they say is fact."

UNIVERSAL EXTINCTION

Our transport rose from the surface of Alpha2, and I noted a very familiar glow coming from behind where the Azdawn compound was located. I tipped the small transport ship to pass over the spot that the compound occupied, and I saw that same lavender color emitted from the ground beneath the ship.

"Atina," I said. "I think we have stumbled on the source of the element that started me on this journey. If we ever need large amounts of it, we now know where to find it. Although I am sure the Azdawn do not wish to share this with us, if it was necessary, we can harvest some of the element for our own use. The fact that we know where to find it might not be too healthy for us. Keep this all to yourself."

We made our way back to our own ship, and we pondered the significance of what had just occurred. Atina said, "I am now convinced that there are alien entities who are trying to assist in the overthrow of the Drezil. All that had occurred in the near past was not a coincidence. Your arrival in a ship that contained the technology needed for interstellar travel, the Drezil's inability to sense your presence, the reaction my father experienced when first exposed to your engine, and the discovery of the structure on Alpha2 were all tied together in some manner."

"Hopefully, this would all lead to the defeat of the Drezil," I said.

Atina needed to trust me now. She needed to infuse my technology with hers and direct Dlano to begin to prepare the resistance members for the upcoming conflict. Leaving him with the Pentemor had been a gamble to see how he would react to his sole presence with the ship. I still had some serious concerns about who or what his agenda might be.

It was imperative that we set out on a voyage to the other conquered worlds in this system. For my part, I viewed all that had occurred as positive proof that the Drezil could, in fact, be defeated by this small collective group of strangers.

The effect that my engine had on those who approached it could only be characterized as mind-altering. The glow it emitted was not of any world that I had ever known or visited. I was becoming convinced that my discovery of the artifact had set about a series

121

of events that were dictated by the entity we had just encountered. I was slightly concerned that I had been manipulated by an outside source, but I also felt a sense of satisfaction that I had been entrusted with the technology which could bring the universe back to a stable footing. The only remaining task was to team with Atina and her father to begin to form a coalition of the resistance supporters from all the conquered worlds into a single massive force that could eliminate the Drezil from their respective worlds. Even though I had some reservations about the Azdawn's ultimate goals, I was willing to use our expertise to help defeat the Drezil. The time had now come for direct action.

Chapter 22

The loading of the Pentemor was nearing completion, so Atina called her father and me to the cockpit to begin planning for our departure. We met in the crowded space, and I said, "Although we are visible to the eye, we will be undetectable by the Drezil's devices and should be prepared to find a plausible explanation for our stealth." With a wave of my hand, I dismissed any further discussion about our invisibility to the Drezil.

Gesturing to Dlano, I said, "It's possible that we might be able to fly close enough to the asteroids we passed on the way here and make them believe that we have collided with one. Any explanation will suffice because they would never think that their technology would fail. What do you think, Dlano?"

"Is there any way we can test the device and see if it provides the cloak that was promised?" Dlano asked.

"Father," Atina said, "we have no way of proving any of the information that was shared with us is true. However, it is obvious that Durell made an interstellar voyage using the artifact he recovered."

Moving to the viewport, I could only shrug my shoulders and say, "Dlano, at some point, you are going to have to begin trusting me."

Dlano squinted at me and shook his head slightly. "So the faith we have put in their technology appears to be warranted. Therefore, we should trust in this new addition to our arsenal which will help us leave our own system and travel to another. I, for one, am going to proceed with our departure from Alpha2 and return to Habordiz as planned."

Grabbing Dlano's arm, I said, "You need to know that I am not buying all that you say you are. There is something you are concealing, and I intend to find out what."

Dlano took a step back. "I understand your hesitancy in accepting me, but as Atina's father, I will always put her needs before anyone else. My plan is that once we are able, we can attempt to get your engine to power this craft at the speeds necessary to provide interstellar travel."

Knowing that Dlano was most likely simply addressing his own needs, I said, "We need to get some sense of the extent of the Drezil empire and the location of all the planets they have overrun. In Hawnl, we have a ready source of this information and might be able to trick him into divulging the locations of the other planets. I'm sure there must be a set of star navigation charts somewhere. All we must do is find them. Hawnl is a braggart, so we can play on his need to feel important and possibly coax the information from him."

Atina skillfully applied thrust to the Pentemor, causing it to lift gracefully off its pad and arch into the airless sky. The return trip would provide the ability to test some of our newly acquired technology to determine if we could control its power. Draping the chain mail over the engine in the hold seemed to increase the level of the hum that was being emitted.

Dlano, however, became extremely tense when the hum increased in intensity and had to move back to the cockpit. Why was he reacting so strangely to the presence of this engine? It was as though his presence was unwanted by the device. Could it be organic? To test its properties, I draped the chain mail over Dlano's shoulder. He immediately returned to his normal self and was able to move about the ship without any adverse effects.

"It appears that the artifact that the entities gave us on Alpha2 has more uses than to provide the stealth capabilities for this ship. If it is as powerful as it appears, we need to continue to test its usages. It must have the ability to form a barrier between your species and the effects of the engine."

I removed the chain mail from Dlano's shoulder. "He would have perished if he moved too close to the engine, but the artifact seems to have given him some immunity to the engine's deadly effects. For the time being, we need to use it for its stealth properties only. If either of you have any other suggestions, please let me know."

Chapter 23

We made our way back to Habordiz and began to plot our strategy for the upcoming trip. First on the agenda was to pry the information concerning the Drezil's locations out of Hawnl so a map could be generated to use as a reference for the trans-universe flight. Dlano was looked upon by Hawnl as an intellectual leader, so it was decided that he would attempt to get the information we required from him. He would be pleased that Dlano had sought him out for some meaningless chitchat. His tongue would be loosened by the gift Dlano would bring—an extremely strong drink that the Drezil enjoyed immensely. It would take a masterful directive hand for Dlano to get the information he needed without arousing Hawnl's suspicions.

Although Atina had total faith in her father and his ability to carry out this touchy mission, I could not shake the feeling that, based on what I had seen when Dlano was exposed to my engine, he might be hiding something from us. Whatever had occurred, the effect that the engine had on Dlano had immediately raised some red flags which I now had the opportunity to investigate. So I went to the Pentemor's hold and collected all the items associated with my engine and moved them to another location in the ship. If anybody came looking for my technology and the stealth abilities that had just been given to us, I was certain they would not find any of the items I had hidden.

The trip was purposely routine, so no alarms would warn the Drezil of the plans for the upcoming mission. We had decided that our break for the trans-universe flight would be better taken on the return trip back to Alpha2 when the ship was empty. The lack of additional cargo would ease the burden on the engine and allow us

125

to maneuver into a position to utilize my engine when we grazed the chosen asteroid. An explosion caused by dropping one of our three fuel tanks should convince the Drezil that we had been destroyed in a collision with the asteroid. After we dropped the tank, I would throttle the engine into place and use its proximity to the Pentemor's main engines to control our rate of acceleration.

Atina and I sat very close to each other in the cockpit of the Pentemor. I said, "The plan that we had devised will not be shared with anyone, least of all Dlano. We know that anyone who knows what we were going to do could be coerced by the Drezil into revealing our intentions. We will implement our plan once you return the Pentemor to her home launch platform and the unloading process has begun. Then our plan would be put to the test."

Dlano looked at the task he had been given with much trepidation. His persuasive abilities were well-known, but he still felt the need to seek the advice of his good friend, Lector. Lector arrived at Dlano's residence shortly after his presence was requested.

The current activities of the resistance cells were the first topic Lector wished to discuss. "Dlano, we are not in any position to start any kind of overt action against our aggressors. It is my opinion that we wait for some time before we try to form a united group of resistance fighters. The Drezil are so busy trying to mount their next planetary invasion that they will not have time to monitor our activities. We can use this time to fortify our position and plan our attack. Hawnl has assured me that our planet is safe as long as we do not try to expel them from this part of the galaxy."

Dlano looked at Lector for a moment, trying to decipher his intent in launching into this support for an entirely new direction. "Lector, when and how did you get access to Hawnl? My opinion was that our unwritten rule stated that we never contact him nor discuss any subject that was associated with their occupation. It appears that you have some privileged access to the Drezil that you have never divulged to any of us."

Dlano grabbed Lector by the arm and spun him around to face him. Peering directly into his eyes, Dlano tried to figure out if he was lying.

"Am I to assume that you are trying to broker your own agenda with Hawnl? If that is the case, I can only assume that you have had a long and fruitful association with him. It is now clear that our inability to carry out any divisive plans to thwart their continued occupation of this world was revealed to Hawnl by you before we had a chance to put them into action.

Lector rose and approached Dlano with his right arm raised as if to physically attack him. "All right, Dlano, so you now know that I have not been entirely honest with you. I was only trying to gain Hawnl's trust so I could pry the information we need from him. I had no intent of betraying you."

Dlano was not convinced. "From this point on, you will be ostracized from the resistance groups and branded a traitor to your people. I would only hope that our brethren will not ask for your life because of what you have done. Your betrayal will never be forgotten nor forgiven."

Dlano felt as though he had just been hit with a physical blow. His friend had betrayed not only him but the people he represented. Without further thought, he made his way back to Atina's residence.

"Ahh," he said, "I see you and Durell are preparing for the upcoming flight across the cosmos."

I looked up from the charts I was pouring over. "Dlano, hello."

"I am ashamed to report that my faith in Lector was not warranted," Dlano said. "He has betrayed our confidence, and my ability to get the information we need from Hawnl has just evaporated. We will need to find some other way to get the star charts we need."

My senses were warning me that I needed to be cautious about putting any faith in what Dlano was saying. *I still think there is something fishy about Dlano and his keen interest in what we are planning,* I thought.

Dlano continued to try to gain information from us, saying, "The only path we are certain will lead to another galaxy is the one that Durell took to get here. So it appears that our first destination must be Earth. If we can find another individual who can supply the information, it may be on Earth."

Atina was beginning to have the same questions about her father as I had. "Father," she said, "Are you trying to tell us that information concerning our plans has been leaked to the Drezil?"

Knowing that he was coming under the scrutiny of both Atina and I, Dlano tried to salvage the trust he was losing from us both.

"I am still shaken by all of this but hope you two can help me deal with Lector's actions. Any damage he might have done was totally his own doing. Although he most likely deserves to pay the ultimate penalty, his death would surely trigger an investigation by the Drezil. We must avoid any inquiries at all costs."

I knew a stall tactic when I saw one. It was obvious to me that Dlano was not only hiding something but wanted to get as much information from us as possible. *Let's just see where he wants to take this but not give him any information about our plans,* I thought.

Dlano continued, "As it is, I would not be surprised if they decided to search this ship because it was recently out of their view. Hopefully, you can conceal your technology during any search which they might undertake. If you wish to confide in me concerning any of your plans, I am at your service. Durell, both you and Atina need to take the lead on any further actions which need to be taken to bring about a full revolution. I feel compromised and have a feeling that Lector will feed me to the Drezil for what I know about his association with Hawnl. You must leave this planet as soon as you can. I'll try to prop up the resistance until you feel it is time to act."

Chapter 24

Hawnl knew something was afoot. His partnership with the rebel, Lector, had proven to be quite rewarding. Bordeth was so pleased with this coalition that he had given Hawnl many additional rewards in the form of access to the elite female population of his world. He could only marvel that Hawnl could have stumbled on this invaluable resource. He instructed Hawnl to send his contact back into the resistance fold and find out what was stirring his curiosity. He was sure that their hold on these inferior beings was so secure that he need not become too concerned with this small distraction. His focus had to be on the next stepping-stone which the Drezil needed to expand farther outward. Earth was in his sights, and he was now ready to send his fleet to bring the planet under his banner.

Very quickly, he would complete this takeover and reduce the population of this green world to only 2 percent of its current level. That was all the caretakers he needed to secure the planet and begin the terraforming process. So it was with little thought that he dismissed the warnings from Habordiz and allowed Hawnl to handle the entire situation. No worse decision was ever made since the Drezil had begun their rampage through the universe. Not only was Hawnl incapable of carrying out his current duties, his lies about the strength of the resistance on Habordiz lulled Bordeth into a sense of security that did not exist. Could Hawnl be the weak link in the chain of command of the Drezil?

I was studying the engine that had powered my craft to this galaxy. The decision had been made to return to Earth because that was the only destination for which we had the proper coordinates.

Knowing that Earth was on the Drezil's hit lit, I was extremely anxious to get back to my home world. As I pondered the possible outcomes of this trip, Atina leaned close into me and whispered, "You have every right to call this entire operation off when we arrive at your planet. It is your home. However, let me assure you that the Drezil are currently bringing their fleet to readiness and are about to move on your world. Once they arrive, they will annihilate the major portion of your people and leave only a skeleton group to serve them as slaves. I don't wish to know what you are about to do, but I need to know if I am going to have to go on without you."

I had considered the consequences of leaving this venture when we reached Earth but had discarded that idea almost immediately. As Atina leaned over to inspect my progress with the engine, I caught a whiff of her scent. I marveled at how my senses were heightened and that I was acutely aware of her presence. During my healing period and the subsequent trips we had been forced to take together, I had grown to respect her talents not only as a superb pilot but as a representative of her species. Although I had not allowed myself to dwell on how I was attracted to her, it was now clear to me that I was beginning to feel more than a passing infatuation for this strong woman.

My mind went back to the conversation we had with the entity on Alpha2. It was as though it had assumed that Atina and I were connected in some way. What had I missed that indicated that we had a future together? Surprisingly, a new thought jumped into my mind. *Could the joining of our different DNA hold the key to the start of a new species?* Where this thought came from, I could not determine, but it was as though my mind had been invaded by some outside entity. There had been something vaguely familiar about the entity we had met. How could it have known so much about us both and our worlds and the technology we would need to defeat the Drezil? His reference to "your future is our past" was intriguing. I could only wonder how all of this was intertwined in the relationship I had with Atina.

While I mulled over the consequences of a Drezil invasion of Earth, I was forced to consider my role in the fight to protect Earth and all its inhabitants from the Drezil scourge. The stealth capabil-

UNIVERSAL EXTINCTION

ities of the Pentemor would keep us hidden but not provide any offensive weapons which could repel the invaders. I understood the military forces on the Earth had some extremely powerful weapons, but I could not think of any way Atina and I could gain access to them. The Earth's defensive capabilities would be overwhelmed almost immediately by the superior offensive firepower that the Drezil would employ. In addition, their ability to map the DNA of all the Earth's inhabitants would allow them to target whomever they wished for one massive blow that would lead to all their deaths. If Atina and I were to have any chance of repelling the Drezil, we would need to intervene before the Drezil had the opportunity to begin their attack. One small ferry ship against the entire Drezil fleet.

Great, I thought. *Nothing like being the underdog. I guess the survival of my entire species is a bit of a challenge for two people, but the entity who sent us on this mission must have an insight that we lack. Hopefully, they are correct in interpreting our ability to control our own destiny.*

The lack of any type of offensive weapons on the Pentemor was concerning to both Atina and me. Without a planned deterrent that could impact the Drezil's ability to carry out their typical invasion scheme, they would have little chance of changing the outcome. I knew in the back of my mind that the tools we were given had more power than was initially visible. Why had Dlano reacted so negatively when he encountered my engine? Was the energy emitted by the device harmful to some species? My observation that the device exhibited some properties which could be characterized as organic might have more validity than I first thought.

The realization that Lector had betrayed them all put a totally different spin on the implementation of their plans. Dlano's position as a respected leader of the resistance was tainted by his association with Lector and might have led to this response to the engine. I was determined to find the truth. I sought out Dlano and requested that he come to the ship and approach the device to see if the same reaction was displayed.

As Dlano entered the hold, the device remained inert, and he did not sense any kind of threat from it. Having provided them with the proof that their group held a traitor in its inner circle and having identified him, Dlano was now viewed by some as a trustworthy member of their coalition. I did not share this opinion. Employing the chain mail to negate the reaction Dlano had experienced was now allowing him to enter and leave the influence of the engine without any distress. His assignment was to ensure that Hawnl did not get suspicious about any of the strange things which were now occurring. When the Pentemor went stealthy and faked her crash into the asteroid, Dlano needed to assure Hawnl that the ship and all aboard had been destroyed. Once he had accomplished this, his only job was to wait for the ship to return, hopefully with good news of a Drezil defeat.

Atina set the launch sequence in motion, and I felt a tinge of fear about our upcoming voyage. My last experience with interstellar travel had not gone all that well, and I was not ready for a reoccurrence of the pain that had racked my body as the acceleration of my sphere built. The method we had devised to control the engine's power seemed to function well, but one could never know how it would perform once we initiated the reaction.

The Pentemor rose from its berth, and Atina skillfully set its course for Alpha2. The slight course deviation in her initial setting would not warrant any scrutiny from the Drezil. The course to Alpha2 had always taken them close to the asteroid, so it appeared to be appropriate for this trip. I released my restraints and slowly worked my way down to the main engine room. The sound of the engines had diminished as we rose above the planet's atmosphere but was still deafening when I approached the hatch. I was preparing to move my engine down the passageway to one that would begin the inter-engine reaction.

My headset crackled as it came to life with Atina's query: "Are you ready to begin to move your engine into place? We are only a few minutes from our release of the fuel tank to simulate our impact with the asteroid. This all has to be timed perfectly if we are to fool the Drezil into thinking we did not survive the collision."

"All is ready," I responded. "Just let me know when I need to move my device into the engine room."

UNIVERSAL EXTINCTION

Atina disconnected the computer auto control system and began to manually make the ship drift toward the asteroid. As the small gravity of the asteroid began to grip the Pentemor, she armed the fuel tank's ejection system. A smothering sense of fear washed over her as she thought of the enormity of what they were about to attempt. Our lives could end in an instant if the entire sequence of events required for this operation did not go off without a hitch.

"My life and that of Durell's are within a hair's breadth of ending. Although I am willing to pay the ultimate price, I'm not all that eager to do so. Hopefully, this plan will take us beyond this galaxy and into the next," she said aloud.

As the Pentemor approached the asteroid, she manually turned the ship so the aft section was pointing toward the surface. With that, she pulled the lever that released the external fuel tank, which easily detached and was pulled toward its impact point by the slingshot maneuver she had performed. She then set the ship on a course which would bring us to the opposite side of the asteroid, shielding us from detection.

"Durell," she said, "initiate the reaction."

I pushed the device toward the main engines. As it rolled down the overhead rail to which it was secured, I felt the unmistakable increase in the acceleration of the Pentemor. Atina had maneuvered the ship to point outward, keeping in the shadow of the asteroid. The ship's engines reached their maximum power output, with the glow emitted from my engine increasing in intensity. The sound it produced was beginning to change in pitch.

Both Atina and I began to feel the effects of the increase in acceleration, which was becoming less tolerable by the second. The only thought running through Atina's mind was *Is this ship capable of enduring these forces?* Her view screen suddenly filled with a vast array of new images, each leaving a visible streak of light which seemed to originate from a point directly ahead of them. Suddenly, the acceleration forces we had felt on our bodies disappeared.

I had moved the device so close to the main engines that the two were now acting as one, with the maximum thrust of the main engines overpowered by whatever force was being emitted from my

133

device. The entire space around me began to expand outward, and I found the hull of the ship was becoming transparent.

Any nearer to the engines and we'll most likely suffer the same consequences as when I first used this engine, I thought. I secured the device to the upper rail and turned to find my way back to the cockpit. What I saw, however, was a clear view of the universe through the now transparent walls of the ship, which made it impossible to find my way back to Atina.

The intercom was still functional, so I asked, "Atina, do you see the same thing that I do? It is though I am moving through the universe without a vessel. I cannot find my way back up to the cockpit, but I am not in any kind of distress. Do you think it wise for me to move the device back away from the main engines to reduce our speed?"

Atina was experiencing the same anomaly but was totally intrigued by the entire experience. "Durell, we do not know how or when the proper time will come to shut down the reaction, but I think the trajectory we set before initiating the engine's thrust will eventually take us to your solar system. If you can close your eyes and try to remember where the passage is to the cockpit, we might be able to solve this problem."

I did as she suggested. I could feel the metallic walls of the corridor and found my way to the ladder which led to the upper sections of the ship. Carefully, I climbed upward and entered the cockpit where Atina was seated. Without any kind of visual reference points, both Atina and I became nauseous. We were, for all practical purposes, suspended in the middle of the universe without any visible clues to our location. I noticed that the point from which the streaming light was originating was beginning to broaden. I was beginning to make out clusters of stars and spiraling galaxies forming on the sides of our main track.

Having no real astronomical knowledge, I was still able to identify each cluster by its Earth-given name. A quiet voice in my mind seemed to whisper the information to me, including a real sense of where we were heading. Any fear I had experienced throughout this

UNIVERSAL EXTINCTION

entire trip washed away, and I was left with the undeniable sense that we were not in the same dimension that our worlds shared.

When was I to stop the reaction? If our progress had been at sub-light speed, the trip to my solar system would have taken many thousands of years. Here we were, however, hurtling through time and space as though we had entered a dimensional vortex which connected our two galaxies. The thought *Reduce your speed* entered my mind. After again closing my eyes, I deftly moved back to the engine room and began to maneuver my device back away from the main engines. As the distance increased, the transparency of the metallic walls of the ship began to ebb.

I could feel the ship beginning to slow. My intercom crackled. "Durell, I can see stars beginning to materialize around us. There is a yellow sun to our left and several large planets which seem to be anchored around it. Our speed is decreasing, but we are still travelling at a high rate. If your planet is within this solar system, we need to discern its location and modify our flight to intersect its orbit."

Chapter 25

The International Space Station

The space station's crew went about their daily tasks with no real thought. Their individual assignments had become so routine that they performed them with mindless familiarity. The sun's rays flashed across the clear ports of the habitat, warming the interior for an instant. As the station rotated on its own axis to create their artificial gravity, each porthole would alternately face the Earth, then the sun, then the blackness of space. The commander of the station, Robert Allen, was a Naval captain whose rank was earned by excellence from the time he was an enlisted man. He was large in stature with a muscular build and graying hair. His spotless uniform showed his pride in his service to the country. His authority was absolute aboard this station. As their station rounded the dark side of the Earth, they began to take snapshots of the moon and beyond with their digital cameras. Each shot covered a small portion of the space around the moon, and they were intended to be used to map the next venture which NASA was about to undertake.

Travel to Mars and beyond had been the dream of all of NASA, and these snapshots would reveal any objects which might derail the mission. Having set the cameras to their auto capture mode, the crew just had to wait until the process was completed and then review the results of the captures. After the cameras signaled that their task was completed, the images were transferred to the computer for review. As each image flashed up on the monitor, the crew cataloged them for storage in the computer's memory. The review of the images by

136

UNIVERSAL EXTINCTION

Captain Allen showed a strange object appearing for a single frame, just outside the crust of the moon. Reversing the sequence, he focused on the frame which held the image.

It appeared to be a silver object which had the shape of a cylindrical mass that was immense in size. He could only guess what they had sighted but moved to reorient the cameras back to the location which had produced the frame. To the naked eye, no object could be seen, but the magnification of the cameras might reveal another image of the object. Captain Allen opened the camera lens so he could have a real-time image of that area of space. Moving the focus point of the camera across the area that had held the object, he found nothing to raise his suspicions. Whatever had been captured in the image was no longer visible and might have been a fault in the device's software.

Whatever the case, he decided to just monitor the upcoming captures for a reappearance of the object. Stowing the camera in its case, he suddenly felt a strange tingling which enveloped his entire body. "What the hell," he called. "Did any of you feel that?"

Several of his crew admitted that they, too, had felt something but could not accurately define what it was. As quickly as the sensation had started, it stopped. During the period that he felt the tingling, he noted that several of his crew seemed to be totally oblivious both of their surroundings and of his presence. Might this be somehow connected to the object he had found on the one frame?

The Pentemor

Our speed continued to decrease as Atina and I began to study the visible planets. The long-range sensors on the ship indicated that the larger planets were located some distance from the central sun, but several smaller planets were closer to the center of this system. I immediately recognized the large planet surrounded by a set of rings as Saturn. In addition, I had further assurance of the identity of this solar system by the discovery of a huge planet which had a large eye-shaped bruise on its surface as Jupiter.

"Home!" I peered intently toward the sun and located a small green sphere which I identified as my own Earth. With a shaking finger, I directed Atina's attention to this planet, Earth, and we began to plot a course which would take us into its orbit. Our speed was finally ebbing to the point where the ship could be maneuvered quite easily. All control which had been lost during our transit to this system was restored, and Atina began to expertly redirect the ship toward the green planet. We were about to meet our enemy and determine the Drezil's plan and timeline for the invasion of the Earth. My only hope was that we could intervene before the mass extinction of Earth's population was to begin.

The DNA cataloging had begun. Bordeth had ordered the fleet to readiness so that after the DNA mapping was completed, they could move forward with the occupation of this planet. The entire crew of the scout ship was well versed in this process and appeared to have little difficulty in the execution of their duties. Their only concern was of a space station orbiting the planet which had momentarily oriented itself toward their location beside a satellite. Their probe of this station had revealed only three individuals aboard. With their DNA mapped, the Drezil moved on to sweep the planet with their detection devices. Without warning, a brilliant flash of light came from the outer reaches of the system. The DNA mapping process was of primary importance to the crew, so this bright flash of light did not warrant any of their attention. This lack of any curiosity would come back to haunt the Drezil soon.

I left the berth area and joined Atina on the flight deck. I had tried to get some sleep but was unsuccessful. Rubbing my burning eyes, I began to assess our current situation. We were approaching Earth, so I reminded Atina, "Remember, this ship might be invisible to electronic detection devices but can be seen with the naked eye. Let's be extremely careful that we only approach from the dark side. That way, we will only appear as a shadow." *The UFO conspiracy believers will have a ball with this.*

Atina waved her hand toward the forward scanner. It was pointed toward the Earth, but it also included an image of the Earth's

UNIVERSAL EXTINCTION

satellite, the Moon. Viewing it from the dark side, I could distinctly see the shadow of a ship in the darkness.

"That is definitely a Drezil scout ship," Atina said. "They are currently cataloging the DNA of all the people on your planet. The process is lengthy, so we might have some time to decide what we are to do. Is there any possibility that your species has any offensive technology we could employ to beat back the upcoming invasion?"

I remembered the suspicions which permeated the different cultures on my planet and the wars that had been fought to maintain each country's way of life. The religious conflicts which had marked the Earth's history were not yet over, and they did not appear to learn from any past mistakes. I was doubtful that any of the leaders of any of the Earth's factions would believe that the attack that was coming would directly affect them. This mistrust could lead to the downfall of all humanity on Earth. I felt a strange detachment from those who populated my home world, as though I was no longer a member of their species but had evolved into someone else. Could two people with one ship intervene with enough force to change the tide of this upcoming invasion? *You're damn right, we can!*

Chapter 26

The ISS1 (International Space Station 1) rounded the Earth onto the dark side, shielded from the sun, and the proximity alarms began to chirp slowly. The crew scanned their instruments but found no indication that there was anything close to them.

Captain Allen was standing behind the crew member who was monitoring the instruments. "Is there any indication anywhere that we are not alone out here? The instruments seem to indicate that something is closing in on our location. Have we suffered a failure in the sensors?" He found himself drawn to the portal which was facing away from the Earth. Shocked by what he saw, he bolted to the main instrument panel to verify his observation. Again, nothing showed up. Moving back to the portal, he verified that, indeed, a ship was hovering just off the port side of the station.

Captain Allen squinted his eyes to better focus on the ship hovering next to the station. Although they were on the dark side of the Earth, a bright aura surrounded the invader, making it hard to stare at it for any length of time. It was of a strange configuration, and Captain Allen ordered all crew members to verify that the ship was next to them.

The ship was shaped like a large football with a bridge visible on the upper side. What appeared to be glass or some sort of transparent material encapsulated the upper side. The craft was too distant to tell if any entities were in the control section. Captain Allen instructed his crew, "Contact the Cape and send them video of what is occurring."

They reported back and informed him, "Sorry, Captain, but all communication with NASA has ceased. Whatever this craft is, it's interfering with not only our communications but also with every electronic and computer system aboard this station. What are your orders, Captain?"

Not having a real sense of all that was happening nor the extent of the influence the other craft was having on them, the captain said, "Let's just wait until we are sure of our situation. Maybe that other ship will help us determine our next move."

Pentemor

Atina and I had not expected to encounter any other ships as we entered orbit around Earth on the dark side. Atina maneuvered our ship into a geosynchronous orbit and was forced to make some radical course changes to prevent a collision with the other ship. I immediately recognized the vessel as the NASA space station which was built in orbit several years ago.

"I think we may have just found our only opportunity to connect with my people and inform them of the danger they are in," I said. "If we can establish some kind of communication with the station, we might be able to sound an alarm and forewarn them of the Drezil ship that is currently scanning Earth." From my experiences in the Navy, I knew that the emergency distress channels were on frequencies 121.5 MHz and 243 MHz. Although the Pentemor did not have a UHF or VHF transceiver, my sphere did. I climbed back to my ship and opened the entry hatch.

I found the radio attached to the bulkhead above my pilot's seat. The system was battery powered, and I knew that it would not have enough power to penetrate the Pentemor hull from inside my own ship, so I decided to remove it and take it up to Atina on the flight deck of the Pentemor. I released the fasteners and removed the radio from its mount. Having secured the transceiver, I moved back to the cockpit.

"Atina," I said. "Is there any way we can attach this unit to your ship's antenna so we can communicate with the space station?"

Atina rose from the captain's chair and walked hesitantly toward me. Her thoughts were beginning to reveal her innermost feelings about me. *Why am I so nervous whenever I am around this man?* But she

141

shook them off and said, "I'm sure we can interface it quite easily with my systems." With that, she took the radio from me and stripped the antenna wires. Then she unplugged the antenna connection from her own system and stripped the wiring as she had with my radio. Twisting the two wires together, she stepped back and admired her handiwork.

"Durell," she said, "try your system and see if we get any reaction from this space station." I set the frequency on my radio to 121.5 MHz and depressed the microphone button.

"This is the starship Pentemor calling the international space station which is off to our left. I am Dr. Durell Dykstra, and I have just returned from an interstellar flight which took me to another galaxy. You and all of Earth are in great danger from a species of invaders known as the Drezil. They currently have a scout ship in orbit around the moon which is scanning the entire Earth and mapping every person's DNA for reasons I will not go into now. Just know that if you do not reply, there will be nothing we can do to help either you or the other inhabitants of the Earth. Please reply on this frequency."

It suddenly dawned on me that I might be speaking in a language that the inhabitants of the station could not understand. "Atina," I asked. "Did you understand what I was saying?"

"No, Durell, you were speaking a language which was totally foreign to me. I think you are speaking in the language of your home planet. They would not be able to understand you if you spoke in the language I imbedded in your brain."

The speaker on my radio crackled to life. "Whoever you are, we are a peaceful vessel with no offensive capability. We are unable to contact our superiors because our communications seem to be malfunctioning. I am Captain Allen, commander of this station. I will need some time to assess what you have said and decide what action to take."

I replied, "You have little time to act on what we have shared with you. The Drezil have already cataloged and mapped this planet's population and will soon start eliminating those who they do not need. Your only course is to let us help. If we act soon, there may be a chance to avoid what will surely be a catastrophic event. We will back away from you so your communications will be restored with

UNIVERSAL EXTINCTION

your superiors. Let me urge you to act quickly. We do not know for sure how to battle those who are about to attack, but there is a good possibility that our combined knowledge might lead to a defense of some sort. Atina, move us back to a higher orbit so they can alert their commanders." The Pentemor moved slowly to a higher orbit away from the space station.

The International Space Station

Captain Allen keyed his communication system and attempted to contact Houston. "Houston, this is ISS1. Request an encoded channel with direct communications with director Charles Bolton. Please advise when this secure channel has been established. Do not ask for clarification as this is a level one top secret request which requires immediate attention."

Upon receipt of the communication request by NASA, an immediate implementation of precast plan was put into place which connected ISS1 to Charles Bolton's secure private line. Picking up the line, Charles asked, "What the hell is so important that you have to use this line, Captain?"

Captain Allen suddenly became really pissed. He needed all the support he could get, and here Bolton was concerned about using this damn line.

"I'm not in any mood to worry about any of these petty issues. Just listen to me and go to the situation room right now." Captain Allen took a deep breath and shook his head as though he was trying the clear his senses, "Get in touch with every major government and military player you feel is trustworthy and call us back as soon as you can. Although you may find this hard to believe, we have been contacted by aliens who insist that we are about to be attacked. This is not a figment of our imagination, and I will provide you with the video which documents the arrival of a craft not of this world."

MICHAEL BRADLEY

Charles Bolton

"I put you in charge of that station because I trusted in your judgment and level-headed approach in a crisis, so I will follow your suggestions," Charles said. "You know it will take a while to bring this group together, so please be patient. In the meantime, I am going to the situation room so we can investigate this further."

Making his way to the privacy of the situation room, Charles tried to digest the enormity of what had just occurred. He opened the small wall safe which held the contact information for the trusted few who he would contact to attend this emergency meeting. His assistant, Margaret Skinner, arrived shortly after he opened the safe.

"Margaret, I have already set up a group call to the individuals listed here for just such an event. Please implement the call procedures and insist that all those listed make great haste in coming to this meeting. Impress on them that this will be the most important meeting of their lives, and their immediate attendance is required."

With that, he made the one call that was mandatory to the president of the United States, Andrew Nelson. "Mr. President, from what I have just been told by the crew of ISS1, we have just been contacted by an alien spaceship which is currently orbiting a few miles from the station. I have called the emergency response team together for a meeting here and expect them to arrive within minutes."

President Nelson had juggled many crises in his time as president of the United States, but this had all the signs of becoming one of the most important calls he had ever taken. He had to trust that whatever was occurring was totally factual.

"The initial message from the alien ship was that the earth was about to be attacked, so it is imperative that we assess the communication in terms of its validity and author some sort of reply. Your input, sir, is essential in this process so we can accurately convey our position in this matter. With your permission, Captain Allen said we will initiate communication directly with the alien craft and try to discern what action we should take."

The president replied, "Proceed in contacting the craft, and get all the information you can on the truth of their statements, their

144

origin, and what they expect from us. Keep me informed of all the facts which come out of your communication with them. I will bring together my emergency response team and begin to assess the situation from this end. Good luck, Charles. I think we are all going to need it."

Chapter 27

Following the arrival of the team members, Charles began to study his possible approaches to this emerging problem. It appeared to him that the situation required an immediate response. Captain Allen had emphasized that the aliens impressed on him the need for immediate action concerning the impending attack, or the outcome would not be favorable to the Earth's population. The team took their seats around the oval table. It gave them all a view of the set of screens which could be focused on any part of the ISS1's interior and exterior.

Having successfully opened a radio link to ISS1, Charles said, "Captain Allen, I am with the crisis intervention group. We would like to see if you can point one of your exterior cameras in the direction of the alien craft you have encountered."

The situation room had filled with representatives from many factions and governments. They were all staring at the large screen which filled the north wall of the room. The control panel began to light up with multicolored lights pulsating in a rhythmic pattern.

Charles had moved to a position to the side of the large main screen. Following what he felt was an appropriate protocol, he said, "We need to see the ship so we can get a real-time picture of what we are up against. In addition, can you reestablish communication with that ship? As soon as we determine the level of the threat presented to us, we will need to communicate directly with them. Are there any questions you have for this group?"

"We have our hands full up here," Captain Allen said. "So we will leave the decision-making chores to you. We are currently swinging our cameras into position so you can view what we see. The craft

146

has moved some distance from us so we could communicate with you. You will only see a telescopic image of the craft which may be blurred due to the distance. When we move closer, all communication will be lost, so we need to find a way to deal with that issue. You should now be able to see the ship, but we have yet to establish a communication link with them."

The screens in the situation room lit up with fuzzy images of the alien ship. It was long and rather large through the center section. The images were not clear enough to identify much about the ship, but it was definite proof that a ship of some sort was in orbit around the Earth.

Charles said, "You would think that with all the advanced technology we have that we could get a clear picture of this ship. Is there any other way we can get a good look at this thing?"

"Charles," Captain Allen said, "we have some shots of the craft which we took when it first appeared next to us. We'll send those down on the secure channel. It will give much greater detail of the ship."

The group watched the screens intently as a clear image of the alien ship came into view. It was extremely large compared to NASA's orbital craft. It had a cockpit on the end which appeared to be the top with a fuselage that was very broad in the center but tapered to a blunt end where it was assumed that the engines would be. What appeared to be the cockpit had clear transparent openings which appeared to give the occupants of the craft a 360-degree view of their surroundings.

Two figures could be seen through the window, but it was not possible to determine their shapes or size. A collective gasp filled the room as though everyone had taken a deep breath. It appeared that whatever they were viewing was unfamiliar to them all. They stood transfixed by the images as the communication link to ISS1 crackled into life, this time with the undeniable change in the voice on the other end.

"We have established communications with the ship, and the voice you hear is that of one of the occupants of the ship," Captain

Allen said. "We will let you take the lead on this from this point on. The entity on the other end is named Durell. He speaks English."

"Alien craft, can you hear me?" Captain Allen asked.

I translated the message for Atina and responded, "We hear you. Have you contacted your superiors? And if so, what are your intentions?"

A new voice came over the radio link. "To the ship in orbit around the Earth, I am Charles Bolton, and I have been designated by our president to be the conduit between our peoples. What is the purpose of your visit to Earth?"

I was shocked. I knew who Charles Bolton was and his position with NASA. I assumed that the president was monitoring this communication and was ready to listen to me. "I am not an alien but a citizen of the United States. Without going into the details of my presence on this ship, I will tell you that we are here as a peaceful emissary of the planet Habordiz, which lies many light-years away from Earth. The message we bring is a warning."

I was desperately trying to find the words which would convey the seriousness of this situation. I shook my head and stared at Atina, begging for some assistance. She offered none, so I forged ahead with the conversation.

"A species known as the Drezil have already conquered and enslaved many worlds across the universe. Their next target is the Earth. They have an ability to read and catalog every inhabitant's DNA. With that information, they can selectively annihilate anyone they wish. They currently have a scout ship in orbit around the moon and are using it to shield their presence."

Charles found it difficult to follow my description of what had occurred and what was about to occur. "I don't know about the rest of you, but I am not willing to believe anything this guy says. We need to plan for a strike on his vessel."

I had warned Atina that these representatives would most likely not believe what we were telling them and view us as enemies. "They have already begun their DNA sweeps," I continued. "If you have any reports that include people feeling strange vibrations which cannot be explained, it is a signature of their DNA probes. If you do not

UNIVERSAL EXTINCTION

act swiftly, I predict that the Earth's population will be reduced significantly with the current 7.4 billion inhabitants reduced to around four million.

I was beginning to impress myself with my ability to quickly put the crisis in a form that they could understand.

"Let me assure you that this is not a time to question the validity of my prediction. Whatever you do, do it quickly. Your time is coming to an end if you don't act now. We will assist in any way that we can, but we are powerless to stop the Drezil without your assistance. And even then, we cannot assure you that they will not prevail."

As the enormity of what they had just learned began to sink in, the entire response team found it difficult to believe all that they had heard. Charles had been pacing the room in slow circles since the crisis had begun. "Durell, how are we to believe what you have just told us without some kind of verification?"

Durell knew that those in charge would require proof that what he was saying was true. He could see no conceivable way to prove his claims, so he decided to bluff his way through. "If you don't act on what I am telling you, you will all die. Make no mistake, the Drezil are coming, and you need to prepare."

Charles responded, "If we are to unite with you for our common protection, we need more than your word that this situation could lead to the demise of most of the inhabitants of this planet. We need time to launch a probe to determine if a ship is hidden behind the moon."

I was getting very suspicious that Charles and his associates were stalling for some reason. "Charles, is there something you would like to tell us? Remember, I am from Earth and have a pretty good idea what you guys are planning. You keep this plan of yours moving ahead, and I will bet my last dollar you will have lost any chance of dodging your fate. It is almost too late already, so you had better get off your pelican asses and do something."

Charles was taken back by the swiftness with which I had seen through their plans. "Without that verification, we could never convince any of our allies that a real danger exists. Is there any other way you could provide proof of the validity of what you have told

149

us? In addition to the lack of positive proof that we are about to be attacked, there is still some hesitation on this group's part in believing that you are of this Earth and that you and your ship are not the real threat. Currently, the government is investigating your claim that you are a citizen of the United States. Much more has to be settled before we can put together any kind of action plan."

Charles finished speaking, only to have a message passed to him from his assistant. "The Pentagon has just reported the sighting of large numbers of alien ships closing on Earth from somewhere beyond the moon. All nations have been alerted of this sighting, and we are preparing to defend ourselves if that becomes necessary. Continue your conversation with the alien ship you are in communication with, and try to assess where they stand in this current environment."

It appeared that what I was trying to convey to NASA was about to come to fruition. The attack was about to begin, and the population of Earth was going to be reduced significantly. Atina and I could now only watch as the carnage began. The Drezil had arrived.

*****

The White House had been put on lockdown at the first sign of alien contact. From his desk in the oval office, President Nelson called his crisis team into session. He began to assess the situation with his best advisors who were at his side from the beginning. It was apparent that something was in the wind, but not having verifiable information, he found it hard to perform any kind of analysis which made sense.

"Gentlemen," he began, "if there is any truth to the information which has been provided by the occupants of the alien ship, we are in dire straits. In my opinion, we would be foolish to ignore the warning they have given us."

They did not have any additional information which would shed light on the situation, so the discussion changed to the identity of the individual who was reporting the threat to Earth. "The principal source of the information was an entity who calls himself Durell Dykstra and who insists that he is a citizen of the United States."

UNIVERSAL EXTINCTION

The president's chief advisor, Benjamin Darring, rushed into the office with his report. "In the past hour, we have verified that there is, indeed, a person of that name who has served in the Navy and lives in Idaho. We have attempted to contact him but have been unsuccessful. It appears that he went missing several months ago and has not been heard from since. It would lend some credibility to this information if one of the occupants of the alien ship was this Durell. Any suggestions about how we should proceed?"

The president pointed to each of the attendees individually. "Do you have anything to add to this discussion? If not, please listen carefully to all of those present so you can help decide what our next move should be."

Each member was polled individually, but no suggestions on how to proceed were given. Having called on the final member of the team, the president said, "It appears that we do not have any real consensus on what action we should take. So this team will continue discussing the situation until we can come up with some plan which might head us in the right direction."

The president had just finished giving his orders when the vice president burst into the room unannounced. "Mr. President, a large formation of ships is approaching the Earth from somewhere beyond the moon. Their speed is decreasing, and it appears that they intend to take up orbits around the Earth. It is imperative that you board Air Force One and take up a defensive posture until the military determines what threat we are facing. Your chopper is awaiting your arrival for transport to the airfield."

Benjamin Darring separated himself from the rest of the group and grabbed the president's shoulder. "We have to leave right now. Whatever is happening, we need to protect you!"

The president was escorted out of the meeting by his security and rushed to the Marine1 helicopter. All other members of the crisis team boarded additional helicopters to meet again aboard Air Force One. The situation was going from bad to worse very quickly, and they realized that the warning they had been given might have come too late.

*****

During the time the advisory group was haggling over what they were to recommend to the president, Atina and I were impatiently waiting for them to do something, anything. We both knew that time had run out for the Earth and that its inhabitants were about to suffer because of the inaction of their leaders. I sat next to her with the radio sitting between us. All we could hear was the crackling of the empty air around us. Even with the immense pressure we were both under, I could not help but feel the same rush that always seemed to accompany any contact I had with her.

Charles was still trying to absorb all that was happening. Although he was not yet convinced about the authenticity of all that he had been told, he had to decide immediately. Was he to trust this Durell person or wait until something developed?

The communication link with us was still intact, so Charles spoke hesitantly, saying, "Our military has sighted a large formation of what appears to be spaceships closing on the Earth from somewhere beyond our moon. Although we do not know their intentions, I assume that these are the invaders you have warned us about. We are totally in the dark concerning their strength, abilities, and agenda, so we would like to beg you for any information you might have that would help us in the case that they intend to do us harm."

I shrugged and looked at Atina, hoping she could suggest some easy way to break the bad news. She just turned her back on me and stared out of the portal. We could both see the enemy ships making their way toward the Earth.

I had not really expected any suggestions from her that would divert what was about to happen. "I'm afraid to tell you that your time has run out, Charles. The Drezil have arrived, and Earth is about to come under a vicious attack that will kill much of the population. It will not be a bloodless end. No great amount of fanfare will accompany the end. No bombs, no bullets, no nuclear devices, just a silent end to those who have already been targeted, followed by a mass attack by the Drezil ships and their attack fighters."

I was finding it increasingly difficult to keep telling these people that they were all about to die. However, lacking any sense that Atina was going to assist me, and knowing that she could not speak

UNIVERSAL EXTINCTION

the Earthlings language, I knew it was up to me to at least try to intervene. To prepare Charles for what was coming, I said, "Those marked for extinction will just go to sleep and never awaken. The only sign of their deaths will be the horrific stench that will envelope all of them as they decay back to dust. The Drezil will intervene with their powerful weapons and burn the planet's structures and the dead in one sweeping action."

Charles was now beginning to believe that the Earth was coming under attack. The delay caused by the president's advisory committee had just been too much to allow for any resistance plans to be developed. The Drezil had no need for any of the Earth's bounty and did not want to be exposed to the decay that would follow their invasion.

Not being able to understand the language of the communication, all Atina could do was watch my facial expression for clues to what was being discussed. The crackling of the poor communication link caused her some concern, but she assumed that I could understand what was being said. *How in the hell am I supposed to assist in this situation if I can't even understand their language?*

I was no longer going to try to ease into the conversation which I knew must take place. "I am sorry we did not arrive in time to help you to defend against the invaders, but we are not sure ourselves how to stop their galactic rampage." I paused to collect my thoughts and drew a deep breath before continuing, "I possess a unique DNA which allows me to be undetectable by their probes, and we can only hope that many more individuals on Earth also possess this same DNA strain. For now, all we can do is watch and try to pick up the pieces when the Drezil have finished their handiwork. Good luck. I hope you will be spared and that we can plan a response sometime in the future."

Chapter 28

The scout ship that had cataloged and studied the inhabitants of this planet moved from behind the moon to a point about halfway between the two bodies. They had studied the Earth's species and determined who would be spared. The template they had used on previous invasions served them well.

Once the preinvasion spy team had returned to the ship, the information about who was to be spared was passed on to the invasion commanders. The heads of governments were spared, along with a group of support staff. All engineers, technicians, and scientists who were required to maintain the planet's infrastructure had been identified and marked for survival. In total, their script called for a total of about four million lives be spared to serve the Drezil. The scout ship had arrived many years ago and had enough time to carry out its mission of selective survival. The choice had been entirely theirs, and they had programmed their assault to proceed as soon as they were given the signal to start. Bordeth had entrusted the scout duties to his brother, Retil, who he trusted implicitly.

"Retil," Bordeth ordered, "make certain that those we have decided to spare from death include the leaders of every nation, especially the president of the United States. Without his assistance, we will not be able to expedite our occupation of many of the countries we must overrun." Bordeth thought, *Even though he is not inclined to think things through, it is only right to let Retil proceed with the invasion plan because he was the one who spent so much time gathering the required information about the Earthlings. He can now put in motion*

154

UNIVERSAL EXTINCTION

the DNA engine which will spell the end for so many of the planet's population.

Retil surveyed his surroundings. He found the side of the moon not facing the Earth to be barren and uninviting. However, when he manipulated his scout ship to a position that gave him a good view of the Earth, he was almost dumbstruck by its beauty. *I can hardly wait until I become the overlord of this planet. Even though its beauty will be marred by our terraforming, I will still have memories of this day.*

After contacting Retil, Bordeth ordered, "Begin the assault. Make sure that all the humans you have designated for removal are dead and burned and that all those we need for planet maintenance are alive."

Chapter 29

President Nelson and his entire staff boarded Air Force One. His face was ashen, and all those present could sense his deep concern. He paused to wonder if he would ever see the White House again. Having ordered the military to a state of full readiness, he could only hope that the ships approaching Earth would not be totally infallible.

Moving to the section of Air Force One which contained the communication equipment, President Nelson told the communications technician to open a channel to his military leaders. His orders were "At the first sign of any hostile action, blanket those ships with every nuclear weapon we have in our arsenal. Do not allow them to get a foothold anywhere in our country on this planet. All other members of our alliance have been given the same orders." Having given the most important orders of his career, President Nelson went to his airborne office to await the fate of the world.

Retil's orders from Bordeth had been specific. In his arrogance, he could not view the outcome in any other light than his total victory over these Earthlings. His stupidity had wormed its way into the equation. He only saw what was on the surface and did not have the brain power to look beyond what he was told by his DNA engine. Preparing to give the order for the kill, he smiled to himself and thought, *I am going to be the greatest Drezil warrior that has ever lived. My brother will no longer be able to treat me as a slave for his wishes. I will be in position to challenge his authority. A new time is beginning for us, and I will take over as the leader of our empire.* With that, he gave the order to begin the invasion of Earth.

UNIVERSAL EXTINCTION

The proximity indicator aboard the Pentemor sounded the alarm as the Drezil armada approached Earth. Atina and I had tried to warn the inhabitants that this was about to occur, but too much time had been taken by the decision makers in their attempt to verify what they had been told. It was now too late. As the enemy ships approached, the Pentemor slid stealthily behind the planet to avoid detection. It was now impossible to communicate with ISS1, but the need no longer existed.

Atina went to the comm center on the Pentemor and began to sweep the frequencies used by the United States Armed Forces. The radio erupted with military chatter that indicated a massive attack was underway. "All we can do now is wait for the final count on how many of your species have survived. We might then be able to set the remaining inhabitants on the right course to join our fight. I know this may be extremely difficult for you to endure, but we have no choice."

As Atina finished speaking, the communication channels being monitored by the Pentemor exploded with so many transmissions that none could be understood. The common message was "We are all feeling a strange vibration within our bodies. Are we alone?" Following the blur of messages, the radios went strangely silent.

Atina moved the Pentemor farther toward the equator. I scanned the surface of the Earth, and all I could see was a mantel of destruction reaching from horizon to horizon. An acidic smoke was beginning to fill the air, moving upward to meet the Pentemor. I felt on the verge of tears as I watched my planet go up in smoke.

"Atina," I said, "we need to do something, anything, to help my people. Take us around the planet until we are near the British Isles. I need to determine just how far this attack has spread."

The Pentemor turned on its side and accelerated quickly, skimming through the contaminated atmosphere. Following my directions, she pointed the ship at the European continent. We came in from the Atlantic Ocean and could make out London well below, and Atina put us in orbit over the city.

We could see fires beginning to erupt throughout the city and found fewer and fewer communication links remained active. I keyed the microphone to send out a general broadcast and said, "For any of you who can hear me, you are under attack by a race called the Drezil. For those of you who survive this initial attack, you must not give in to any of the demands of your attackers. Do not agree to anything they bring up, no matter how good it appears."

I was beginning to find it difficult to speak because of the emotions I was feeling after seeing so many of my countrymen die. I knew, however, that any help we might provide would be in the form of advice only. Now was not the time to try to start any kind of resistance.

"They are killing most of your species and will leave only a few of you as caretakers of this planet until they are ready for complete occupation. At that time, they will kill the rest of you. Go anywhere you can find shelter from them. They can read your DNA and will be able to detect your location if you do not find a way to hide from them. Go underground, under the sea, inside your mountains, anywhere that might give you some shelter from their probes. Do this now, wait until you are contacted, and pray to God that you survive this onslaught."

The radio chatter increased again, this time to a crescendo. Cries for help flooded the airways. Atina piloted the craft to a position hovering just above the ground and over Washington, DC. I could see fires beginning to spread throughout the city. The Drezil ships began to open fire on the city, targeting anything that moved. Thousands of small fighters strafed the entire city, destroying all that man had built in this center of democracy. All that would be left was a smoldering ruin that was testament to the Drezil's superior power.

Both Atina and I assumed that those spared the carnage would include the president and his staff as all other planetary invasions had excluded this group. Only time would tell if the Drezil followed their typical template. I knew I was in no mental condition to provide Atina with any suggestions on how to proceed.

President Nelson settled into his assigned seat and ordered the aircraft commander to get airborne as soon as possible. Cries for help were coming from all parts of the globe, with each reporting massive deaths from an unknown cause. China seemed to be the country most affected. Their population was falling by the millions each passing minute. The ruling body was still in power, but it appeared that they would not have many people to rule. If there was any group totally unaffected, President Nelson could not determine who that might be. His mind went back to the warning that had come via ISS1 from the alien ship which orbited Earth. *Could they be correct? Was this Durell a citizen of the USA? Could he and his associate bring some action to bear that would stop this killing?*

Having given his orders to the military, President Nelson pushed Ben Darring to the side of the comm room to allow him to access the communication equipment. He asked that a link be opened to allow him to talk directly to the alien ship. Once the comm link had been established, he took the mic and pressed the transmit key. "This is the president of the United States. I do not find it necessary to validate what you have told us. Durell, I am now assuming that you are indeed a citizen of this country and wish to help us deal with this current situation. If there is any advice you can give us in dealing with the invaders, please give it to me now."

Crossing to the forward viewport, I scanned the Earth for the last time, knowing that it would be devastated very soon. Although I was not known to exhibit my emotions easily, I felt the single tear running own my cheek. I knew I could never abandon the Earth or those humans left alive after the attack by the Drezil. "Mr. President, I do not believe that you had the ability to respond to our warning in time to do anything that would have changed what is currently happening. What we advise you to do now is to ride through the worst of this carnage and have a plan to regroup after the Drezil have done their worst. You cannot stop them, not now anyway."

The enormity of what was about to happen had finally impacted me. Pointing to my home planet, I said to Atina, "I am about to experience the same emotional death spiral as you did when your planet suffered the same fate as mine. I have no idea how you survived this trauma, but I will be leaning on you to help me get through this tragedy."

Atina came to my side and took my hand in hers. "I know exactly how you are feeling right now, but you have to move beyond the grief you are feeling and just get killing mad. You now have all the motivation you need to blow these Drezil assholes off the face of the universe. Now let's get going before they can move to their next target."

"President Nelson," I said. "The Drezil will send a single overseer to govern what is left of the Earth's inhabitants after their attack. All the heads of state will be ordered to assist them in keeping order." I could not continue without taking several deep breaths. It was almost becoming too real now that my planet was about to be attacked.

Knowing that what I was telling them was almost unbelievable, I said, "Do as they ask, but do not lose hope because we have a plan which might end the Drezil's occupation of your planet as well as all others in their hijacked empire. The worst is yet to come for you. Watch, learn, pray, and hide. We are going to wait until their fleet has retired, and then I will contact you again. Until then, good luck."

Now what am I supposed to do? President Nelson thought. Slamming his fist on the control console, he tried to vent his fury. "I cannot believe that as strong a country as we are that we can do nothing to defend ourselves. It appears that I will be the last president this country will ever have. God help us."

President Nelson closed the communication link to the Pentemor. Dropping his head into his hands, he began to ponder what his next order should be when he felt Air Force One make a sudden lurch to the left, followed by an extreme dip of the nose. The aircraft began to pick up speed as it plummeted from forty-one thousand feet toward the earth below.

"What in the hell is going on?" President Nelson screamed.

The intercom scratched to life with the steward saying, "Mr. President, the flight crew are all dead. There is no one left up here to—" The intercom went silent. The aircraft continued to plummet downward, rolling on its back as it made its death plunge. There was only silence from the crew. The president began to pray because that was the only thing left for him to do. His family had joined him in their attempt to escape the invader's wrath, and now they all clung together, awaiting the end. The altimeter reached zero with a thun-

UNIVERSAL EXTINCTION

derous explosion, killing all on board which, of course, included the president of the United States.

The Drezil had just made another huge mistake. Retil had trusted the members of his crew who had identified which humans were to be spared. He forgot that a typical Drezil did not have the ability to think beyond the specific orders given. They had entirely forgotten to include the members of the president's flight crew, who had just been killed. "Kill all of those inept crew members who allowed this to happen," he ordered.

The most important country on the Earth now had no leader and very few options of identifying any group that could assist the Drezil in controlling the remaining population. It appeared that this invasion was now ripe for rebellion. A perfect scenario for creating an atmosphere of revenge for the Earthlings. Could this be the beginning of the end for the Drezil?

Chapter 30

The fleet of Drezil ships began to strafe every city and town on the face of the Earth. Although this show of force was not necessary, because of the use of the mapped DNA of the inhabitants, it was ordered by Bordeth to convince the remaining humans that any resistance would be futile. Their many thousands of ships began their assault on the illuminated side of the planet, moving around the sphere as the sun turned night into day.

Their progress on this rampage was swift, completely obliterating all who had been marked for death. They only bypassed those places which Retil had marked as containing humans who were to be spared.

As their onslaught continued, the face of the Earth began to get covered with a thick smoky haze which only enhanced the Drezil's environmental terraforming process. As each country fell, the surviving population could only watch in horror as their family, friends, and neighbors all fell without uttering a single sound. Atina and Durell had predicted that there would be no mercy shown, and none was. The planet was now the property of the Drezil empire.

Bordeth was beside himself. He viewed his campaign screen and knew that Retil had not carried out the battle plan as he had ordered. Opening a comm link to Retil, he said, "What have you done? We have always been successful because we had the help of the planet's leaders. Now you have managed to kill the leader of the most powerful nation on this planet. Your punishment will be severe when you get back here."

UNIVERSAL EXTINCTION

Retil answered, "How could I predict that this leader's aircraft would be flown by inhabitants who were not excluded from death? You are asking too much of me, and I think it might be time for me to take control of this invasion. If you aren't going to lead, I will."

Bordeth was not amused. "Retil, you have now gone too far. You will do what I tell you to do or face the same fate as those on the planet you have just attacked. You are to become the overseer of this planet, but that can change if you continue to oppose me. Do not test my resolve."

If they could quit squabbling and put their power struggle to rest, it did not seem to be too big a hurdle for them to find someone else to take the president's place. Their control always relied on their ability to have absolute control over the defeated planet's inhabitants. His senses told him that Retil was not right for the overseer's position, but as he was family, he decided to allow him to continue as the initial plan had been drawn. Maybe another fatal mistake? The Drezil's total inability to see the whole picture was setting the stage for their demise. In the evolution of the universe's story, the last piece of the puzzle was bringing together a coalition of members of conquered worlds. Then their combined numbers and knowledge would end this black chapter in the life of the universe.

Atina brought the Pentemor within communication range of ISS1 so I could speak to Captain Allen, if he was still alive. "ISS1, this is the Pentemor. Do you have a copy?"

The immediate response was "Yes, Durell, we hear you. Some of the crew of this station have avoided the fate of those on Earth for some reason. We have all lost our families, friends, and colleagues who were directing us from Houston. What are we to do now?"

The tension in Allen's voice could be cut with a knife. It was obvious that he was in no mental condition to make any rational decisions, so I left him with this last. "Captain Allen, we know what you are going through right now. I have family on Earth, and they are all, most likely, dead from this attack. My colleague, Atina, has seen her home planet be devoured by the Drezil just as you have witnessed. Be assured that this is not the end. Many cells of resistance exist across the universe, and we are going to attempt to solidify their efforts in an offensive which we believe will drive the Drezil out of the universe. The damage has already been done to our home planets, so we need to see what resources we still possess and begin to move forward."

I could tell that Allen was frozen in fear and grief. If I could not bring him back into this fight, he would prove to be useless to the resistance effort. To get his undivided attention, I began to yell at him. "Although we all know the horrendous casualties we have suffered, now is not the time to lay back and drown in our sorrow! Quit acting like a three-year-old and take command of your station. We are looking to you, Captain Allen, to spearhead the resistance effort here on Earth."

I could feel his anger beginning to boil over. His voice fell several octaves. "I have lost everything that was precious to me, so any way I can hit back at these assholes will be okay with me."

"Be very careful as you begin to build your resistance groups, Allen. Keep each cell very small, and only have group representatives meet with you. If you are discovered, it will mean immediate death for you all. Atina and I are now going to return to her home planet so we can begin to contact other worlds who have been forcibly occupied. No contact from us will be possible until we return to this world."

"Durell," Captain Allen radioed. "We are stranded up here with no way to get back to the surface. Is there any way you could assist us? We need to get our dead crewmates home."

Atina and I were standing in the control room, looking at the space station which was not more than a hundred yards away. I passed the request on to Atina, who said, "Durell, we can get them back if we can find a shadow in the Drezil's probe coverage. It will be where no one has yet been affected by the DNA scan."

"I understand," I said. "When do you think we can do this?"

"As soon as we can. Their coverage is becoming planet wide as we speak. Tell the crew of the station to don their space suits and stand by for us to pick them up. You understand that we are taking a chance on being discovered, but I understand how we need to get them home so they can begin to prepare for a counterattack."

UNIVERSAL EXTINCTION

I relayed the information to ISS1 and prepared to receive the crew. Captain Allen and his executive officer, Commander Rice, entered the airlock leading to empty space. They took one last look at their former home, knowing that it would soon burn up in a reentry ball of flame. The distance to the Pentemor was only a bit over a quarter mile, but leaving the station without any type of tether made it seem miles away.

I had opened the hatch and strapped myself to the Pentemor. I could see the two figures only a short distance away, moving freely through the space between the two craft. As they approached, I cast a nylon line toward the leader. Grasping the rope, Captain Allen knew that they were going to safely cross the void between ISS1 and the Pentemor. Captain Allen, Commander Rice, and the last remaining crew member had tethered themselves together before stepping out of ISS1, so the single rope pulled them all directly into the Pentemor's open hatch. The hatch closed behind them, and the pressure indicated that the air was now breathable. I knew that with their helmets on, they could not hear me, so I gestured for them to remove their suits and follow me upward toward the cockpit.

As we entered the cockpit, Atina said to me, "This entire plan is now at the mercy of our ability to take these individuals down to the planet without being discovered by the Drezil. Do you have any idea how difficult it will be to evade their sensors?"

Captain Allen was stunned by the technology that he saw aboard the Pentemor. The cockpit was equipped with devices which he had never seen. He and his crew had just stepped into the future of space travel and found it difficult to absorb the jump in technology which had just come to the Earth.

Atina and I had not yet figured out how we were going to accommodate the entire crew of ISS1, so I just shook my head and pointed to the area which had the berthing quarters. "You will all have to share these spaces until we arrive on Earth. Please allow us to set the ship on a course which will take us to a safe place. I cannot take the time to explain all of this to you, but be assured that we are doing our best to help you."

165

MICHAEL BRADLEY

"Atina," I asked, "does it seem strange to you that they were not able to detect us during this entire invasion? The stealth technology which was given to us on Alpha2 must be working extremely well, but our current position has been stable for too long."

"Yes," Atina said. "And since we are still visible to the naked eye, we need to be careful how long we remain static."

"So we need to move fast. Once we have secured the ISS1 crew, we need to immediately head down and land them in the best possible location, possibly the underground Cheyenne Mountain Complex which might have had enough shielding to protect the occupants from the Drezil probes. If they agree, we need to establish a low orbit and get them to their new home as soon as possible."

Captain Allen returned to the cockpit. The two individuals who were flying this ship both appeared to be humanoids. "I am Captain Allen, Commander of ISS1. My executive officer and I are the only commissioned officers left on board. Who are we privileged to meet?"

Speaking perfect English, I said, "I am Dr. Durell Dykstra. This is my colleague, Atina. She is from the planet Habordiz, which was invaded some time ago, so she knows all the trauma you are currently experiencing. She neither speaks nor understands English, so I will translate for you."

I could sense Captain Allen's distrust of me. I knew I needed to convince him of my authenticity. Hoping that he had the ability to connect the dots, I said, "I am from Idaho and had served many years in the Navy as well as another career as a college professor, hence the title of doctor. We cannot afford to delay in getting you to the surface, so we will not continue with our introductions any further. Just know we are here to help, and you need to begin to bring together all the planet's resistance members."

Captain Allen nodded. But I could still sense his uneasiness.

"When we return," I said, "hopefully we will have a strong coalition of planets to launch a counterattack against the Drezil."

Atina approached the Cheyenne complex and was careful to steer the Pentemor away from any location which would give anyone eyesight of her ship. "Durell," she said, "we cannot spend any time discharging these individuals. We are taking a horrendous chance as

166

UNIVERSAL EXTINCTION

it is. Tell them to go to the hatch immediately. We'll open it as soon as we are stable on the ground. They need to stand clear of us so we can immediately get back in orbit."

After I translated Atina's command for the ISS1 crew, all I could say was "Good luck to you all. I cannot tell you how it was determined that my DNA was not traceable by the Drezil, but as soon as I can find out what test will show that, I will pass it on to you. I cannot be the only human who has this same DNA protection. Until we return, do your best to bring together all of those interested in breaking free from the Drezil's control. Goodbye. And again, the best of luck."

Now that all those present knew exactly what was going to happen, Atina pointed the Pentemor toward the center of the planet. Manipulating the controls, she scanned the screens to determine where her landing point would be. "Durell, I need you to identify the landing location. Please point to our destination on the navigation screen."

Scanning the screen, I located the position of the Cheyenne Mountain Complex and placed my finger on that spot. "Atina, use whatever techniques you have to avoid anything that might give our position away. I trust in the stealth technology we have been given, but we still must remember that we can be seen visually."

Atina moved the control stick in several directions. She skillfully maneuvered the ship to a position next to the entrance of the complex.

With that, we all felt the unmistakable lurch of the Pentemor as it settled onto firm ground. Atina immediately activated the hatch, swinging it open so the humans could leave the ship. They dropped to the ground and waved to Atina and I, and they quickly made their way away from the Pentemor. When Atina felt they had moved a safe enough distance from her craft, she began her ascent back toward Earth orbit.

"Atina," I said, "we have now done all that we can here on Earth, but we still don't have any map of the universe that would help us determine where the other conquered worlds are located. A new plan is now needed to allow us to bring together a coalition of fighters."

Chapter 31

Dlano

It now seemed that Dlano's failure to get the star maps from Hawnl because of Lector's betrayal was having a devastating effect on our plans. He desperately needed the charts to identify the other Drezil-conquered worlds, or there would be no chance to mount any kind of opposition. The ability to defeat the Drezil had been given a death blow. Dlano knew the importance of the information that Hawnl possessed and that without it, the resistance would be powerless to mount any kind of opposition. The only way he could see to get the maps was to coerce Hawnl into providing them for him. To this end, Dlano called Lector to meet with him immediately.

"Lector," he said, "we all know what you have done. For your own personal benefit, you have betrayed your people. It has resulted in the deaths of many of your friends. We are now going to give you a chance to redeem yourself. If you betray us again, it will be the end of your life."

Dlano knew that no matter what Lector did, he was doomed. His betrayal was unforgivable, and it would be up to Dlano to take care of this problem.

Dlano continued, "You know that the Drezil are going to kill all who remain on this planet so their terraforming can be completed and they can repopulate Habordiz with their own kind. So if you wish to live, your only course of action is to assist us in getting the information from Hawnl that we need to find the other conquered

168

UNIVERSAL EXTINCTION

peoples. This will be your only chance to redeem yourself and rejoin our fight. What is your answer?"

Lector appeared stunned by this invitation to rejoin the resistance after what he had done. "Dlano, I have regretted my association with Hawnl from the offset but could find no way of getting out of it. Now that you have given me this chance, I willingly accept and will assist in any way that I can."

Dlano was hearing what Lector was saying, but he did not believe one word that he was saying. *I need him to get to Hawnl, but how far can I let him go before I have to take care of business?*

Lector was desperately trying to salvage his life. "Although my fear for my own life led to my association with Hawnl, I no longer fear for myself, only for our species. Even at the cost of my own life, I will get the information you need. We will have to be extremely cautious because Hawnl may have a brain the size of a pea, but he is not totally stupid. If he senses that we are after those maps, he will order the death of all of us. Now exactly what do you need?"

"Lector," Dlano said, "there are star charts which contain the locations of all their conquered worlds. We need those charts so our emissaries can contact each world's remaining population and begin to form a coalition for a massive retaliatory attack on the Drezil. It should be apparent to you how important this is. No matter what it takes, you must copy those maps so we can begin to contact each world and gather as many participants as we can."

The irony of the situation was truly staggering. From a confessed traitor, now Lector had the future of the entire universe in his hands. Without his assistance, they would all perish as the Drezil moved from world to world, taking all they could for their own benefit.

"Now, Lector, let's formulate a plan that will get us those charts."

Hawnl had no respect for the remaining occupants of this planet. He hated the atmosphere, heavy with oxygen and nitrogen. He yearned for his home planet and had lulled himself into a state of apathy. He neither cared for the Drezil's expansion plans nor his mandated position as overseer of these people. So when Lector offered him his friendship, he grabbed at it immediately. Unknown to Hawnl, however, was the plan to gain access to the star charts

169

which would enable the resistance to begin to bring together the entire galaxy against the Drezil. The arrogance of the Drezil elite in allowing these charts to be on Habordiz at all was testament to their disdain for the remaining occupants of Habordiz. They were unknowingly setting the stage for the upcoming battle.

Chapter 32

As Atina pointed the Pentemor skyward, I looked back at the Earth, wondering if I would ever see it again. We passed the Earth's only satellite, and I could not take my eyes off the Earth, my home. As it faded into a bright blue spot, Atina said, "Durell, we are returning to Habordiz with the hope that the charts we need will have been copied. In the meantime, we need to try to force a modification of my DNA so that I will be as undetectable as you."

Now my antenna really went up. I had gained a great amount of trust in Atina, but this request was way beyond the trust issue. Atina could die if we attempt to modify her DNA. My feelings for her were beginning to affect my willingness to put her in danger.

I had to admire her willingness to put her life on the line.

"My suggestion is that we infuse some of your blood into me and hope it has the desired effect. If you have any other suggestions, please let me know."

Not knowing anything about how this DNA modification was going to affect her, I could only say, "There is a chance that might work. There is also a chance this could kill you. However, we need a backup plan in case it doesn't." I crossed the cockpit and grabbed Atina, spinning her around to face me. "You must know by now that I have some deep feeling for you and that I cannot agree with any plan that might put you in danger. You know we are eventually going to have to face and recognize the truth that we are growing closer by the minute. I have never thrown the word *love* around easily, but I think we are headed in that direction"

171

Atina was caught completely off guard by my revelation. "I have been having some unusual feelings coursing through my body when I am close to you. I have never been so attracted to a male as I am to you. However, now is not the time for us to delve into our personal attraction to each other. The time will come for that. Right now, we need to move forward with my DNA modification."

Knowing that I could not completely forget what was just discussed, I gave Atina a full man hug and released her. I felt that I needed to offer an alternative method of transferring my DNA. "My DNA is imprinted on more than my blood, and if the transfusion fails, we have yet another method to investigate. Our species passes our DNA on to our offspring during the mating process. I know that there is danger in mixing our DNA in this manner, but if you and I mate, there is a chance that we can succeed in the DNA transfer. Being a newly regenerated male, option number two is quite attractive to me. If you feel repugnant about such a union, I will understand completely."

Atina was not totally caught off guard by my suggestion. Our species were linked, and she had felt a growing attraction to me as an outlander. Procreation had never entered her mind, but now that I had suggested we consider it, she found herself pleasantly intrigued by the prospect of our union.

"Durell," she said, "I sincerely hope that the blood transfusion gives me the ability to avoid detection by the Drezil. We will not know if it works until my father runs his tests. We must assume that it did not work as we approach Habordiz, because even though the Pentemor is stealthy, I may not be. If, after my father has tested me, we find that I am still detectable, I agree that we should try the alternative method you have suggested. I am not sure how to go about it, so I would rely on you for leadership in our union. Again, this will be a last resort to pass your DNA on to me."

I was never a real fan of needles, so the prospect of giving some of mine using a syringe was not all that attractive. Atina opened the medical cabinet and found all the equipment needed to do the procedure. She smiled at me and pulled on some sterile gloves and

UNIVERSAL EXTINCTION

attached a needle to the syringe. "You're not afraid of a little needle stick, are you?"

"You're really enjoying yourself, aren't you?" I said.

Atina wrapped a rubber band around my upper arm and had me squeeze my hand into a fist. She ran her finger over my inner arm and found a suitable vein to tap. Inserting the needle deep into my arm, she pulled the plunger back and drew some of my blood from my arm. Although I was not having second thoughts about what we were about to do, I was, nevertheless, becoming very nervous about the actions we were about to take. Although similar, could our DNA be different enough to cause her harm?

"Durell, you will have to inject me with your blood. If anything happens to me, you will have to continue this journey on your own. I cannot tell you how to proceed, but your ability to control the Pentemor will be tested. You must get us back to Habordiz, or all will be lost."

Atina motioned for me to take the copilot's seat next to her. She pointed to the navigation screen and traced a path outward toward the area of space which we were about to traverse.

"It's too late for us to turn back, so prepare to engage your engine," she said. "Hopefully, we will survive the trip, and I will not suffer any bad reaction to the injection."

As the Pentemor raced outward from the Earth, I could see several definable planets as we passed the blackness of space. I knew we had to complete the injection of my DNA if Atina was to have any chance of avoiding the Drezil.

I took the syringe we had prepared from my blood draw, inserted the needle into her arm, and pushed the plunger down, forcing my blood into her vein.

Atina felt the new blood coursing through her body, which made her feel dizzy and disoriented. "My vision is starting to tunnel, and I feel very shaky. Help me!"

I picked her up and laid her on the large bed in the sleeping quarters. Her condition worsened, so all I could do was watch over her.

173

"Atina," I asked, "do you feel like you are going to lose consciousness? If so, I will not know what to do, so fight any feelings of tiredness. You must stay awake until your body acclimatizes to my blood and DNA. I will be here with you until that happens."

"Will I survive this trauma, or will I just go to sleep and never awaken? I feel like death is closing over me, but I am going to try to push it back until I am used to this new DNA."

"Durell," she said, "I am feeling better now. Better than I have felt in my life. I think my body has accepted your DNA and will hopefully become undetectable by the Drezil. Let me rest for a while, and I'm sure I will be ready for our interstellar journey."

I waited for several hours, pacing the cockpit floor in circles while Atina slept. The Pentemor coasted outward from Earth's solar system, passing the large outer planets Jupiter, Saturn, and Uranus. I was tempted to try to use the controls which Atina so deftly manipulated while piloting the craft, but I decided it would only be a testament to my insanity to do so. All I could really tell was that we were on course for the outer reaches of the solar system, gaining speed with each passing minute.

I had decided to wait until Atina was awake and stable after the infusion to engage the engines for our jump to her planet. Reviewing what we had just done and the dangers it presented, I was aware that messing with DNA structures was way out of my area of expertise. If there had been any other option open to us, we would have taken it. *Actually, there was option two, which I would have preferred, but we never needed to go there.*

I valued Atina to a point where I would have gladly given my life for her, but in this instance, she had to do this on her own. I was encouraged that she had begun to feel much better before she went to sleep. But until she woke up again, I would still be apprehensive about what we had done. Watching her sleep, I began to realize how much this alien woman meant to me.

My god, I thought. *Have I fallen in love with her?*

Chapter 33

Dlano waited, albeit impatiently, for Lector to complete his mission. *Would he betray us again?* he wondered. *Is the entire resistance effort in jeopardy of being discovered?* The thought that all their lives now were in the hands of a known traitor did not give him any solace. The wait was going to be excruciatingly long, but he could do nothing to speed up the process.

Dlano began to consider his daughter's journey and the danger he had put her in. *As soon as she returns, we are going to reassess the direction we have taken,* he thought. *Even though I may be ordered to do so, I will never again ask her to be involved in such an insane journey, not knowing whether she made it to the other side or not. If we get the information from Hawnl, we will just have to find another way to use it to our benefit. I would expect that the Pentemor should be back soon, but I cannot wait for their arrival to implement our plans.*

When Lector returned from his audience with Hawnl, he seemed quite proud of himself for offering to help, considering that Dlano had terminated his membership in the resistance group. Dlano asked, "Lector, did you get the documents we require?"

Lector responded, "Dlano, not only did I get the star charts, I also got the summary for their entire expansion plan. I found the next world on their list is a place called Earth, and that invasion is already taking place. You were correct. Our time is limited."

Dlano was surprised that Lector had been successful in getting so much information from Hawnl. As a double agent, he was extremely talented.

175

"Our planet is set for their complete takeover in the very near future," Lector said. "I was foolish to think that Hawnl would keep his promises to me. My life should be forfeit for what I have done, but I beg you to let me try to make amends for my betrayal. My life is in your hands, but one other piece of information came into my hands."

Dlano walked up behind Lector, knowing what had to be done. However, Lector was not yet finished with his report.

"The Drezil are not all involved in this universal rampage. There are groups on Nepapile and Alpha2 who oppose Bordeth in his campaign to rule the universe. Although their opposition has not yet been openly exhibited, they are in position to be of help to us. I know how to contact them. I will not hold any of the information I possess hostage for my own life, but again, I beg for another chance to clear my name. I also got a sense from Hawnl that you and he have some connection that I could not define."

Lector finished speaking, so Dlano quickly reviewed the information he had presented to him. "Lector," Dlano said. "You have done an extremely good job, and the entire resistance membership owes you a debt of gratitude. However, the trust we had in you is now gone, so I have no option but to kill you." Dlano then shot him in the head. Knowing that Hawnl would know that Lector was no longer alive, Dlano shrugged and said, "Looks like you just had a horrible accident. Any associations I may have with the Drezil cannot be revealed. I'll have to explain this personally to Hawnl, but I sense that he will not be all that concerned about your demise."

Chapter 34

The news concerning the attack on the planet Earth could not have been better. Other than a lack of report from the central part of a country called the United States, all had gone well. The loss of the United States president and his staff should not cause undue concern according to Retil. Bordeth could only heap praise on his brother for the magnificent job he had done in securing Earth as the Drezil's next stepping-off point.

Retil was so proud of himself that he had no doubt that the overlord position would be his. He knew that the successful invasion of Earth was the key to overrunning many planets that had been untouchable up to this point. In his communication with Retil, Bordeth gave him additional instructions.

"Now that we have the Earth as a part of our empire, make sure that any surviving inhabitants are under your total control. Our sensors indicate that we have annihilated over seven billion of these Earthlings, and the remaining humans will exert the required influence to give us the control we need. There are not enough humans left to concern us, and their level of intelligence is not high enough for them to do anything but accept our total domination. Any individual who does not accept your total authority is to be killed immediately. That should send the message that we are their masters in every way."

Retil ended the communication link and could only feel a glow of satisfaction that he had been entrusted with the overthrow of this planet and had done so with little effort. The terraforming had begun many years ago and was beginning to turn this planet into a suitable home for his own species. He now had to inventory all those left alive and set the final solution plan into motion. He smiled, knowing that all the members of this subspecies would be killed very soon. In his arrogance, he failed to realize that this species had the innate ability to spring back from the most horrific circumstances and find ways to survive. In addition, he was totally unaware that all those individuals who had been deep underground in the Cheyenne Mountain Complex were still very much alive. They were soon to be joined by a leader who had been given a look into other conquered species' plans for ending the Drezil's rampage. Retil's tenure as overseer was going to be short-lived.

*****

Atina woke from her sleep refreshed and ready to take on the challenges that were ahead of us. She had gained a newfound survival instinct that made her realize that she and I possessed an immense power that could spell the end of the Drezil.

She sat up too quickly and experienced the nausea that came with vertigo. Looking around the spinning room, she saw the interior of her ship with a new set of eyes. The spinning sensation she was experiencing wound to a stop, and she saw me looking at her with a concerned expression on my face.

"Durell, whatever your DNA brought to me, it has enhanced my need to take this battle to the Drezil. We have solved the interstellar travel puzzle and can now bring more planets into our fight. If Father has managed to get access to the location of the other worlds, we can now begin our journey to build a force that will push the Drezil back to their home planet. Let's make ready to engage the engines and jump back to Habordiz."

Atina desperately needed to get acquainted with her new self. Moving to the cockpit, she settled into the pilot's seat and took the ship's controls into her hands. The controls felt familiar, and she had the urge to engage the engines to start their interstellar flight. "I think the human need to survive no matter what the circumstances has been infused into you by our DNA merging. I will start the engines as soon as you are ready. I am anxious to begin to free my planet from

UNIVERSAL EXTINCTION

the Drezil, even with the chance that we might not be successful. Are you ready to begin?" I asked.

"Let's get underway," Atina said. "Our destiny is in those stars, and I'm ready to begin this journey." Having completely recovered from the DNA procedure, Atina pushed the Pentemor's throttles to their full position. "Durell, engage your engine."

The engines began to push our craft outward and away from Earth's solar system, and the familiar array of kaleidoscope colors and light began to form. Atina and I no longer felt the effects of the acceleration which had incapacitated us on prior occasions. As our speed increased, the transparency of the ship's hull began to occur. We stood in the cockpit monitoring our progress, and a low-level light began to appear off to the left of our current track. A noticeable deviation from our direction seemed to be taking place.

The sounds emitted by the engines were taking on an uncharacteristic rumble that seemed to increase as we veered farther off our course. Something or someone seemed to be redirecting our craft to an unknown destination. I pondered the option of shutting the engine down but had not received any quiet directions to do so like before. I was beginning to place much trust in the entity that seemed to be offering the subtle directions.

"Durell," Atina said. "Do you have any idea where this ship is taking us? I have a feeling that we are not on the same trajectory back to Habordiz that we followed when traveling to Earth."

Shrugging, I responded, "We have most certainly deviated from our original course. Why, I cannot tell, but there is nothing we can do about it, short of shutting the engines down. I think that would be a serious mistake."

I ran down to the engine room and carefully began to move my engine away from the main propulsion. I expected the thrust we were feeling to start to reduce, but it did not. We had lost control of the engines.

Returning to the cockpit, I said to Atina, "I'm not too sure that we could interfere with this voyage even if we wanted to. Those quiet directions we have been hearing are silent right now, but my guess is that we will learn our destination and the reason we have changed course very soon."

Having turned our destiny over to whomever was the architect of this mission, we settled down in our respective seats to await our fate.

We both felt the slowing of our craft as soon as it began. The walls of the ship began to materialize, and the kaleidoscope of colored bands into which we were traveling began to widen, change in intensity, and finally terminate in the soft glow of a lighted aperture. Our craft continued to slow so all the anomalies which had accompanied our interstellar flight dissipated. We passed through the lighted aperture and were again in normal space-time.

Atina rose from her seat in the pilot's chair and looked intently at the new space that was surrounding us.

"Durell, I do not recognize any of the planets or stars I see. We have not returned to Habordiz, so our ability to contact my father is no longer an option for us. Any star charts he might have gained access to are now unattainable for us. I think our entire plan has just been defeated. I see no way we can possibly mount any kind of opposition or rebellion against the Drezil if we cannot return to Habordiz."

I intently studied our surroundings. I could not find any star cluster that I recognized as either associated with Earth or Habordiz. The two suns that occupied this solar system were surrounded by six planets which appeared to be very Earthlike. We had travelled to an entirely different galaxy for reasons we could not understand.

"Durell," came a mental voice. "We have brought you to this sector of the galaxy so that we can assist you in your mission to rid the universe of the Drezil menace. There are several habitable planets in this system, which is why we have taken up residence here. Those of us who escaped the Drezil's onslaught gathered all our remaining population and fled our home worlds."

How can I hear and understand this message when there is no one anywhere around that I can see? I think I had better listen to this guy.

"We selected this cluster of habitable planets because we knew that there was nothing of interest to the Drezil here. We are housed

UNIVERSAL EXTINCTION

in an armada of sphere-shaped ships orbiting the fourth planet from the system's sun. Most of our population has been spread across all the inhabitable planets in this system to make it harder for us to be detected. We know how curious you both must be concerning our ability to communicate with you and would invite you to visit with us as you did on Alpha2."

Both Atina and I heard the message and could only stare at each other in utter silence. Neither of us had expected any such communication, especially from the entity we had encountered on Alpha2. Although I had no knowledge of how the entity was communicating with us, I had the feeling that my thoughts could be read by our mentor.

I asked, "We have no idea what we are supposed to do. Are we to travel to the fourth planet and communicate with you in person, or do you want to continue to keep us at arm's length?"

The thought came immediately back. *You need to do nothing but bring your ship to our location. If you do not concur, we will send you on your way to your original destination, Habordiz. Do you wish to collaborate with us?*

I knew we had no choice in this matter. I glanced at Atina, and she gave me an approving nod. "We are proceeding to your location immediately," I said. With the decision made, Atina set our course for the fourth planet.

She plotted a course that took us on a meandering trip through the systems planets. Arriving at the fourth planet, we saw a large spaceship which was in high orbit around the planet. The ship was of a design neither Atina nor I had ever seen. It was made up of what appeared to be many small units joined as a complete craft. There seemed to be no consideration for architectural design, only the need to join them as one. It had many projections protruding from a central core that did not seem to have any discernible purpose. It was colorless and appeared to be cold and uninhabited. If any word could describe its overall appearance, I thought it might be *scary*. We approached the craft and saw a light which appeared at one end of the ship, revealing an opening hatch which had a runway of sorts beyond its doors.

181

Again, I heard words in my head. "Please release your ship to our control so we can bring you safely aboard."

"Durell," Atina asked, "do you think it is safe for us to proceed?"

As no alternative seemed available, I said, "Release your controls. We need to follow this path to its end so we can find out the direction we are to take."

Atina slowly took her hands off the ship's controls. The Pentemor slowed to a stop as if waiting for the new directions it was about to receive. We felt an undeniable lurch as our craft began to move toward the opening in our benefactor's ship.

Our ship entered the alien craft, and we both felt the immense energy rush that had accompanied our previous encounters with this entity. It was as if our adrenalin was being released in massive doses. Although we both felt the same sense of euphoria, we reacted quite differently to its influence.

Atina experienced an overwhelming sense of attraction toward me while I seemed to become much more attuned to our current situation. When I glanced at Atina, I noticed a strange expression cross her face.

"Durell," she said. "We have yet to address the situation which exists between you and me. When we entered the influence of our current benefactors, I felt an undeniable attraction to you. I think it is time for us to investigate our relationship because I feel we have a destiny which is tied to an intimate relationship we have yet to explore."

I knew that we would need to determine what the future held for us both, but I was not yet ready to give in to the temptations I had concerning our eventual union.

Atina seemed to be dwelling on our personal relationship instead of the task at hand. "I know that now might not be the time to begin to assess our relationship, but at this moment, I can only say that there is no doubt in my mind that I love you. If this comes from some reaction to the stimulus we are currently feeling, I still cannot deny its reality."

I was not totally confused. I had expected her to address the tension which had developed between us for some time. "Atina, I

UNIVERSAL EXTINCTION

will admit I have developed some very strong feelings for you during our association."

Atina started to feel a rush of heat envelop her body, starting from her head and coursing throughout her body. Her face took on a brighter shade of red, which seemed to be happening at the same time as her other outward signs of emotion.

What in the hell is happening to me? she thought. *Am so disturbed by this man that I cannot control my physical reaction to him?*

"If the circumstances were different," I said, "I would try to entertain a deeper relationship with you. However, our current situation demands one hundred percent of our combined attention and skill, so any personal issues we may have must be pushed to the side so we can address our status. Once we have some sense of direction, we will have more freedom to interact on a personal level."

Our discussion came to an end, and we felt our ship settle into its berth, followed by the sound of the engines powering down. Atina initiated the atmospheric analysis to determine if it was safe to open their hatch.

"Durell," she said, "the air outside is breathable, and the temperature is beginning to stabilize at a level compatible with our needs. The gravity is almost the same as that of our home planets. In my opinion, we are being urged to leave the ship. Do you think that is advisable?"

"There is no doubt that this entity wishes us to leave our ship," I said. "I, for one, am becoming increasing desperate to find our way back to Habordiz. I think we really need to put some eyes on these dudes before we commit to any of their suggestions. They might be exactly opposite to what we are looking for."

Because of our inability to determine how we had been spirited away from our original course, I was extremely hesitant to move forward without more information on this entire affair.

"Until we have evidence that they are not what they appear to be, I think we should follow their lead. As we are a team, we need to be on the same page with decisions of this importance."

"I have a sense that those who have taken us under their wing can be trusted," Atina said. Extending her arms in frustration, she

183

said, "Also, it isn't as though we have any other alternatives. I totally agree with your assessment and feel we should put our faith in them." With that, Atina initiated the egress procedure which opened the lower hatch and extended the ladder to the floor of the hangar.

*****

Rotan had been following Durell and Atina during their travels to Earth and their subsequent attempt to return to Habordiz. His last meeting with them had been on Alpha2, and it had led to a concerted effort on his part to formulate a plan for the defeat of the Drezil. Viewing their tentative departure from the Pentemor, he was overcome by a sense of admiration for their willingness to jeopardize their lives to assist in the defeat of the Drezil. After their craft was gently placed on its berth in the hangar, Rotan saw a ladder extending from mid-ship to the floor of the hangar. Noting two individuals exiting the craft, he directed his staff to meet with them and take them to the central core of the massive ship that he called home. Rotan knew that there was a distinct possibility that these two individuals held the key to the survival of the entire universe as they all knew it. He didn't know how or what they could do to quell the Drezil's occupation. All he knew was that the remaining members of his species were going to provide any assistance they could to Atina and Durell. It was imperative that they share their technologies and configure some sort of weapon that would put an end to the Drezil menace. They could not overtly employ any weapons themselves but knew they could depend on these two aliens to do their work for them. If they kept their true goal a secret, they could assist Durell and Atina in defeating the Drezil.

*****

Two shrouded individuals met with us and escorted us down a long circular corridor which was transparent in some sections and opaque in others. I decided to hang back a bit to see where this was

UNIVERSAL EXTINCTION

all headed. Turning toward me, Atina gave me a quizzical glance. We were really in a foreign place this time.

The corridor opened into a large room containing large numbers of strange devices being tended to by many humanoids.

"Durell," Atina asked, "what do you think these guys are doing? I get the feeling we are being shown some sort of devices which could be of use to us."

We could see many other humanoid individuals who were performing whatever duties they had been assigned. We reached the end of the corridor, and a large section of the wall slid out of our way and into a slot in the side of the hallway.

"How cool it this, Atina? Just like *Star Trek*. The only thing missing is the swishing sound."

Beyond the corridor, we were ushered into a cavernous room which had no discernible ceiling. Once we stepped inside the room, individuals, furniture, lighting, and many exit points began to materialize.

"Atina," I said, "I think we have found our benefactors. Let's have them take the lead and see what they propose. It is obvious that they have a keen interest in us and our mission to rid the universe of the Drezil. If this plays out like our last encounter with Rotan, we need to say nothing, just let them communicate their desires to us through telepathy."

The space we had entered continued to become populated by additional objects, and we were taken to a central kiosk located high above the main level. Here, we were met by several individuals, including Rotan. Each being was surrounded by a bright white haze which I could only assume was some sort of shield used by them as protection.

Rotan spoke first, saying, "We are here to formulate a plan to stop the Drezil's advancement and force them to abandon the worlds they have conquered."

I sensed there was much more to this meeting than was immediately apparent. Having been dragged all over the universe by this guy, I was not too keen on following his lead. I had the same feelings that had enveloped me when I first touched the artifact in Africa so

185

many years ago. Even though I was skeptical, it was as though I had some strange connection with all the entities who had accompanied Rotan to this place.

Rotan continued, "It now appears that we need to come together as a viable force to put an end to the Drezil's aggression." He then said directly to me, "In truth, we are not only similar, we're the same species—humanoids."

Atina turned her back to Rotan as if to send a message that she was an important part of this team and did not appreciate being ignored. I said, "No decisions of any kind will be made without Atina's input. We are a team, and all decisions will be made with that in mind."

Having received his dressing down from Atina, Rotan could only continue addressing us both. "Many years ago, our forefathers salted the universe and its habitants with our DNA to ensure our survival. Your survival was not of great importance to us then, but it is now. Your planet was not the first in your system to receive our DNA. In fact, the planet you refer to as Mars was our original introduction point, but as you well know, the atmosphere on that planet was not sustainable after the Drezil attacked and destroyed the planet's ability to remain habitable."

Chapter 35

Looking into the distant past, it became painfully obvious why only a single planet in our solar system was inhabitable by humans. During their initial rampage through their own galaxy, the Drezil had come into possession of an extremely powerful weapon. Although they did not initially know how to use it or what the consequences of setting it off might be, they had identified a planet in a distant solar system which seemed ideal for a test. It was perfect for their intended terraforming and should make an ideal stepping-off point for further expansion in this solar system. There was also a blue-green planet a bit closer to the central sun, which was going to be the next planet to attack. Many millennia in the future, the Drezil's descendants would live to regret the decision to direct this weapon at this system.

Zamae and her spouse, Bestue, had just completed work on their newest research paper which attempted to document and legitimize their observations concerning an alien presence that had been detected far out in space beyond Mars's atmosphere. They were both respected astronomers, so their paper's impact on the Martian society was immediate. Other entities began to realize that their planet might come under some type of attack, which led to a rally call for their military and civilian resources to provide some sort of response to any threat that might come.

It all came too late because the alien force was composed of an overwhelming number of ships and warriors who were intent on the occupation of the planet for their own species. The aliens' normal approach to the assimilation of a planet and its occupants into their empire did not prove to be viable because the DNA of the planet's

187

species was not yet mapped. So the conquering force, led by a lizard-like individual named Palad, decided to use an untested weapon which they felt would annihilate all life on the planet while conserving its assets for their own use. He ordered the fleet to move closer to the planet under siege and to arm their ships' weaponry. Although he had not communicated his intentions to his commander, he was overjoyed by the prospect of capturing this planet intact and without any of its inhabitants rebelling against him. At the same time Palad gave the command to deploy the weapon, Zamae and Bestue had detected the movement from the aggressor fleet and had sounded the alarm throughout the planet. Their feeble defenses were put on alert as the senior politicians began to argue about ways to communicate peacefully with the aliens.

Not knowing what effect the new weapon would have on the planet and its occupants, Palad continued his attack, which he assumed would kill all life on the surface of this globe. In addition to discharging the untested weapon from his own ship, the combined strike force of all his other ships began to flood the planet with their own death force. The additional power of the untested weapon aboard Palad's ship, combined with the other ships' weapons, caused the planet's atmosphere to suddenly begin to electrify into a death-spewing plasma which ignited with explosive force, destroying the majority of Palad's armada. The explosive gasses began to expand beyond Mars's gravity's ability to restrain them, so Palad ordered his remaining ships to a higher orbit.

The expanding plasma force was further enhanced by the oxygen which was the lifeblood of the planet's inhabitants. The atmosphere began to explode into a nightmare of hellish red flames, and all Zamae and Bestue could do was hold each other, knowing that they were about to die. The oxygen-rich atmosphere burst into a cascade of fiery columns, which detonated everything on the surface of the planet before exploding outward, taking the entire planet's protective atmosphere with it.

Palad viewed the results of his attack. *How will I explain this to my superiors? I have rendered this planet totally useless for our occupation. My only recourse is to mark this solar system as uninhabitable for our species and never return. If anyone ever finds out what I have done, I am sure I will be executed. Best to take what remains of my fleet and return home. I'll just tell them that we attempted to test the weapon on an uninhabited planet, but it caused an explosion that crippled the fleet. I had the only weapon of this type which we possessed, so I will just recommend that we never again seek this destructive force because we cannot control this much power. It will only destroy more of our fleet if we attempt further tests.*

The shattered fleet headed out of the solar system, with only a few of Palad's associates noticing the bright blue planet orbiting closer to the system's sun, but none of them wanted to challenge Palad's decision about further exploration of this system.

Chapter 36

Rotan knew how the past mistakes made by the Drezil had shaped the history of this solar system. He felt the need to explain this history so Atina and I would be better suited to understand why no species had yet to confront the Drezil and try to defeat them.

"Atina," I said, "I think we have found the key to our survival here on this huge spaceship. This human being in front of us seems to have many of the answers we have been searching for. Let's just see where this is all going."

Rotan continued, "It is our opinion that the Drezil abandoned their attempt to colonize your solar system under the false notion that Mars was the only inhabited planet in that system. Long ago, the Drezil attempted to invade Mars, but they only managed to destroy the planet's environment by using an untested weapon which stripped away the entire atmosphere."

"Okay," I said to Atina. "Now that mystery is solved. We have known since our first probes visited Mars that life on that planet had existed in the past, but not to this extent. I suppose we owe the folks on that world thanks for keeping the Drezil off our backs for as long as they did."

A large hologram suddenly appeared in the center of the room with a planet like Earth rotating at its center. Small explosions could be seen coming from its surface. As we stared at this apparition, Rotan moved to the side of the display opposite us.

"It wasn't until your species began to experiment with nuclear power and orbital space travel that they became aware that you existed," he said. "You were viewed as an easy target for their aggres-

UNIVERSAL EXTINCTION

sion and were marked for immediate assimilation into their empire. I know that you are unaware that your species and ours are, in fact, quite similar."

What a joy, Atina thought. *Another species of super males.*

"We waited until you were viewed as a valued addition to our efforts before we contacted you. To put it bluntly, we are the same. Although we, as the parent group, initiated your birth and growth, you have become a unique, strong, and valued asset. It is now time for us to bring this fight to the Drezil's home."

*****

Back on his own planet, Bordeth had long been aware of the fiasco which had led to the destruction of the planet Mars. Although he had never informed Hawnl of his knowledge of the only use of the weapon, subsequent tests would not be possible unless they could procure additional weapons. So following the attack on Mars, Hawnl was totally in the dark concerning the existence of the weapon, much less it's power. He would only be told much later after he was up for assignment as an overlord. His only option was to disavow the existence of the weapon and never attempt to use it again.

Bordeth had called Palad to his residence. "If we reveal what you did to the planet Mars, my time as the leader will probably come to a bad end, and your life would be forfeit!" he yelled. "Let's keep the past in the past. We'll go after the remaining planet, Earth, very soon."

The preferred atmosphere of the Drezil was composed of methane and carbon dioxide, so it was much more susceptible to ignition than an oxygen-rich atmosphere. Bordeth knew that the weapon could be used against them if it were ever discovered. For this reason, after he informed Hawnl of the weapons existence, he had sworn him to silence, threatening him with death if he ever divulged its potential. He then forced Hawnl to take a position in an out-of-the way planet named Habordiz as its overseer. Although he thought knowledge of this weapon was now controlled, unknown to him, several other officers knew that it had taken part in the destruction of Mars and knew of the weapon's potential.

Among those who knew of the weapon's existence were Madille, Hawnl's brother, who was the leader of the Drezil resistance group. His position on the salt planet, Alpha2, put him in daily contact with many of the workers who were from Habordiz. In addition, he had heard rumors of another alien entity who was on Alpha2 who could communicate directly with the human resistance groups on many of the seized planets.

His name was Rotan. However, Madille had no way of contacting him. His dilemma, however, was whether to chance revealing the existence of the weapon to the humans and place his own species in jeopardy of being annihilated. His only recourse seemed to be to find some entity that could act as a go-between and offer a guarantee that the weapon would not be used against his own people. Could this Rotan be the key to stopping the expansion of the Drezil and returning the seized planets to their rightful occupants?

Chapter 37

Dlano had long ago given up any hope that Atina and I had survived our intergalactic journey to Earth. His inability to communicate with Atina telepathically was almost iron-clad evidence that she was deceased. He knew that if any further progress was to be made in ousting the Drezil from their system, he would have to take a proactive role in his position as leader of the resistance. The betrayal by Lector had left him extremely wary of all the resistance members, so any action he took would have to be kept secret. He had formulated a plan which would allow him to take over Atina's salt route and put him on Alpha2, where it was rumored a sympathetic group of Drezil opposed to the genocide of humans and other species resided. It seemed the only recourse he had, so he began to plan for his first ferry trip to Alpha2.

Dlano sat in his office on Habordiz's launch facility and ordered his ground crew, "Bring the Lasser out of her hangar and prepare her for launch. It is evident to all that Atina will not be able to take this trip."

Dlano's preparations for his departure were complete. Hawnl had given his wholehearted approval of the plan because he knew that Dlano's departure would make the remaining population much easier to control. The brilliant flame from Dlano's ship flashed upward into the night sky, so the remaining members of the resistance could only surmise that Dlano had totally abandoned them and their cause. Dlano, however, could only think, *If I am successful in this venture, I may be able to bring some hope back to my people that their time of slavery might be coming to an end.* Dlano, however, failed to define exactly who his people were. With that thought still ringing in his head, he settled down for the long boring ride to Alpha2.

Completing the long trip from Habordiz, Dlano's ship descended to its berth on Alpha2. He was totally unaware that he was being monitored very closely by an entity that he was yet to meet. *I'm not too sure why I took on this search, but something has been pushing me in this direction.*

Since his experience with the engine on the Pentemor and its numbing effects on him, he had been unable to formulate any plan on his own, but he seemed to be prompted to action without knowing what or where he was headed. After he secured his ship, it was no different. Without knowing why, he decided to investigate the far side of Alpha2. The crew that was responsible for unloading his craft were hard at work, but it would take the better part of an entire day to complete their task, so his excursion would not cause any undue concern for the Drezil. Dlano knew where and how to gain access to a helicopter. He had used it before on this planet. He hoped his new sense of adventure would not raise any concern on the caretaker's part.

He gently maneuvered his helicopter upward, rotating it over to see his ship cradled in its offload site. He could not note any alarm or concern from the crew, so he leveled off and headed away from the site. The site disappeared behind his helicopter, and he accelerated to a higher altitude to gain a better view of the planet's topology. It was completely barren of any signs of life or civilization, just a solid mass of salt-covered hills and valleys. His trajectory took him quickly to the side of the planet which was almost directly opposite of his ship's location. Scanning the surface of the planet, he noted what appeared to be a structure of some sort on the ground.

Although he was sure he was seeing something solid and real, it began to shimmer as though it was either transparent or a figment of his imagination. In any case, he decided to put down as close to it as possible. Whether he was responding to some subtle suggestion or his own curiosity was unclear, but he knew he had to investigate this apparition.

UNIVERSAL EXTINCTION

Donning his protective suit, he unclasped the seal on his craft and stepped down to the surface of the planet. His feet sunk slightly in the dusty soil, and a plume of dirt swirled into the airless vacuum. He then saw what appeared to be a door embedded in the structure.

"What is the ominous humming sound?" he asked out loud. Of course, only the occupants of his helmet could hear him. "Wait just a minute now. I can tell that sound is kind of coming from everywhere." *I wonder if I'm talking to myself because I'm scared out of my wits or if I am just naturally weird.*

He could also hear an audible hum coming from somewhere, presumably within the structure itself. He was just beginning to look for a handle or knob which might allow him to enter when a door suddenly opened, revealing a dark interior.

Oh, oh, I think I have just really stepped into it. I guess I have no choice but to cooperate with whoever is running this show.

He was prompted to enter, and without hesitation or thought, he stepped into the structure. As soon as he had cleared the hatch, it abruptly slammed shut, leaving him in total darkness.

"Remove your helmet," came a command. Without knowing why he was being ordered to remove his life-saving helmet, and without considering the consequences, he removed his helmet and was met by breathable and cool air with a mist of water vapor. The darkness was pierced by a bright light emitting from another door which slid to the side to reveal a corridor lined with small openings. He moved down the corridor to a spot which seemed to be a junction for several tunnels that were identical to the one he currently occupied.

Having followed all the suggestions he had been given, Dlano was now getting extremely concerned about his health. Could this be a trap which might end in his death? Dlano said, "Whoever you are, I need some answers about why you have called me here."

The response was "I am Soute, and I have been directed by our leader, Rotan, to apprise you of what is about to occur. The planet Earth has been overwhelmed by the Drezil forces and is now in their control. That means that Habordiz is about to be sterilized of all human life so the Drezil can begin to completely change the envi-

195

ronment to suit their needs. Atina and Durell are alive and currently working with Rotan to formulate a plan to defeat the Drezil."

Soute finished his introduction to Dlano, and a figure appeared behind him. Dlano immediately took an offensive posture. *Have I been drawn here just to be killed by this enemy,* he wondered? *They are alike, and I guess I cannot expect any mercy from this one. Like an idiot, however, I left the only thing I had that could be used as a weapon on Habordiz. I am going to do my best to give a good accounting of my species and try to defeat this Drezil even though I am going to die.*

Dlano assumed the posture of a warrior, seemingly ready to repel the enemy's attack. In a language he should not have understood, the alien Drezil said, "I am Madille."

"I belong to a group of our species who wish to put an end to the violence which our leaders have brought on the many planets we have enslaved. We have knowledge of a weapon which could be used to end any further expansion of the empire. We know that it will mean that many of our species will die but have accepted that this will be the price for our leader's insane conquests."

Bullshit, Dlano thought. *As usual, we are being set up for another takeover. Not this time, bucko!*

"This weapon was responsible for the destruction of all life on a planet in the solar system occupied by Earth. Mars, as it is known, was a vibrant planet that supported millions of inhabitants until one of our commanders tested this weapon."

Dlano could not believe what he was hearing. "Are you telling me that you have this weapon of mass destruction and have not yet used it on us? I find it hard to believe that you and your species could care less about us. I cannot figure out why you would give it to us."

Madille continued as though Dlano had not heard a word. "The weapon caused a catastrophic explosion of the planet's atmosphere, leaving it without a viable source of oxygen for the inhabitants. It has never been used since because it makes the target planet totally uninhabitable for any species."

Dlano could not really process all that he had been told. If he had been given a doomsday device, what was he supposed to do with it? He needed to get back to Habordiz as soon as possible to clear his mind.

Madille said, "Without any conditions, we will help you construct and train you in the weapon's usage. We know that you have every right to detest our species, but we are willing to put this weapon in your hands, hoping that when you retaliate against my species, you will spare our home planet. The mentor who has assisted us in this decisive move wishes to remain anonymous. He has informed us that you are not a savage people, and you will do what is right for all of us."

Soute's voice sounded clearly in Dlano's head. "Now that you have access to the weapon which you have procured from the rebel Drezil faction on this planet, you may be able to put an end to the Drezil madness. It will be your challenge to prepare the Habordizite people for the upcoming battle."

Dlano's head was overflowing with information. He could not determine where all the subtle pushes had come from that led him here. He thought, *Way too much responsibility has been placed on me. Even though I know who is behind all this activity, I cannot reveal the source, nor can I ask directly for help.*

Soute crossed the room to join Dlano and extended his hand. "We have been actively directing you since your experience with the engine in Atina's ship. We have no doubt that you, in collaboration with Atina and Durell, are capable of spearheading the fight to defeat the Drezil."

All that had just occurred left Dlano dizzy with questions. Although he had been placed on Habordiz to monitor the status of its occupants, he was totally unaware of the progress that the Drezil had made. How could Atina and Durell have survived their journey, and why had he heard nothing from them?

"Soute," Dlano began. "What do you want me to do? I am willing to help in any way that I can, but I do not see what I might bring to the upcoming battle."

After Dlano finished his questioning, Soute placed a liquid tablet into his hand. He immediately felt a tingling sensation that enveloped his entire body.

"Your DNA has now been altered to make you undetectable by the Drezil. You have been given the information necessary to build the weapon which will end the Drezil's tyranny. You will need to travel to your home world, where we will begin to prepare you for the upcoming war."

Now Dlano was totally confused. "Why are you gifting me with all this powerful technology, Soute? I have absolutely no idea what to do with it or how I am to break the Drezil hold on my planet."

"Dlano, you will find that Atina and Durell will contact you and join you in this preparation. To cover your disappearance, you will launch your ship at the appropriate time, after which you and your ship will just disappear from the Drezil sensors. You will not be detectable and can travel back to Habordiz without any fear of Drezil interference."

With that, the area around Dlano began to dissolve. The disappearing shell began to pulsate with a lavender hue, and streams of brilliant light began to shoot upward as though the shell of the structure was releasing itself to space. He hurriedly put his protective helmet back on in time to see his breath begin to turn to a steamy fog. After the structure was gone, he was left standing alone on the salty surface of the planet without any evidence that the structure he had visited ever existed. He moved to his helicopter and started to carry out the instructions which Soute had given to him.

Chapter 38

We left our mentor's encampment, and Atina and I sat comfortably on the flight deck of the Pentemor, streaking at light speed toward Habordiz. Now that we had a clearer picture of the stakes involved in any attempt to overthrow the Drezil, we were both prepared to do whatever was necessary to bring the battle to the Drezil's home turf.

Just the knowledge that a weapon existed that could render the Drezil powerless was enough to push us both forward. We had been told about a weapon which was used against Mars a long time ago.

"Atina," I said, "the weapon which destroyed Mars appears to be a viable resource which we can use to bring the Drezil to their knees. It seems that we have been given an opportunity to build this weapon which would change the balance of power in our favor."

The weapon which would be built using the information Dlano had been given was the game changer we had been seeking.

Atina said, "I do not view any option other than the complete annihilation of all the Drezil who occupy planets they enslaved. Our intention is not to cause genocide for their entire race, so we will try to leave their home planet untouched. We would, of course, warn them that our intentions would be to end this war as quickly as possible and allow any of their species who wished to leave to do so. We wish only to exterminate those Drezil who have propagated this insanity.

"This entire plan is based on the suggestions we have been given from our benefactors. The trust we are putting in them may come back to bite us in the ass. They have assured me that the connections we have with the peaceful Drezil who reside on Alpha2 will lead us to the construction of the weapon we need. Can you see any other way for us to proceed?"

Atina's head had been spinning since Rotan had begun to educate us concerning the evolution of the Drezil menace. "I don't have the ability to think rationally right now, so I will let you, Durell, take the lead and determine what course of action we should take."

"Rotan, we are prepared to do whatever is required to construct this weapon and put an end to this war. What is required of us to begin the next phase of our saga?" I asked.

Having been convinced that we were the key to ending the Drezil's insane campaign, Rotan said, "You will now need to travel back to Habordiz and meet with Dlano. My colleague, Soute, has given him the information that will be needed to construct the weapon. Although he knows that he has this valuable knowledge, he is unsure of how to use it. You can utilize what he knows to further your quest. Dlano will share what he knows with you at the appropriate time."

Neither Atina nor I knew what Rotan was preparing for us. "We really want to assist, but please give us more to work with than you have already provided," I said. "We cannot operate in the dark forever."

"For your part, you will need to have the ability to communicate telepathically. Without your knowledge, that ability has already been given to you both. You have been using it without realizing it. Your travel to Habordiz will begin soon. Your ship has been modified to allow your travels to occur interdimensionally."

"Holy crap," I said to Atina. "Almost instantaneous travel between our source and destination using the Pentemor. She is now a true intergalactic starship. Just what I need to get home a bit quicker."

Soute commanded, "From now on, you will refer to our species as Azdawn, which is the name given to us millennia ago. We still do not know where we came from but assume that we are not from this galaxy."

Several individuals who seemed to be of the same humanoid species as Rotan suddenly appeared next to him. Their posture was

UNIVERSAL EXTINCTION

of extreme reverence, and it was readily apparent that Rotan was a powerful leader.

"As the leader of this group, I have full authority to deal with you as I wish. Although we are a peaceful species, we need to partner with you so the Drezil do not continue to annihilate this universe. You are free to leave our planetoid as soon as you are ready."

Having completed all our business with the Azdawns, we were ushered back to our ship to begin our first trip with the new propulsion system.

When we entered the flight deck of the Pentemor, we were greeted by a completely new array of controls, instruments, and furnishings. Not only had our benefactors rebuilt the entire engine room, they had also made the crew's quarters into an extremely comfortable cabin. The Pentemor had become a showpiece, fit to lead the entire fleet we were about to inherit.

Neither Atina nor I had any problems understanding the new controls. "Is there going to be any issue with the division of power between us as we move forward?" Atina asked.

"We each have our own special abilities which will allow us to work together as a team. You will take the lead in your areas of expertise, and I will take the lead in mine," I said.

With that, Atina moved to her seat in the captain's chair and began to set the ship into its launch configuration. The familiar hum from the engine took on a completely unique frequency, which confirmed that the newly made changes had taken effect.

Moving the new throttles into their takeoff setting, she said, "Durell, make sure you are belted in securely because I do not have any idea what to expect from this new configuration."

The Pentemor began to slowly glide upward. The engine seemed to respond immediately to any input given by Atina. She had no idea where to point the ship, but something or someone had given her subtle instructions with which her body began to comply. She tipped the craft and pushed the throttles forward as the ship began to point toward our destination, Habordiz.

However, now, instead of light changes and color arrays, a total darkness enveloped us, and the engine began to whine as though

201

injured. I stumbled to the viewport and tried to make sense out of what I was seeing. If fear was part of this trip, I had met that requirement. Atina came quickly to my side and grabbed my arm, as if trying to gain some strength from me. Looking at her, I could tell that she was very upset.

"Atina, do you know what the hell is happening?" I asked.

Her face showed the same fear, or should I say panic, that was consuming me. She turned to me, and I could tell that she had absolutely no control over this situation.

"I have no idea what has just occurred, but I can only speculate that we have entered the transitory dimension to which Rotan referred. It is obvious that we lost control of all this a long time ago. I believe that faith in our mentors will help us through this. He said that our travel to Habordiz would be almost instantaneous, so let's hope he was accurate."

As Atina finished speaking, the ship was flooded with an extremely bright white light, indicating our arrival somewhere. Where were we? The ship was quiet and motionless.

"Atina, could you spin the ship so we can get some visual cues about where we are?" I asked.

The ship slowly began to rotate, and the planet Habordiz came into view. We were in a high orbit above the planet, directly in line with one of the polar caps.

Our ship floated lazily over the polar ice, and I had a moment to study my shipmate thoroughly. I had long since come to realize that there was more to our association than the problems that currently faced us. Namely, the Drezil. I felt a strong attraction to Atina since our meeting and had considered approaching her on a more intimate level. My reluctance to do so was fostered by my inability to determine how she might respond to my advances. Also, I was a chicken when it came to approaching women in a romantic way.

Enough, I thought. *I have much more important matters to deal with, so this distraction must be put to rest. I must put these feelings aside and focus purely on the upcoming fight.*

"Atina," I started, "we need to do whatever it takes to meet with your father. He has been given new insight into this mission and has

UNIVERSAL EXTINCTION

been rendered undetectable by the Drezil. Set a course for your former launching site so we can contact your father and request his assistance. He has the information necessary to construct the weapon we need. All we need to do is meet with Dlano and assist him in building and deploying the device. He will be waiting for us when we arrive."

Atina broke orbit and set a course that would take us to meet with Dlano to begin the final phase of our quest.

*****

Dlano could remember nothing from the time he entered his ship on Alpha2 until he awakened in high orbit above Habordiz. The polar caps were swimming directly below his ship, and he felt as though he had just arisen from a long welcome sleep.

Whatever the entity he had encountered on Alpha2 had done was totally unknown, but it appeared that they had done exactly what they had said. He was uninjured and filled with a newfound desire to take the lead in his species battle with the Drezil. He put all his trust in the entity's instructions and broke orbit to slowly land his craft in a remote location on Habordiz. The location was securely out of sight of all those who service the spaceport. Leaving his ship, he made his way the short distance to his home. With a new dedication, he began to call together those members of the resistance that he trusted.

This cell of the resistance was composed of many of the learned members of the Habordiz elite. Those who had been left after the Drezil purge made up the nucleus of the planet's scientific genius. They were joined by several members who were fighters in the Habordiz armies and had knowledge of battle strategies. Together, they formed a cohesive group which could effectively plan any resistance measure needed once the Drezil's weaknesses could be found.

Dlano addressed those elite members who had been brought together in his lab and said, "The call has been made, the stage is set, and we are about to embark on the greatest mission of our lives. We will be joined by an entity of great age and power who will direct us in our fight against the Drezil. They informed me that they cannot take direct action against the Drezil but will rely on us to implement

203

the plan which will negate the Drezil's ability to ravage the universe any further."

Bandde, a high-ranking member of the resistance, spoke first. "I know you have gone to great lengths to meet and join with those who have provided you with the weapon which will supposedly end this war. However, how can we be sure that they and you are not leading us down the road to destruction? If this group is so powerful, why don't they take care of the Drezil themselves?'

Those assembled could sense immediately that Dlano had become extremely irritated by Bandde's query. "Look," he said. "If any of you have any better suggestions about how we can defeat the Drezil, step right up. Our benefactors come from a society which does not allow any violence, regardless of the consequences. If there are any other dissenters, you are welcome to take my place." Hearing no opposition, Dlano continued, "They will not be able to keep any of the planets they have enslaved and will be forced back to their own planet. Each of you may be called on to make the ultimate sacrifice, but I have been assured that we will prevail. I have knowledge of a new weapon which will render the Drezil vulnerable to our attacks. I have been given the knowledge necessary to construct this weapon and will be trained in how to use it after it is constructed. I now know for certain that we will be able to take the fight to the Drezil on their own turf."

Bandde asked, "How is this all supposed to come together? We are only a small group, and we cannot act alone. If we can find some support elsewhere, I am willing to put my life on the line, but I will not join with you without assurance that we will have support."

"I am just waiting for the entity to give me additional information before we proceed," Dlano said. "Please be patient, and above all, our plans must remain unspoken. If the Drezil ever get any idea of what we are about to do, we will never be able to carry out this invasion successfully. Now return to your homes and await my call to arms."

Having shared the plan with the resistance, Dlano could only wait to be contacted. Whomever was designated to give him further orders was totally unknown to him, but he had an idea that it just might be his daughter.

Chapter 39

Atina and I climbed the steps that led to Dlano's residence. We were met by a jubilant Dlano, who grabbed Atina in a huge bear hug. I looked through the door and noted several individuals milling around the room with no discernable duties. Not wanting to interfere with the reunion, I busied myself by studying the small group who seemed to be desperately trying to ignore me.

He had been convinced that she had perished, and it was as though she had been brought back from the dead. "Thank God you have survived," Dlano said. "Soute told me that you both were alive and had met with Rotan, his commander. I have been given the information necessary to construct and deploy the weapon which should put an end to the Drezil's madness."

Atina knew all that Dlano was telling her but tried to downplay her participation in the entire series of events. She knew exactly where this was all headed but hoped that the new ability she and I had been given could remain unknown to everyone until the time was right.

"Father," she said, "although you have been given the plans to construct the device which could end the Drezil's occupation of all the planets they have taken, you do not have the ability to use it. Either this entire group accepts Durell and I as the leaders, or no offensive will ever materialize."

Atina," Dlano said, "I have been told that you two are going to lead us in this battle and that you have been given some additional abilities which will assist us. Given that you have not been forthcoming with any information concerning the battle plans you will follow, we have no choice but to accept you both as our leaders and follow you." Dlano sighed deeply. "Our ability to negate the Drezil's scanning of our DNA will make a great difference when it comes time to implement our attack. My ship is not far from here and, like yours, cannot be seen on their detection devices. It can, however, be seen by the eye, so I will make sure it is well hidden. I suggest you do the same with your ship."

I was now more suspicious of Dlano's intent. Moving to a position where I could monitor Dlano's response, I said, "I have some real reservations about revealing our plans. We know that Lector informed Hawnl of the resistance's internal structure, so I will not expose our goals to anyone associated with your group. Like it or not, Atina and I will keep any plans we may have to ourselves."

Dlano's face turned red with the frustration he felt. He had assumed that his position as Atina's father would give him the ability to be a trusted partner in the planning of the war with the Drezil. "You cannot mean that I will not be part of this planning process," he said. "I will not allow you to move forward with whatever plans you have without me." He stood quickly and stormed out of the room.

The Pentemor had been used as a model for several cargo ships which formed the nucleus of Habordiz's fleet of transport vessels. Their construction was almost identical to the Pentemor, so it was assumed that they could all be modified to accept the new interstellar engine which had been installed by the Azdawns. Each ship's engine room was prepared to receive the new engine by placing lead-lined panels on all walls. This was an effort to reduce the effects the engine might have on the crew members of each ship. The material used was harvested from Alpha2 on a previous trip made in the Pentemor. The glowing substance could be easily separated into small pieces, each having the ability to power the crafts. The ships were each modified, and a fleet of eleven interstellar ships began to emerge. The resistance now had the tools to begin ejecting the Drezil from their planet.

The time had come to immunize all the fighters to destroy the Drezil's ability to read and control their DNA. Dlano had taken a sample of my DNA long ago and had developed a serum that could alter the Habordizites' DNA to make it impossible for the Drezil to

UNIVERSAL EXTINCTION

use it as a weapon against them. Those who were treated would just seem to disappear from the Drezil scans for no apparent reason. It was decided that now was the time to utilize the serum, even though we were taking the chance that the Drezil might immediately begin to question the disappearance of much of the population. Dlano, however, had no such fears because he knew that Hawnl was so lazy and stupid that he would not be able to process what was happening fast enough to sound any alarms.

*****

Hawnl knew that something was afoot. The sudden disappearance of several of the Habordiz inhabitants had not gone unnoticed. The failure of Dlano to return from Alpha2 finally convinced Hawnl that he needed to investigate these latest occurrences and assess the possibility that the resistance members were up to something. Hawnl was about to put his query into motion when Dlano, Atina, and a stranger abruptly entered his chambers. He was shocked to see them all because his information led him to believe that Atina and Dlano were both either missing or dead. His inability to scan any of their DNA also caused him much concern.

Dlano began the conversation. "Hawnl, this is Durell, a traveler from the planet Earth. He and my daughter, Atina, have journeyed to Earth and witnessed the genocide perpetrated there by your species. That planet's population was almost eliminated in the final attack, but we now know that whatever plans you have for the future will be unsuccessful. We are here to inform you that the Drezil's days of conquering other species have come to an end. You will be given no choice."

Hawnl appeared shocked at the audacity of this infidel.

"We demand that you give us the star maps which indicate the location of all the worlds you have assimilated. If you do not comply, we have constructed and are ready to deploy the same weapon you attempted to use many eons ago in your attack on the planet Mars. Your home planet will be the first target if you do not agree to our demands."

Moving behind Hawnl, I knew that I had to intimidate him into compliance. I said, "After we have destroyed your world, we will move on to all the planets you have conquered. Any planet which has had the entire population killed so you can terraform it to support your own species will be our next targets. We intend to wipe your species from the entire universe if you do not provide us with the information we need. In addition, your own life hangs in the balance." I could tell that Hawnl was getting extremely nervous by my very presence behind him. "We have nothing to lose and will end your rampage in any way that we can. Although we are not willingly brutal, we will take whatever measures that are necessary to reach our goal, which is a universe without Drezil rule. What is your answer?"

Hawnl could not believe what he was hearing. "You have all just signed your own death warrants. I am going to contact Bordeth and request that our fleet return here and put an end to this uprising. You will all be taken and interrogated until we determine who is responsible for this insanity. Now leave before I take matters into my own hands." Hawnl finished speaking, and he saw a weapon of some sort appear in my hand. It shot a lead projectile, hitting Hawnl in his left chest. His body crashed to the ground, leaving him stunned and unable to move.

"Hawnl," I said, "you are only the first of your species to feel the pain which will be the price for your sins. You will not communicate with anyone and will provide us with the information we have requested. If you fail to do so, the pain you feel right now will be insignificant compared to that which I can inflict on you."

Hawnl finally began to sense the seriousness of his predicament. He began to shake and mop his scaly brow because the perspiration was beginning to fill his reptilian eyes. It was not often that a Drezil closed both sets of eyelids. This only occurred when they were extremely afraid.

I knew he was afraid of me, so I pressed my advantage. "You are a coward, and I will give you what all cowards deserve—a slow and painful death. Do not test me. You and your peers have just destroyed most of the human population on my home planet, Earth, so you will get no mercy from me. Both Atina and I can tell what you

UNIVERSAL EXTINCTION

are thinking, so do not try to deceive us. Now for the last time, give us the information we desire."

Hawnl said aloud, "I have stored the maps you desire in a safe place whose location I will reveal to you if you promise me that I will be allowed to go free. In addition, if your rebellion is successful, I wish to be named as the absolute ruler of what remains of my species."

Hawnl felt another blast of pain, this time in his right upper chest. The human had discharged his weapon again. "You are in no position to demand anything," I said. "Either you bow to our wishes right now, or I will continue to shoot you."

Hawnl saw his green lifeblood oozing out of this new wound, and he realized that his choices had just been diminished to one. "Please," he whined, "do not discharge that weapon at me again. I will provide the information you have requested. It is in the cabinet above my communication device."

I moved to the side of the room which housed the communicator and felt inside the cabinet. To my surprise, I grasped a large round canister which was open on one end. "If this is not what we need," I stated, "I will kill you." Inspecting the contents of the canister, I found a set of star maps on which many planets were highlighted, indicating that they were under the control of the Drezil. "Atina," I said, "We now have a complete set of directions to allow us to begin our journey to reclaim this universe. I see no additional need for Hawnl's assistance. Dlano, do you concur?"

Without responding to my query, Dlano emptied the weapon into Hawnl's green scaly body. He wailed from the pain of the damage done to his body, and he fell to the floor of his opulent quarters, dead. As his green life ebbed from him, I could only assume this creature's final thoughts were about his own stupidity. *Now I am sure that I have shown Atina and Durell how trustworthy I am,* Dlano thought.

Bordeth's communicator chattered with Hawnl's familiar code. Taking the handpiece from its cradle in the instrument, he said, "Hawnl, I do not have time for your nonsense. I am quite busy with my newly acquired female companion. She is showing me things I have never experienced before. If you leave me alone, I may loan her

209

to you. So if this is not an extremely urgent emergency, leave me in peace."

The answer was a totally unfamiliar voice. "Bordeth, my name is Durell, and I come from Earth, one of the planets your warriors have conquered. I am going to give you only one warning before we unleash a hellish attack on your planet."

This is so cool, I thought. Knowing that Atina could read my thoughts, I could not help but to show off a bit. I had seen this scene play out on so many hero movies, I couldn't pass up the chance to put on a bit of swagger. *Maybe I should try to scare the hell out of this guy.*

"We have acquired the same weapon you used to destroy the planet Mars. As you know, this weapon will render your entire planet uninhabitable for any species. If you do not call all your occupation forces back from all the planets you have devastated, we will begin by destroying all life on the planets you have taken for your own."

I knew that Bordeth had no intention of giving up without a fight, but nevertheless, I felt it necessary to give him a chance to surrender.

"We know the locations of all the planets in your empire and are now ready to begin forcibly removing your kind from our universe. If you comply with our demands, we will spare your home planet. It will, however, be marked as a pariah, not unlike the leper colonies which were once part of my home world. You will never again be allowed to roam the universe, and all your offensive tools will be remitted to us. You have one hour to respond. Oh, by the way, Hawnl has been neutralized, so you will contact me to notify us of your decision."

Bordeth was dumbstruck. How could these rebels have gained access to the weapon which could end the Drezil's dominance in this universe? In the deep recesses of his puny mind, he knew he should investigate this new threat, but his arrogance led him to become extremely defiant to the extent that he would not even consider the rebel threat to be genuine.

When Bordeth called his war group together, he had only one message for them: "Call together all your ships and exterminate all native life on the planets we have taken. Leave not one humanoid alive. Ravage each planet for its valuable resources, and then move on to our next targeted worlds and do the same. We will drive all species out of this universe and kill any who resist. Go now and carry out my orders. *Those who choose to oppose me and my army will pay dearly for their arrogance*, he thought. *Let's see what they can bring to this fight.*

It became obvious that Bordeth did not believe them because the hour had passed without any contact from the Drezil. After configuring the weapon on all the available Habordiz ships, Atina and I assigned targets to each ship, saving the Drezil home planet for our own attack.

The brilliant trails of white-hot exhaust from the Habordiz's rebel ships faded into the heavens as the attackers began their separate journeys to their assigned targets. Each had on board the necessary weaponry to carry out their task and the capability of interstellar travel. The Azdawn had ultimate control over who could discharge the weapons to ensure that the power contained within their ships was not used for any purposes other than those which they deemed necessary. Having been equipped with the technology to provide instantaneous travel across the universe, their trips would be extremely short. There could be no doubt that the Drezil would be taken totally by surprise at the swiftness of the rebel attacks. Atina and I delayed our departure to allow Dlano time to brief all the homebound resistance members to take total control of Habordiz. No Drezil were left to oppose us, so our task would be relatively easy. Only those local inhabitants who had sided with the Drezil during their occupation would be singled out for punishment. After Dlano had completed his tasks, he boarded his ship and, along with several of his companion's ships, began the journey to their assigned target, Noedif Prime.

Chapter 40

Of the four planets that the Drezil had totally terraformed to support their own needs, Noedif Prime was the largest and most prized. They had long ago eliminated the indigenous population with a savage attack that left not one native alive. The source of their weaponry came from an electromagnetic pulse that caused all human DNA to separate and dissolve, leaving them as pools of flesh and bone which slowly disintegrated.

The Drezil had formed a society of sorts which was closely monitored by Bordeth and his henchmen. The leader of the occupying force was Thyzzez, a formidable Drezil who had given the final order to kill all the humanoids on the planet. The warriors who had taken this planet were rewarded by preferential treatment when it came to housing, food, and entertainment.

The years had been good to them all. Their lazy lifestyle had resulted in an apathetic attitude which left them in a state of total denial when thoughts of a revolution by the humanoids surfaced. Their slovenly lifestyle included mass consumption of their favorite beverage, which had a mind-dulling effect on them. It was as though they were all inebriated most of the time and did little to better themselves or the planet they had conquered.

They had long ago abandoned their defensive weapons and would never be able to repel any offensive attack. Their stupidity was beyond belief, and they were very quickly sinking into a mind-numbing lifestyle. Therefore, the small crafts that appeared above the planet did not cause any real concern among the Drezil leaders. They could only surmise that the ships were from their own home world and most likely here to present gifts and praise for the great work they had done. Little did they know that their existence was about to be terminated.

The beauty of the planet before the advent of the Drezil was breathtaking. From space, it appeared to be covered with lush green vegetation, blue-capped mountains, and aqua oceans that stretched throughout the entire planet. Now it had a dull brown cast that effectively hid all of its beauty. This was the prize of the empire, and Thyzzez had been granted the honor of becoming the overlord because he would not hesitate in killing the remaining humans to terraform the planet when the time came.

Thyzzez gave the order to prepare the welcome for their visitors. "Gather all our comrades for a feast with the visitors who have just arrived. I will personally meet with them and give them the hero's welcome that they deserve. They must be here to do the same for us. All I am waiting for is their communication so I can direct them to the proper landing site."

He then began to try to contact the newcomers. Although it seemed strange, Thyzzez was not really concerned when several other small ships suddenly joined the other craft that had initially been detected.

Dlano heard the request for communications which was issued from the planet. He called all his captains in his fleet to assess the situation and plan their next move. They had orders to annihilate all Drezil life on this planet and would carry out these orders. The only item up for discussion was the time and manner of their attack.

Addressing his fighters, Dlano said, "We have caught them totally by surprise. They must think we are emissaries from their home planet, so we can proceed with the battle plan without fear of any offensive action on their part. I am the commander of this entire armada, so my ship will begin the initial attack." Continuing his communication with his armada, Dlano said, "Do not deceive yourselves concerning what we are about to do. This will be total genocide of all Drezil inhabitants on this planet. In addition, our attack may well leave this planet uninhabitable by any species, including our own. Without this extreme show of force, we will have little chance of defeating the Drezil. So I will take responsibility for the initial attack, hoping that it will be all that is needed to accomplish our goal. If further action is required, I will order you all to use your ships and weapons to complete the decimation of the Drezil."

"Although we have been given implicit directions concerning the weapon's use, I am ordering all ships to move well away from the planet before I discharge it. I have a feeling that we are too close to the planet and might be caught up in the explosion that is about to occur. If I move my ship too far from the surface and the weapon malfunctions, we will move closer and try again. My daughter, Atina, and her partner are currently preparing to begin their trip to Andop to ask that the Drezil surrender so we are not forced to take this drastic action to force them out of all the worlds they have taken. If they are not successful in convincing Bordeth to stand down, we will all move forward with our assignments."

Chapter 41

Atina awaited our planned time for departure from Habordiz and said, "Durell, I am ready to begin our journey to Andop, the Drezil's home world. Our assignment is to be ready to destroy all life there if Bordeth does not comply with our demands. You will need to give the final command."

"Atina," I said, "we are about to do something that will give us nightmares for a long time. I know this is necessary, but I need your approval before I order this attack. Help me come to terms with what I am about to order."

Telepathically, Atina answered, *We have been given no choice in this matter. The Drezil have sealed their own fate, and you and I are just the trigger to set to initiate their destruction. No matter how this turns out, however, remember we have some unfinished personal business. Now let's get this done.*

I walked over to Atina, who had taken her seat as the pilot and commander of the Pentemor. I rested my hand on her shoulder to convey my solidarity with her.

"My father has travelled to Noedif Prime and will destroy the Drezil who have taken that planet for their own. Hopefully, when Bordeth is informed of our invasion, he will relent and bring his entire force back to Andop, leaving the planets they have taken to their indigenous populations. We cannot do anything for the former inhabitants of the four planets that the Drezil took over as they have killed all the native population, but we can ensure that those planets are again inhabited by humanoids. As soon as we arrive in orbit above Andop, I will wait only a short time for Bordeth's response before we unleash the weapon."

215

Chapter 42

Thyzzez was mystified why he had not received an acknowledgment from the visitors. His continued attempts to contact them were without any success, and he began to wonder if he had misinterpreted their intentions. He was about to contact his senior officers when a bright light began to appear above the planet.

As the light grew in intensity, a low moaning sound began to resonate throughout the atmosphere. The sky, typically brown from the methane-heavy clouds, began to take on a fiery red appearance. At its outer edges, the red hue seemed to be turning a brilliant white as the methane and oxygen atmosphere began to ignite. A curtain of white-hot destruction began to expand rapidly across the face of the planet, robbing the inhabitants of the life-giving atmosphere that they had so carefully terraformed for their own survival.

Thyzzez slowly realized what was occurring when he began to feel the effects of the atmospheric explosion as it shook the entire planet. His skin began to blister, and he was unable to focus on anything around him. He was confused about what was happening and could not understand why all of this was occurring.

The planet's atmosphere ignited totally, causing a blast wave to expand outward. It carried with it the totality of the Drezil occupying force, including the entire planet's living population as well as all they had built. The planet became uninhabitable very quickly.

The surface smoldered from the heat generated by the blast, and it began to turn a dark chocolate brown. Where there previously was life and an inhabitable planet, there was now nothing more than a charred rock which was completely dead. The first death blow had

UNIVERSAL EXTINCTION

been delivered to the Drezil. It was now up to Atina and I to inform Bordeth that we had struck this fatal blow and could repeat the attack on Andop if Bordeth did not bend to our demands.

All Bordeth's perverted activities were about to come to an end. He had been threatened by someone who threatened to annihilate him and his empire if he did not surrender to their wishes. His lavish lifestyle had isolated him from the day-to-day management of the Drezil holdings. He was untouchable, or so he thought.

He was confused. He had attempted to contact Thyzzez on Noedif Prime but had no success. He was considering sending a ship to that planet to assess Thyzzez's situation but was slow in acting. His inability to make quick decisions was about to catch up with him.

Pacing his command center, Bordeth tried to make sense out of what was happening. For some reason, he felt the need to don his ceremonial uniform as though he was getting ready for a celebration. He had no idea he had just put on his funeral garb.

While considering what action to take, his communicator sprang to life with an unfamiliar voice. "Bordeth, this is Durell, and I represent the resistance forces of the planets you have taken. We have invaded and destroyed the planet Noedif Prime along with your entire occupying force. The planet is now uninhabitable by any species. We gave you warning of our intention, but you have not yet responded to our demands. We will not wait long for you to surrender your forces and bring all your occupying armies back to this planet. We are aware of your treacherous nature and know it would lead you to try to counterattack us if you are given enough time to do so. So we give you no time to plan for your reprisal. Either you capitulate immediately, or we will destroy this planet and all who reside on it. We await your communication."

Bordeth went into an amphibian rampage. Screaming at his command officers, he said, "All your heads will be on the line if any of this is true. I will not take this laying down." He then began to stomp his feet, and green drool ran down his scaly chin.

"How did this happen?" he ranted. "Where did these humanoids get the weapons to make such demands on me? Noedif Prime is too far for any visual assessment of its condition, but I am not going to take the word of this inferior human and surrender my entire force."

His inability to contact Hawnl on Habordiz was concerning, but he could rationalize any number of reasons for the silence. Hawnl was such a lazy lout that he was most likely just ignoring Bordeth.

Without any other trustworthy information to act on, his response to the threat was "Whoever you are, I will not take what you say as true. I command you to depart from here immediately. If you do not do so, I will instruct my forces to destroy you and any supporters you may have. In addition, both Habordiz and Earth will soon be rid of your infectious species."

The message was received by Atina and I just as a massive group of Drezil ships was detected launching toward the Pentemor. I pressed the communicator button and said, "You have just sealed your own fate. The ships you have just launched will be destroyed, along with your planet and all who reside there. We will follow this attack up with the destruction of your remaining outposts on the twelve worlds you have taken. They will be warned just as you have been. Hopefully, they will have better sense than you."

With that, Atina energized the weapon. The atmosphere morphed into a deadly, plasma and the ships which had left the surface began to ignite, one by one, in a white flash of heat.

The same destructive force that had destroyed Noedif Prime was unleashed on Andop with the same results. Bordeth felt the first tremors begin to assault the planet, and he could only hear the death screams emitting from his fleet as it was destroyed, one ship at a time. He saw a bright light beginning to appear above the planet. The light grew in intensity, accompanied with a low moaning sound which began to resonate throughout the atmosphere. The sky, typically brown from the methane-heavy clouds, began to take on a fiery red appearance. At its outer edges, the red hue seemed to be turning a brilliant white as the methane and oxygen atmosphere began to ignite. A curtain of white-hot destruction began to expand rapidly across the face of the planet, robbing the inhabitants of their life-giving atmosphere.

UNIVERSAL EXTINCTION

Bordeth slowly realized what was occurring as he started feeling the effects of the atmospheric explosion that shook the entire planet. His skin blistered, and he was unable to focus on anything around him. He was confused and could not understand how all of this was occurring. The planet's atmosphere ignited totally, and the blast wave expanded outward. Bordeth's last thought was, *What the hell happened?* Then he exploded as the temperature on the planet's surface shot up by thousands of degrees.

Atina had moved her ship to what she thought was a safe distance before the weapon was activated, but the shock wave caused by the planet's destruction shook her little craft, causing it to tumble farther away from the destruction zone. The Pentemor shuddered from the effects of the blast wave, so it was only by luck that it was not destroyed. Pentemor began to tumble outward from the flaming planet in an erratic series of loops that started to tear panels from the ship. The first to go was the engine's fairings, followed by one of the Pentemor's exhaust nozzles. Had the ship been oriented toward the exploding planet, it, along with its inhabitants, would have been a casualty of the planet's demise. Atina's caution in moving farther away from the planet had saved them from certain death. The craft righted itself, and Atina and I gaped in astonishment at the results of the weapon's power. The ever-expanding cloud which contained the atmosphere that used to surround Andop was white-hot while the planet's surface was quickly turning a grayish brown color. Never having seen destruction at this level, we could only watch in awe as an entire civilization was vaporized before our eyes.

"Atina, I am deeply concerned about the Azdawn's failure to warn us of the effects the weapon would have on our ship. Had you followed their directions, we would both be dead. Why did they tell us that the safe distance was much closer than we experienced? We need to seriously consider our relationship with them. I am also concerned about why Dlano did not warn us of the dangers of remaining too close."

The cloud dissipated, the planet came into focus, and it appeared that only death was awaiting anyone who approached it. The Drezil menace was injured severely, but we knew that this war was not yet won. There were still any number of additional Drezil who could counterattack if they could piece together a new command structure. It was imperative that we move quickly to squash any attempt by the remaining Drezil to reorganize. Our plan had taken this into consideration, and we had already placed resources close to all eleven remaining planets infected by the Drezil menace. After witnessing the power of the weapon, neither Atina nor I were going to be quick to support further action that might cause complete genocide of the Drezil species. Only if it were necessary would the weapon be used again.

The Azdawn had provided all the resources necessary to bring about the fall of the Drezil empire; however, they could not and would not take an active role in the war. Long ago, their culture had abandoned violence as a method of problem solving but knew that these humanoids could never defeat the Drezil without offering the same treatment as they had received. However, the Azdawn support and willingness to continue to provide access to the weapon was tempered with their need to remain as nonviolent bystanders. They had given two humanoids the tools and power to lead this fight but still retained control of the use of that power. They were relying on these two individuals to use great care in dispatching their ships to the planets which were taken by the Drezil. If no further action was required to bring this war to an end and the Drezil could find another unoccupied planet to colonize, the Azdawn would render the weapon useless.

Following the attack that destroyed Noedif Prime and Andop, the rebel fleet was instructed to return to Habordiz. Those ships stationed around the remaining eleven planets which the Drezil had taken were awaiting word from Dlano before they moved forward with unleashing the power they possessed. Their only action thus far had been to destroy the Drezil satellites which surrounded each planet. Without these devices, the planet's overseers could no longer control the native populations.

The Drezil, on the other hand, were desperately trying to reach Bordeth for orders concerning what they were to do. Madille, located on Alpha2, had been made aware of the destruction of his home planet. He had been asked by the resistance leaders to communicate with those Drezil who held the remaining conquered planets. Opening a communication line with the leaders of each of the eleven planets, he informed them of what had occurred and warned them not to make any aggressive moves toward the rebels. His most urgent message was sent to the three remaining planets that were populated only by the Drezil. He knew that these planets were the next to be targeted for destruction. He had brokered a deal with the rebels which would allow his species to colonize one of the planets they had taken. If there were none left after the battle, the Drezil would either fight until their entire species was wiped out or be forced out of the universe. Although many of those who were left after the destruction of the home planet might have viewed him as a traitor, Madille could only try to save those who remained on the conquered planets. His intent was to meet with each of the planet's overseers and convince them of the futility of continuing to resist the rebels' demands.

Without the leadership offered by Bordeth, the remaining Drezil commanders were unable to forge a functional command structure. The only top-level leader they could turn to was Bordeth's brother, Madille. The Azdawn had utilized him in their plot to overthrow the Drezil by allowing him to believe that the weapon they had provided could only be used by the humanoids who had visited him on Alpha2. He was totally unaware that his entire species was on the verge of being annihilated. It appeared that the Azdawn had their own agenda which did not include the Drezil as members of this universe. The Drezil were going to suffer greatly for their attack on the Azdawn so many millennia ago. The revenge the Azdawn sought was about to be carried out. Their intention was to completely wipe out the Drezil species. Their inability to carry out any violent actions forced them to find a surrogate who could be trusted to use the weapon and advance the Azdawn's chances to take control of all the inhabitants of this universe. Once they had completed all their objectives, they intended to reestablish their species as the masters of the entire universe. The enslaved species could then be used to fight whatever battle presented itself.

The willingness of the humanoids to carry out all the actions which would eventually lead to the Azdawn's domination was of incalculable value to them. Their only concern was that I might see through their entire scheme and turn the power and talents they had given me against them. To ensure this did not take place, they had failed to tell Atina and I that the weapon would not only destroy any target planet but also any ship which was in orbit around the planet. They knew that the destructive power of the weapon, when used on Andop, would kill both Atina and me.

Chapter 43

They had prepared well. The humans were moving forward with the plan of attack they thought was their own. The Azdawn knew better. They had been the authors of this invasion from the start. Their telepathic ability had placed the entire battle plan in Atina and my heads. We had passed it on to Dlano and the other resistance commanders.

I knew something was behind all the offensive success we were experiencing. I had a real sense that whoever was behind all that was happening would require payback for the assistance we received. *If we are not careful, we will be tied to some entity that we will regret ever meeting. No free rides!*

The Azdawn's need for revenge had not been met by what had just occurred on Noedif Prime and Andop. To satisfy their agenda, the entire Drezil species would have to pay.

Dlano knew exactly what the Azdawns had in mind. Strangely feeling the need to be honest with his companions, he said, "They had no intention of stopping the slaughter with one or two of the Drezil's captive planets. They are intent on destroying the entire species. If we do not wish to do the Azdawn's bidding, another species will be called on to complete the task. Then all who had knowledge of the construction and operation of the weapon would be destroyed, along with the Drezil."

Even though the Azdawn's roots were the same as the Earthlings and all other humanoid species, they would have no hesitation in enslaving the entire human race. They had no idea that the power they had given us would be the catalyst for a new advanced species that would be called on to bring the treacherous Azdawn to their

223

knees. They had forgotten one major element in the evolution of the universe's species—the humans—and they shared a common DNA which made them a singular species. The Azdawn had evolved into a more advanced society than their human brothers and sisters, and they had no idea that Atina and I held the seeds which gave us the potential of evolving into a race which could be much more powerful than the Azdawn.

They had given Atina and me the ability to foster an advanced race which could eventually become universal peacekeepers. All that was needed now was a union between us. We could then pass our unique abilities on to our offspring through our shared DNA.

The Pentemor made a comfortable sanctuary for Atina and me. She casually set our course for Habordiz and initiated the trans-galaxy engine. I watched her as she skillfully set all the controls as if it was second nature for her.

"Atina," I said, "would you be upset if I told you that my admiration for you goes well beyond the bounds of friendship? We have shared many difficult moments and have always let our personal feelings take a back seat to our duties to the rebel cause. I think it is time to end that."

Atina gave me a look that I could not decipher. "You do not need to put into words what we both already know is fact. There can be no doubt that some very deep feelings exist between us, but I do not believe now is the time to pursue our own agenda. Let's try to focus on what has just happened and figure out how we are to proceed from this point. Our arrival at Habordiz might be met with a celebration. But remember, we are not done with our crusade.

"Durell," Atina said. "Have you been able to deal emotionally with what we have just done? Destroying an entire planet along with its population is not something I ever thought I could do. How have you managed to continue functioning considering what we have just done?"

I could only respond, "I am a warrior. I have served in my own country's military and understand that sometimes, the destruction of your enemy is the only way to bring about peace. If you cannot deal with the brutal side of war, you might want to stay home next time."

UNIVERSAL EXTINCTION

Atina was infuriated. "How dare you address me like that. I have put my life on the line many times and have proven my will to do the most adherent things to bring about the salvage of my people. Don't you dare call my commitment to this war into question. You can't get rid of me that easy. No matter what my feelings are for you, I am a dedicated warrior to our cause."

Our conversation came to an end with the sound of the engine's thunderous ignition preparing the ship for arrival at Habordiz.

Our ship settled gracefully on its home pad, and word came from Dlano that the remaining Drezil on the other eleven conquered planets had agreed to the resistance's demands. They would move all their remaining population to the planet Yucholl, which had been one of the first taken. It was large enough for them and could be monitored easily by the humans. Dlano had been appointed as ambassador and chief negotiator for the humans and was already preparing for his journey to meet with the Drezil to iron out the details of the surrender.

Atina and I, on the other hand, had received a heroine and hero's welcome from the freed inhabitants of Habordiz. We exited the Pentemor and were spirited away to a platform high above the launch site. Even though our planet's population had been decimated, a huge crowd was gathered to celebrate their newly earned freedom. Neither Atina nor I were at all comfortable being the center of this attraction, but we felt we had to submit for the sake of those gathered.

"If there is any compensation for my collaboration in this entire affair, my only wish was to return to Earth and help to rebuild my own planet."

Sensing my discomfort, Atina asked, "Durell, what in the hell are you thinking? We have defeated the Drezil, so you should be ecstatic. Instead, I seem to get the feeling you are not at all happy. So what's up?"

I could feel a tenseness coming from Atina. She turned toward me with a wanting look on her face and with a single tear coursing down her face. How could I tell her that I needed to get the hell out of here and figure out how to get back to Earth?

225

In my newly acquired telepathic voice, I said, *Atina, we are not the same as when we began this adventure. We have been given power and abilities which have never been exhibited by other humans. I do not know where we are to go from here, but I guarantee you that if we do not remain together, we will never be able to find peace. You and I have been given genetic abilities which may be the source of a new species of human. We both know that our lives will never be the same as when we met, but I need you to trust me. I have had some strange feeling about the Azdawn and their actual agenda. Their lack of warning concerning the safe distance above the planet needed to survive the weapon's blast has lit a fire of distrust in me. We need to be extremely careful from this point on in our dealings with them.*

I could see that Atina was shocked by the substance of my message. She had known for some time that our mutual attraction was growing stronger with each passing day. She had contemplated many times the ramifications of a physical union with me but had never seriously considered what the outcome of such a union might be.

"Durell," she said, "even though we have not actually discussed the consequences of a physical union between us, I know deep down that we are definitely capable of producing an offspring. We should not even consider moving ahead unless we both agree to the consequences of our actions. We could be responsible for creating a new human species."

Her reference to a new human species left no doubt that she saw our association as more than a partnership. The thought of producing an offspring which would possess our collective genetic blueprint was just beginning to gel in my mind.

"Atina," I asked, "am I to assume that you are suggesting that we come together as partners and begin a life as a couple? If that is the case, I need to tell you that I have not only come to respect and admire you, but I think I have fallen in love with you. If your feelings are the same as mine, I think I would be open to a future with you as my partner."

Atina walked over to me and put her arms around my neck. I could feel her hot breath on my neck and the slight touch of her lips.

UNIVERSAL EXTINCTION

"Durell, you can have no doubt of my feelings for you. I am open to anything you might desire to do with me."

We both understood and accepted the unique nature of any relationship we might join in. The enormity of what was beginning to occur began to impact us both, and each of us offered ourselves as a willing participant in the creation of the new life which would eventually form the nucleus of an advanced human species.

Atina's culture had long ago abandoned any physical contact for the purposes of procreation. "Durell, I am willing to enter a physical union with you. I know you will respect my right to abandon the insemination process at any time. I was never picked to reproduce, so I am completely unschooled in this alternative impregnation process."

"I have participated in many physical unions throughout my life, many for the sake of pleasure only. I think you will find that our sex act will not only be pleasurable but will result in the birth of a new life. I know what will be required of us to consummate this union and will lead you through the entire process. Atina, I want you to be absolutely certain of what we are about to do. I am totally committed to you and the offspring we will be producing. Now is probably the best time to tell you that I love you and want to spend the rest of my life keeping you safe. If you feel the same, you have to tell me."

Atina answered, "Durell, I love you. I trust you and want to join with you. Our lives have been connected from the first time I saw you."

We had now agreed to carry out the act which would create a new advanced race of humans. Atina knew that I could lead her through what would be required to produce an offspring that would join our worlds.

She looped her small arm in mine and followed me into the confines of our sleeping quarters. She felt a strange rush of excitement that was totally foreign to her. "Durell, my heart is beginning to pound, and I feel hot flashes coursing through my body. Is this normal even before we get physical?"

I could only take her arm and turn her toward me. Kissing her, I said, "What you are feeling is your sexual desire beginning to send your body messages which you have never experienced before. You do not have any control over this, so just let it happen."

Had we known what was about to happen in the universe, we might have been less likely to continue with what we had planned.

Atina felt a disturbing invasion of her psyche. Even though she had mentally prepared herself to become the mother of a new human, she was beginning to have dark thoughts concerning the direction we had mapped for ourselves.

Even though I had sensed the subtle changes in her, I was totally unaware of her inability to filter out the changes which would eventually have a devastating impact on her relationship with me. She had been so focused on completing the mission we had undertaken that she had failed to note the changes in her dedication to the human cause. A dark cloud seemed to be turning her thoughts toward a more violent approach to problem-solving.

She was just beginning to feel the pangs of mistrust in me, which were coming from messages she was receiving telepathically from some unknown source. Could she be becoming a puppet for the Azdawn? Had Atina and I knew what the future had in store for us, we would never had considered producing an offspring with the abilities that were well beyond that of any human or Azdawn.

Chapter 44

The room was semi-dark with light coming only from three candles set on a table next to one of the beds. I led Atina to the bed. I could read her mind, and I knew she was afraid. *What is this going to be like?* she thought. Her only knowledge concerning procreation was from the studies she had completed in her younger years. She had never been exposed to the physical act of love, so she was concerned not only about how it was going to feel but also what the period of gestation was going to be like. She and I were about to create a new life that would carry our combined DNA and, most likely, be much more advanced than all other humans. Her fears were mounting, and I motioned for her to lie back on the bed. As she did as I asked, she heard me telepathically tell her, *Atina, do not fear what is about to occur. In my society, what we are about to do is commonplace and considered extremely enjoyable by both participants. You have never joined physically with another human, so be prepared because you will initially feel some pain, but it will quickly dissipate into a glow of pleasure. I will not rush or insist on continuing if you do not wish to do so. Are you ready to begin?*

I closed the entry door to the bedroom. Atina knew that the time to back out of this arrangement was long past, and she was becoming increasingly stimulated by the thought of joining with me. She pressed her lean body fully against me, and I knew the time had come to face our destiny.

Atina's eyes darted toward the bed. Her shoulders slumped in resignation, knowing that she was about to change her entire future. Hands shaking, she began to loosen the buttons on her blouse.

Although her fears were still present, Atina said, "I trust you, Durell. I will try to follow your lead, but please remember that I have never been inseminated and will be extremely nervous once we begin."

With that said, Atina removed her clothes. Once she was completely naked, she slipped between the rough sheets which covered the bed. Having slept here many times, she could not believe how different it felt now that her intention was something other than sleeping. The cool air had chilled her, and she noted that her breasts had become very taut with the nipples becoming extremely firm. Her body was rigid, as if waiting for some sort of punishment.

Seeing the perfection of Atina's slim body, I could not help feeling a rush of desire as I caught my first view of her naked. Her skin tone had a slight olive tint. I wondered why I had never noticed her beauty before, but my primal senses told me to take this woman for my own. My only desire now was to have her completely. Just before she slipped between the sheets of the bed, I saw her shiver from the cool air. I was amazed by her toned body and the effects the cool air was having on her.

Atina had long ago decided that when the right time came, she would tell me how she really felt about our partnership. *Is now the time for me to open my heart to this man?* she thought. *I want our union to be one of love and not due to our mutual physical attraction. Any offspring that may result from what we are about to do should be the product of my love for this man.*

Following Atina's lead, I removed all my clothing. She reluctantly gazed at my muscular body. Although she had seen many pictures of naked males and never reacted to them, this was an entirely new experience. She could only marvel at the new sensations which were coursing through her body at the sight of this magnificent male. She could sense the pheromones I was producing, which caused a rush of desire to invade her body, beginning at the junction of her legs and moving quickly upward towards her brain.

I slipped between the covers next to her, and the heat from my body begin to light a fire within her. Her body turned to this new heat source, and as her breasts touched my chest, she gave way completely to the wanton desire that had taken control of her. She was

UNIVERSAL EXTINCTION

now completely comfortable with what was about to happen. She wrapped her arms around me and whispered into my mind, *I am ready. I love you and want to join with you in the creation of a new life.*

The moment that message came into my mind, another louder voice said, *Stop!*

Atina heard the same message at the same time. We were both taken aback, but our natural need for procreation could not be silenced. As we came together, we did not have any thought for the consequences of this moment. The far-reaching impact of our union would be felt throughout the universe.

Chapter 45

Atina had always pondered how she would react to being pregnant. As a child, she was taught that procreation was simply a matter of mechanical insemination which led to the continuation of her species. After she and I had bonded physically, she had to reevaluate her entire education concerning her sexuality. She had been warned not to proceed with her union with me but had not heeded this advice. Now she was being subtly urged to abandon her association with her own people as well as me.

The Azdawn had placed one of their kind close to Atina and me throughout our entire adventure. He was one of the high-level leaders of the Habordiz resistance and was part of the group who designed and carried out the attack on the Drezil. Atina knew him as Dlano, whom she understood was her father. His proximity to Atina allowed him to telepathically inject ideas into her mind which would eventually lead to her abandoning all her trusted allies. The final message she received was to join him in a journey to the new home of the Azdawn. Had she known what was to occur shortly, she would have never agreed to abandon her allies and join with the Azdawn. Rotan's ship, the Imnadda, was dispatched to Habordiz to bring Atina and Dlano to the Azdawn's adopted home, the planet Simiri 86.

When I left Habordiz, Atina was pregnant. Our single sexual encounter had led to several more insemination attempts, one of which had been successful. Although I was very conflicted about what I should do, I knew I needed to return to Earth as soon as possible.

232

UNIVERSAL EXTINCTION

"Atina," I said, "I do not wish to abandon you, but I have extremely important things to do on Earth, so I need to depart here as soon as I possibly can. I promise I will return as soon as I set the Earth's rejuvenation in motion. Please forgive me for what many may view as abandonment, but I have no choice."

Atina answered, almost too quickly, "I know you have much to do, so I see no problem with your departure. Don't worry about me or our child. Although I have never given birth, I am actually looking forward to the experience. When you are ready to return and become a part of our new family, let me know well in advance of your arrival. Now go while you still can."

Okay, I thought, *what in the hell does she mean by that? Things are getting out of hand here. Maybe my return to Earth might not be a bad idea. Something very strange seems to be happening to Atina. Could this be the result of our sharing our DNA through her insemination? Whatever the case, I have to get out of here!*

I utilized the Pentemor for my journey home, and it, along with the engine that had powered us throughout the universe, would become the template for the construction of a fleet of interstellar ships. My main goal at present was to gather all the engineering minds available from across the entire planet to build the armada of ships which would be utilized to thwart any future attacks on the Earth. With that in mind, I contacted my new friend, Captain Robert Allen.

My ship slowed as it approached the Earth, and it returned to normal space, leaving the now familiar trail of ionized gasses behind which faded from the rainbow of colored sheets to an invisible trail of electrified plasma.

The view from the cockpit revealed an entire solar system that seemed unchanged from the last time I had seen it. Sliding between the planets, I found myself approaching the Earth at a decreasing speed. As Earth came into view, I was almost overcome by the devastation I viewed below.

It was almost painful to stare out the cockpit windows and look toward the Earth. There was a mantel of gray and yellow gas circulating around the planet which almost blocked my view of the surface.

233

Smoke and ash were still rising from the unchecked fires that went unattended. It appeared that the Drezil attack had not only caused immediate death and destruction but also left a legacy of damage which could not be controlled by the remaining population. The decaying of all those murdered humans who had been killed, along with the plants and animals killed, left the air heavy with a stench that would last for months.

I skillfully aimed the Pentemor toward my destination outside the Cheyenne Mountain Complex, and my communication device crackled to life. "Durell, this is Captain Allen. We have prepared a landing site for you on the northeast side of the complex's entrance. You will find a crew there who will assist in the care of your vessel. Please meet with me as soon as you can so we can bring you up-to-date on the status of our recovery efforts."

I responded, "I have located your position and will instruct the Pentemor to land where you have suggested. It is good to hear from you, and I have some news of surprising developments that could make our restoration efforts much more important than we had initially thought. I will see you shortly." With that, I keyed the landing instructions into the Pentemor's computer and sat back for the landing to be completed.

After the landing sequence had brought the Pentemor to a gentle landing, I was almost overcome by the emotions which flooded my body. Since I had last visited my home world, I had participated in a war which had resulted in the death of millions of living beings. My planet was now safe, but few of my fellow humans survived the Drezil invasion. I would have a new offspring soon, and my mind was wrapped around my love for the alien, Atina. I was unable to clearly focus on what I needed to do from this point forward.

I was taken by my greeters through the entrance of the Cheyenne Mountain Complex. My initial impression of the inside of the structure was one of total astonishment. The air was cool and damp. The huge door that closed behind us as we entered was composed of several feet of titanium and locked not unlike the bank vaults I had seen before. I was ushered into a small alcove cut from one of the stone walls. Inside, I found Captain Allen and his executive officer.

UNIVERSAL EXTINCTION

"Durell," Captain Allen said. "It is good to see you. We are in the initial phases of formulating a plan that will bring the entire remaining population of Earth under a single governance that will have only one goal—the defeat of any alien race which tries to invade this planet. You will be a major player in this effort, and we hope you will agree to become the commanding officer of the entire fleet we will be constructing. Your arrival here in the Pentemor will speak volumes to all who agreed to join us."

I personally did not care to impress anyone and made that clear by turning my back to those who had arrived. I felt there was way too much to worry about what anyone thought about the importance of my participation in the resurrection of the Earth's society.

I responded, "The experiences I have had lately with other entities has left me with an extremely suspicious attitude and little trust in any species other than our own. I have little faith in any of the partnerships which were formed during our fight and eventual defeat of the Drezil."

It would come as a surprise to all my new companions, but I had abilities which they would find astonishing. *I think I should be careful about using any of my new talents in the view of anyone here on Earth.*

"Captain Allen, even though both Atina and I were given many enhanced powers by the Azdawn, I am becoming increasingly alarmed that these gifts might have been given only to assist them to reach their final goal. What that agenda might be has yet to be determined, but take my word for this. They are a self-serving species who cannot be trusted. The only thing working in our favor is that the Azdawn could not negate any of the powers they had given to us."

I was trying to give Captain Allen only enough information to satisfy his curiosity without revealing all the new abilities I had.

"Our telepathic abilities have always been part of our species' capabilities. We had just not been able to exercise them. Atina is still on Habordiz and carrying our child, so we will have to await the arrival of our offspring to see how our combined DNA affects the child. In the meantime, I am at your disposal."

235

Captain Allen had taken command of the remaining inhabitants of the Cheyenne Mountain Complex as soon as he arrived. There were few upper-level government officials left alive anywhere in the world, so the only conceivable route was to establish a new government which would initially be under military rule until a plan was formulated to determine who had survived and how many inhabitants were still alive on the planet. To this end, Captain Allen requested that all the remaining military officers and civilian leaders meet at the Cheyenne Complex to try to form some sort of governance. His initial plan was to utilize my expertise and knowledge of the disaster and consider appointing me as a coleader on the planet. The recovery of humanity had begun.

The meeting room was cavernous. As with all the Cheyenne Mountain Complex, it was hewed out of solid rock. The structure would allow it to withstand the destructive power of a nuclear bomb. The large conference table located in the center of the space was adorned with flags from the many countries whose representatives were attending this historic gathering. Cheyenne Mountain had provided an ideal shelter which shielded its occupants from the carnage experienced around the globe.

Although the DNA mapping process initiated by the Drezil had proven successful for the majority of the planet's occupants, those housed in the underground complex had escaped the Drezil's probes. The solid granite walls of the structure glowed a pale white and had the appearance of polished wet stone. They completely shielded everyone inside from the probes as well as most other electromagnetic media, including the TV and radio announcements which had given a complete pictorial summary of the entire attack. Those housed within the structure's innards had little knowledge of the scope of the devastation which had decimated the planet's population.

"When we inform those housed in this complex of the scale of the devastation outside, we may have a real problem on our hands. Everyone here will insist on leaving to check on their own families and friends. We cannot allow them to leave, so be prepared to use force if necessary."

UNIVERSAL EXTINCTION

The representatives took their seats at the conference table, and Captain Allen introduced himself and me to the gathering. "Let me make myself perfectly clear," he said. "Although there are few of us left to govern this planet, we must come together as a single entity to salvage our species. We can no longer fight among ourselves as the enemy will take advantage of any weaknesses they discover. The attack we experienced that took away so many of our friends and families will not be the last if we do not become proactive in the construction of a fleet of ships which can ward off any future attacks."

Although we had put an end to the Drezil menace, there was no guarantee that they acted alone. We had to form a close-knit group to plan our future.

"Make no mistake, the Drezil are not the only species which has designs for the Earth," I said. "Although we have yet to pinpoint what species will be the next threat to our way of life, we know there was an entity behind the Drezil's attack on us. With all this in mind, we have declared martial law within the United States and are committed to building a fleet of interstellar ships."

Looking at the assembled leaders of the world, I could not help but be concerned about our ability to bring this group together as a singular focused group. It was imperative that the entire population of the Earth had a single goal in mind.

I pointed to the group and said, "You will all have an important part to play in the resurrection of our species."

Having said my piece, I turned and walked to the portal and left the room.

Captain Allen waited a few seconds after my departure. He turned to the assembly. "It is our opinion that we could and should be viewed as the leader in this effort and be given the authority by all of you to declare a unified martial law that includes all countries on the face of this planet. All who join in this communion of nations will be included in the creation, testing, and manning of every ship we complete. Those who opt out of this new governance will be left to fend for themselves."

Many of those present seemed to take a step backward, as though they were trying to remove themselves from the entire process of reclaiming the Earth. The foreign representative turned to Captain Allen and pushed him off to the edge of the crowd. Captain Allen was so surprised that he initially could not react to the disrespect. A short time later, he crossed swiftly to the foreign representative and hit him square in his jaw.

He said, "Our only hope to defend this planet and our species from any further assault is to band together into a formidable army which would initially be defensive in nature. Any of you who want to join this guy on the floor, feel free to step forward. Where this will all lead is a question that remains unanswered, but I assure you that any further insurrection will not be tolerated."

The crowd of attendees shuffled forward, pressing against the raised platform which Captain Allen occupied. Hands began reaching out, trying to touch him as though he had just become a messiah.

"The planning for this endeavor has been initiated by Dr. Durell Dykstra, who has seen and been a major player in the defeat of the Drezil. His expertise and close connection with leaders from other planets will serve as the stimulus for our reborn race to be a power to be reckoned with. He will become the commanding officer of the fleet we intend to construct. Speak among yourselves and your constituents in your home countries, and be prepared to give us your answer in two days."

Chapter 46

It had always been my intention to try to ascertain what had happened to my family and friends during the invasion. With that in mind, I took my leave from Captain Allen and Cheyenne Mountain and headed for my former residence in Idaho. I had a newly acquired talent for flying both fixed wing and rotary-wing aircraft, so I was given access to a Cessna 310 twin engine aircraft for my trip home. Leaving Wyoming, I was able to get a clear view of the aftermath of the attacks which were perpetrated by the Drezil. I flew over Montana and noted the lack of any other aircraft as well as little activity on the ground. It was as though all the inhabitants of this sector of the country had left. My main concern, however, was the status of the small valley which contained my hometown. Circling the valley, I could see little activity, no automobile traffic, and no discernable life, only a dark brownish gray cloud which hung over the city. I felt a rush of sadness when I began to consider that so far, all the evidence I had seen indicated that no life was left here.

I approached the small airport which served this area and attempted to contact the tower for permission to land, but I received no reply to my transmissions. Having no recourse, I set my aircraft down, hoping there were no objects on the runway which would cause any damage.

Taxiing towards the small terminal, I spun the aircraft around 360 degrees to see if there was any activity. Not seeing any other aircraft moving, I went directly to the terminal and parked as close as possible to its entry. After the engines slowly spun to a stop, I exited the aircraft over the right wing and moved toward the terminal.

239

There was a distinctly foul odor which made the air very heavy. The stench was almost overpowering, so I made a mask out of my T-shirt and wrapped it around my face, hoping for some relief. *My god, what am I getting myself into? I have witnessed so much death in the past that I really don't know how much more I can stand. Hopefully, the stench in the air will dissipate soon.*

Approaching the terminal, I saw what appeared to be human remains scattered throughout the building, lying on the floor, slumped in the seats surrounding the exit door, and scattered around the tarmac. They were unrecognizable as humans, and they all appeared to have died in the not-too-distant past. The silence was almost deafening. I skirted the building and found more deceased individuals who appeared to have been headed for the small parking lot which served the facility. With my apprehension building, I found a pickup truck which had been opened just before the event that killed all those at the airport. The entire series of events which had just occurred left me trembling, my hands shaking uncontrollably. The keys were still in the ignition, so I climbed in and attempted to start the truck. After several tries, the engine finally came to life with a roar. Still, I couldn't shake the morbid realization that the carnage I was witnessing could have been avoided if Atina and I had warned Captain Allen sooner.

Steering the truck out of the airport parking lot and onto the road leading down a hill to the central part of the town, I noted that the river that bordered the west side of the city was a strange blue-brown color. Having spent many hours playing in these waters, I knew that something catastrophic had occurred which had tainted the water. Moving closer to the river's edge, I noted a strong odor which I associated with rotting flesh. Had so many creatures, both human and animal, been killed that the water could not absorb their bodies?

Enough, I thought. *I have to stay on task and investigate my own family and friends' well-being.* I then set my sights on the route I had taken so many times in the past, my way home.

The town was decimated. No living being was encountered on my way to my house and workshop. Rounding the final corner, I saw my home untouched by whatever had caused the death of all

UNIVERSAL EXTINCTION

those who had populated the town. The front door was still locked, and the shop doors were closed but not latched. I entered the house to the odor of decaying food and mildew. I found all my belongings where I had left them, with only a dusting of dirt covering every part and piece of my residence. The many months I had been away had changed little, and I could almost believe that I had just stepped back to the start of this journey. Having viewed all I could endure, I made my way out to the unlocked shop.

Memories rushed into my head as I viewed the roots of the vessel Rachell and I had constructed. In one corner of the large shop, I found what appeared to be human remains. The hair was still intact, and I could tell that it had belonged to my assistant, Rachell. A wave of sorrow flooded my psyche, and I knelt to offer my respect and sorrow to the person who had trusted me when there was no real reason to do so.

Rising and moving to the workbench, I found an envelope which contained a letter from Rachell. It read:

> Durell, I have waited for a long time for you to either return or to somehow contact me concerning whether our experiment either failed completely or was a success. The last thing I saw of you and our ship was a brilliant flash of rainbow light which seemed to streak outward from this planet. For some reason, I have had a reoccurring dream that you have survived our insanity and are going to return to me soon. There has been a report that an entity has been discovered outside our atmosphere, and we are awaiting their contact to ascertain if they are friend or foe. We also have reports of people just falling to the ground dead on the European continent. Not knowing what this is bringing to us, I have penned this letter to you in the hopes that you will return to this shop in the future, hopefully to find me here to assist you in any other ventures you might undertake.

With that, I will just say that my admiration for
your talent and courage is without bounds, and I
sincerely hope we meet again.

I struggled to emotionally deal with all that I had just experienced. I now knew that my entire adventure from the time I last left this shop had somehow been orchestrated by someone other than myself. With Atina possibly pregnant and currently living on Habordiz, I knew that any action I might take would have to be done without her assistance. I knew that many of the successes we had experienced were due, in large part, to her planning. I knew I would need to locate another individual to join me in the construction of the defensive system which would be needed to protect the Earth from any future invasion. With that in mind, I contacted Captain Allen with a request to begin the search for the most qualified individuals who could play pivotal roles in the future of the Space Agency.

Chapter 47

Morning broke over the mountains in Wyoming, and Captain Allen and I met to discuss the options that we might have based on the delegate's answers. The attack had left many major countries totally devoid of any leadership. China, India, and the Arab nations were the most severely affected as they had little to protect a large portion of their population. Russia had lost most of its military bases and was without any usable defensive capabilities. It was left to those individuals who had taken shelter deep in the Wyoming complex to formulate a plan to bring together all nations and form an alliance which would be the foundation for a new offensive space fleet. The need for both defensive and offensive capabilities had been proven by the destruction left in the wake of the Drezil's attack. New ships with interstellar voyage capabilities would be powered by copies of the engine which took Atina and me on our quest and would be structurally based on the Pentemor. The ship was positioned in a tight orbit around the Earth and was available for study by the engineers who were designing the ships which would form the nucleus of Earth's space fleet.

Adel Harvey had collaborated on the construction of the International Space Station in the years before the Drezil invasion. Her 5'3" stature enhanced an appearance which had caught the attention of many men. Her blond shoulder-length hair always looked a bit unkempt and continually fell onto her face, causing her to shake her head from side to side to clear her eyes so she could see. She never dressed to attract men, but her natural beauty stopped them in their tracks. Although she was a stunningly beautiful woman, she had managed to dodge all attempts to persuade her to enter any kind of personal relationship. Her life goals did not include any associations which would distract her from becoming the best aerospace engineer in the world. Her future was certain in her own mind, but she was about to see her plans take a total departure from the direction she had initially set.

Adel was a superb engineer and understood the urgency of the task before her. She would be asked to play a major role in the newly formed Space Agency. Her mentor, Dr. Nicholas Ray, had groomed her for just such a challenge. She had the innate ability to visualize a project from its inception to completion. In this case, the cursory examination she had given the Pentemor allowed her to envision a new and better ship that would be the pride of the universe. The design and construction of this new addition to the interstellar travel community would be the envy of all. Her vision was a large sleek vessel which could carry a minimum complement of one hundred souls. It would have to be constructed in space as its very weight and mass would be impossible to lift from the Earth's surface. Even though she had my engine to utilize as the power plant which would allow the ship to perform interstellar jumps, the sub-light engine she had designed would be utilized in normal flight.

When Adel and I first met, I felt an intense attraction toward her. *Could she be feeling the same attraction?* I thought. Having never been attracted to any of the opposite sex, she was not ready to deal with anything except the job she was asked to do. However, she felt a hot blush as we shook hands for the first time. Noting that I held onto her hand just a bit too long, she pulled back to assess what was going on. Her engineering mind was trying to deal with this attraction as though it was an engineering problem.

Even though I was distracted by the immense job that was before me, I felt extremely at ease with Adel and instantly trusted her. She, on the other hand, had always been slow to accept anyone into her design and construction community who had not proven their worth. We began the task which would lead to the entry of a new ship into our space fleet, and it was assumed that we would move from the design phase of the project to initial construction in a short time. It was soon very evident that the task we had undertaken was much more involved than anyone had ever imagined.

"Adel," I said, "we are fortunate to have a functioning ship which will reduce the amount of engineering required to build our new fleet of ships. You have already been up to the Pentemor and given her a cursory examination. We have now brought her down to her new launchpad so you can examine her at will. The Pentemor will serve as our template for our construction."

Adel's visit to the Pentemor totally overwhelmed her. She could not believe the technology which was contained within the skin of this ship. Although the greatest surprise was yet to be unveiled, the size and construction of the ship took her breath away. Its skin was extremely thin, made of some material that seemed to flex very easily when touched. It was silver in color and polished to a brilliant chrome-like finish.

Dropping down from the cockpit of the Pentemor toward the engine room, I saw the distinct signs that Adel was beginning to experience some type of distress. "Adel," I asked, "are you feeling okay? Several people who were exposed to my engine became extremely ill and were forced to retreat from it. If you begin to feel strange, please let me know."

Adel continued to make her way to the engine room. As she got closer to the engine room, she began to feel a dull ache beginning in her stomach and radiating upward toward her head. She approached the hatch which separated her from the engines, and a sense of fear took over her mind. She slowly backed away from the hatch.

She turned to me and asked, "How could this be? I have never been affected by any device like this before. I know that examination of this engine must be done, but how am I to carry out my duties if I cannot enter the engine room?"

With that, she retreated to the flight deck, at which time the annoying feelings, both physical and mental, faded. "Adel, I think we need to get out of here so you can tell me exactly what you were feeling." We exited the ship as quickly as possible so she could feel safe.

"Durell," she said, "I have just had the most unpleasant experience ever as I tried to enter the Pentemor's engine room. I became nauseous, and a real sense of fear took over my mind. I had to leave that place and was not able to open the hatch leading to the engines." I had heard this same story before, and I knew exactly what had happened to Adel.

Adel and I returned to the Cheyenne Complex. Turning to her I said, "Adel, you have experienced the power of the interstellar engine which resides in the belly of the Pentemor. Without modifying your DNA, you will never be able to examine the engine nor be able to duplicate any of the systems which keep it under control. In another situation such as this, an individual who reacted the same as you received an injection of my blood which modified his DNA enough to allow him to touch the engine. If you are willing, I will offer you the same procedure. We never noted any bad effects from the injection, but as you know, any procedure has its risks. Would you like to proceed with this?"

Adel found all that was occurring to her was coming much too fast for her to digest. "Durell, I need some time to think this over. I am not a person who jumps into something without researching it thoroughly. I am dedicated to this project but will look for some other method which will allow me to do my job. My first thought would be some sort of suit which could block the engine's effects on me. I will inform you with my findings as soon as possible."

I answered, "I share your concerns but must impress on you the urgency of the task we have accepted." I was beginning to become irritated with how Adel seemed to be trying to dodge any involvement in this project. Pointing directly at her, I said, "We are going to proceed with the design and construction of the first of our ships and will not wait for you to complete your research. I know you're the best mind available to lead this team, but I cannot agree with your willingness to move slowly. We will begin a search immediately for your replacement. Your expertise will be greatly missed."

Adel was taken back by my response. I had not been abrupt nor offensive but had just stated my case and dismissed her. *How could he have come to this dismissal so quickly without even giving me options?* she wondered. *I think I might have overstepped my bounds with Durell. Could it be that there is much more to this man than I initially thought?*

If he feels that there is little or no time for me to research other options for protection from the engine, I might have to reassess my decision.

I had purposely thrown cold water on Adel concerning her membership in the design group. I wanted her to understand that everyone was taking some chances by just being part of the group. The sacrifices made by all who had been involved in the defeat of the Drezil left no room for any participants who were not totally committed to the defense of the Earth. If Adel wished to dictate terms which would result in any delays in the project, she would just have to leave the project. I hoped, however, that Adel would reassess her personal needs and agree to receiving the injection which I was offering.

I was considering what to do about Adel's vacated position when she came into my planning room. She seemed to be unsure about what she was supposed to do or say, so I gave her the opening she seemed to need. I motioned to a chair in front of me and gestured for her to sit.

"Adel," I said, "we are really going to miss your expertise. I would like for you to reconsider your decision to leave our group."

"Durell," she answered, "I do not wish to leave this group. I understand the sacrifices that have been made to pave the way for this entire project. If my continued participation requires that I have this injection, I will allow *it*. My only request is that you be present when the procedure is done."

Adel offered her arm as a gesture to signify that she was ready to proceed with the procedure.

I was overjoyed by Adel's decision. "I appreciate your willingness to proceed with this process. I will make preparations so we can complete this right now." I did not want to give her time to question her decision, so I immediately took her to the infirmary, where my blood would be drawn and injected into Adel.

Dr. Wainwright was called to the infirmary to perform the transfusion. When Adel and I arrived, he directed us to a sterile room where the technician was awaiting us. Although she had not initially questioned the wisdom of proceeding with this infusion, she had committed to it and would not back out. I took my place in the chair where my arm was outstretched to receive the needle which would take the sample. I began to realize the significance of what we were about to do. Once my blood had been injected into Adel's veins, we would be sharing more than my DNA. My past experiences had taught me that the sharing of my DNA had much more consequences than allowing for approach to the engine. Once the infusion was completed, I intended to closely monitor Adel's response to it to determine if she had any new skills or abilities. Feeling the stick from the needle, I knew it was too late to back out. If our blood proved compatible, Adel would receive the DNA-altering plasma.

Adel moved to the technician's chair and presented her arm. Having already taken a sample of her blood to test for compatibility, the stage was set for the injection. She winced noticeably as the needle broke through her skin and entered her vein. As the fluid began to course through her, she felt a rush of heat explode completely through her entire body. Her senses immediately began to sharpen, allowing her to almost see the new DNA begin to alter her own. The space around her began to fade into a bright white light, and she dropped into a deep sleep.

I immediately became concerned as Adel slumped forward in the chair. Taking her wrist in my hand, I found her pulse had shot upward to over two hundred beats per minute. Lifting her arm away from her body, I noted that her skin had taken on a deep bronze hue.

Not knowing what was happening to her, I picked up her featherlight body and moved her to the bed in the corner of the room. When I lowered her to the bed, she stirred and opened her eyes.

"What happened to me?" she asked. "I feel really warm, and my vision is a bit blurred. Whatever your blood has in it, it has suddenly enhanced all my senses. Even though my vision is still blurred a bit, I can begin to see much better than when I was wearing my contacts."

She flexed her arms and noted a new tautness to her muscles, and she felt as if they were regenerating themselves almost instantaneously.

"I can feel a new power deep inside my body. I am becoming extremely tired and need to sleep. Will you look over me until I awake, Durell?"

UNIVERSAL EXTINCTION

"Adel, don't fret about your safety. I will stay with you until you awaken. Maybe you have sensed that I am beginning to care for you and would never put you in danger. Sleep assured that you are safe. I guess my DNA has given you some of the fabulous feelings I deal with all the time. Enjoy them. I do!"

Chapter 48

Had Atina known what was to occur shortly, she would have never agreed to abandon her allies and join with the Azdawn. Rotan's ship, the Imnadda, was dispatched to Habordiz to bring Atina and Dlano to the Azdawn's adopted home, the planet Simiri 86.

After the Imnadda had settled gently onto the landing pad on Habordiz, Dlano requested that Atina join him in his home. Before Atina's meeting with Dlano, he had already been given orders from Rotan concerning the journey back to Simiri 86. When Atina entered, she felt the undeniable urge to join her father in a journey to a destination that was yet to be defined. Not knowing the source of this sudden need to join her father in leaving Habordiz, Atina began to feel her attachment to me begin to fade. She now felt that a new future awaited her and her yet-to-be-born child, which did not include any of the associations she had established during her adventure with me. The fact that I would be returning to Habordiz in a short time not only was of little concern to her, but she felt that she was going to intentionally avoid any contact with me in the future. For some unknown reason, she was scuttling her entire previous life, including the father of her child, to follow her father to a new home and life.

Atina was not yet beginning to show any signs of her pregnancy. She and Dlano boarded the Imnadda for its return journey to Simiri 86. Atina felt a fleeting moment of regret that her life was taking such a sharp turn away from me and our planned future. Regardless of any plans she had previously considered, she willingly boarded the craft and settled in for the short ride back to Simiri 86. The uneventful trip would end in the total enslavement of Atina for use by the Azdawn.

Atina and Dlano were greeted upon their arrival by several individuals who seemed to be important figures in the Azdawn hierarchy. They were escorted into a large building with corridors which led in several directions, all terminating in brightly lit rooms whose interior layouts were completely obscured. Dlano left Atina to follow a small group who disappeared into a room to one side of the main corridor. Atina was led to a different area of the complex and ushered into a small room which was equipped with many foreign-looking devices that seemed to have some medical purpose. All but two of the men in her group exited the area. She was left with only two of the young men who indicated that she should sit on an exposed upholstered ledge. The thought came to her. *Relax, let these men prepare you for what is to come. Do not resist the procedures that are about to take place, and be assured that no harm will come to you.*

Atina felt herself beginning to fall into sleeplike state, which left her totally aware of what was happening to her but not having the ability to intervene in any way. She was slowly lowered to the table which had been slid next to her, and soft straps were attached to her wrists, immobilizing her arms and chest. Two bottles of some sort of liquid were hung from an apparatus several feet above her head. Her mentors then inserted a needle in each of her arms and opened some valves to allow the fluid from the suspended bottles to begin to enter her body. A warm wash of sedation coursed throughout her, and she began to slide into a comfortable coma-like state. She was not totally comatose when she saw her caregivers usher two figures into the room. They stood beside her, and through her hazy, unfocused vision, she noted their nakedness, and she now knew what was going to happen to her. Her caregivers readjusted valves controlling the dispensing of the liquid into her arms, and she drifted into a peaceful sleep which blocked out all the activity around her. She would have been horrified if she had known what the two individuals were doing to her.

Atina awoke slowly to find herself wrapped in a luxurious blanket which clung to her body. Her senses were beginning to come alive, and the pain in her midsection started to send searing flashes of electric shocks up her spine and into her brain. Her arms ached where the needles had been inserted, and the bruises on her thighs and lower abdomen were testament to the abuse she had suffered.

What has happened to me? she wondered. *Why am I experiencing so much pain? I was assured that no harm would come to me, but I now feel that I was deceived. The messages which appeared to come from nowhere do not seem to be trustworthy. I am beginning to think that my decision to abandon Durell and my previous life was not my own. Have I been duped? And if so, by who? Could my father be a part of what is happening to me?*

Atina began to drift in and out of consciousness. Tubes had been inserted into her stomach, and life-giving slurry of liquid was continually injected into her. The room she was in seemed to continually rotate between light and dark as the days and weeks passed in a seemingly endless parade. She noted that her stomach had begun to swell, and she sensed movement within her body. She was visited on a regular basis by white-robed figures who were occasionally accompanied by her father, Dlano. Time seemed to have no real meaning to her, and she could not tell how long she had been held captive. Her only hope was that whatever they were doing to her would soon come to an end.

Chapter 49

Adel slowly recovered from the procedure which was destined to modify her DNA. All her senses returned to normal, and she began to feel a strange warm rush throughout her entire body. Although it was not unpleasant, she was concerned that it was an abnormal feeling which she had never experienced before the infusion of my plasma. She arose from her chair feeling a new strength course through her body and with a newly gained clarity of her vision. There could be no doubt that something incredible had happened to her, but it would be some time before she really realized the extent of the changes which had occurred.

I reached for her as she stumbled to stand and prevented her from falling. She felt my firm, muscular hands and arms wrap around her and knew the intense feelings she experienced were an indication of her infatuation with me. Slowly lowering her into a nearby chair, I felt her warm body shudder and her arms tighten around me as though she was trying to prolong our closeness. *Could she be the reason for my inability to concentrate?* I wondered. I was experiencing feelings that I long ago put aside in order to initiate the alliance which would eventually lead to the formation of the new Earth Defense Administration. In the recesses of my mind, I knew that my allegiances should be to Atina, but these new feelings cast a shadow on my past relationship. I knew I needed to return to Habordiz as soon as possible to deal with the confusion I was now experiencing.

"Adel," I started, "I will need to take the Pentemor and return to Habordiz to finish some business that I left incomplete. I need you to complete your studies of the ship as soon as possible so I can make the trip back. I will be as brief as possible and should return to Earth very quickly. Please gather your crew to complete your designs."

Adel was caught completely off guard by my orders. She had sensed some connection that was forming between us and could not determine why I had decided to return to Habordiz. "Durell," Adel said. "I will, of course, do as you have directed, but your departure will be untimely at best. We need your leadership to get this design and construction completed, but if you absolutely must go to Habordiz, we will do our best to move forward."

Having informed me of her feelings about my departure, she called her team together and began to study the Pentemor's secrets. Following the precise in-depth study of the Pentemor, Adel and her team began the process of designing the next evolution of an earth-based interstellar ship. I was given the go-ahead for my immediate launch to Habordiz.

I was preparing for the launch of the Pentemor, but I had a strange feeling, as though I was abandoning all my colleagues in the pursuit of my own personal agenda. The Pentemor had been brought down to the planet's surface to allow for a much closer examination. The ship sat in its cradle flooded with the bright light from the powerful spotlights that lit the launch site. Its exterior had been polished to a mirrorlike finish, making it appear as a blunt-faced dart pointed to the heavens.

I activated the boarding ladder and climbed into the interior of the ship. It seemed familiar and comforting to again be on board the ship that had played such an important role in saving the universe from the scourge of the Drezil. I made my way to the cockpit, noting the low-level hum coming from the engine room, indicating that the jump engine was active. It was all too familiar. Atina and I had flown this craft as a team, and I now felt her absence. She had taught me all I knew about piloting the ship. Now I was on a mission to find her and return to Earth. I took my seat at the controls and initiated the start sequence, bringing the primary launch engines to life. The engines lit, and the Pentemor belched a stream of liquid fire and smoke as it began to rise off the launchpad.

UNIVERSAL EXTINCTION

I skillfully pointed the craft upward and away from the Earth's surface and set a course for the trans-dimensional launch window beyond the moon. I knew from prior flights what to expect as the craft neared the jump site. The intergalactic engine had been silently idling since the Pentemor's launch, but now I pushed the throttle into the first detent and felt the acceleration of the craft begin to push me deeper into my seat. The familiar kaleidoscope of plasmatic colors began to appear in front of the ship as it entered the dimensional tunnel which would lead me to Habordiz. As in past flights, I felt the tremendous force of the engine begin to push me toward unconsciousness.

Chapter 50

Atina slowly drifted back into a conscious state. She felt no pain, and her stomach seemed to have shrunk back to its near normal size. The restraints which had held her captive were no longer secured, and she was able to sit up and examine her surroundings. *What has happened to me?* she wondered. *I feel as though I have been severely abused in some way. How long have I been in this condition, and who is responsible for what has occurred to me? I don't think I can trust anyone here, and I hope I can find some way to return to Habordiz.*

Scanning her surroundings, she noted a group of individuals who had just entered her room. Her father, Dlano, was in the lead and came to her bedside with a rush. He hugged her and began to express his sadness over what they had put her through, but he assured her that what had been done would save an entire species.

Not having any idea what had occurred, Atina began to quiz Dlano for details of what they had done to her. It was obvious that Atina was more than upset. She was livid. "Father, I know that something terrible has been done to me, and I want to know exactly what you and these others did," she demanded. "You had no right to impose any actions on me that might affect my health and welfare. You know I am pregnant with Durell's child, so you had better be honest with me. Now what in the hell did you do to me?"

Although he had been warned not to divulge any of the details of what had been done, Dlano said, "Atina, you have been granted the privilege of giving birth to a new species of Azdawn which will be the seed that will bring us back to our former glory. I am an Azdawn, and I was placed with you shortly after your birth. Your biological

256

parents were eliminated to allow me to enter your life. Your offspring, a male and a female, will grow to lead us into the future. Even though we do not yet know why you still show signs of being pregnant, we will now only monitor your health and allow you to be free to roam this new planet as you wish."

Atina was shocked by what she had just heard. She started to massage her stomach, trying to find any sign of new life within her. "You dirty son of a bitch! None of you had any right to use me like this. You have ruined my chance to have a child with Durell, and for that, I will never forgive you." Unable to control her emotions any longer, she slapped Dlano hard across his face. "I cannot believe any real father could do this to their daughter. I now hear that you are not related to me in any way and may have been party to my real parents' death. I disown you."

She was shocked beyond words to learn of her forced pregnancy and the birth of not one but two babies. Dlano's admission that he was an Azdawn explained a lot. She had always known him as her father, but now, all the questions which had plagued her concerning the strange voices that had directed her had been answered. Dlano was not her real biological father but rather an Azdawn who had been placed with her to influence her life's direction.

The gestation period for the hybrid children Atina had produced was four months, so there was no need for the Azdawn to continue to monitor her health. Had they followed her medically, they would have noted that her hormones were those of a pregnant woman.

She started to consider how she was going to escape her captors so she could bring the child within her womb to full term without the Azdawn's knowledge. She was now able to move around the facility with no restrictions. Mapping out a plan to escape was her primary goal, but she did not realize that Dlano was closely monitoring her every thought. Atina's plans for her escape began to take shape, so Dlano knew he had to intervene. She was needed to continue to produce more hybrid Azdawns to repopulate their species. After consulting with Azdawn leaders, the decision was made to move Atina to another location, a minimally occupied planet called Emporia 8.

There, she could wait until her body was ready and able to accept another Azdawn mating session.

The Azdawns had given both Atina and I some special abilities which, unknown to them, had begun to evolve on their own. Although Dlano could not sense it, Atina had clouded his mind and hidden the pregnancy she shared with me. Had he known that Atina still carried another child, he would have immediately moved to terminate her pregnancy. Of all the mistakes that had been made by the Azdawns, this was the worst. The fuse had been lit for their ultimate defeat.

Chapter 51

The Pentemor lurched violently. Having made many trans-dimensional jumps, I knew immediately that something out of the ordinary had happened. I felt the sudden deceleration of my craft, and the colors associated with the dimensional travel faded quickly into an inky black universe. Peering out of the cockpit windows, I could not discern anything recognizable. I seemed to be in a space completely devoid of any structure or stars. Then, as though a curtain was sheered in half, a space opened in front of my ship. The rift grew, and the Pentemor was drawn into the opening, revealing a brightly lit enclosure which seemed to be dimensionless. The Pentemor came to rest on a small sliver of metal which jetted from the side of a mammoth structure that appeared seemingly out of nowhere. I heard a hiss of air which began to build in volume approaching a loud roar that indicated some sort of atmosphere was beginning to form outside my ship.

The cockpit windscreen suddenly fogged over from the outside because of the moisture within the new atmosphere. The sound began to subside slowly, and the fog dissipated. I felt some sort of motion and turned to see that my craft was slowly being drawn into the inside of the structure. After the aperture closed behind the ship, I could begin to make out physical shapes of buildings. My ship was deposited on a glowing platform which omitted the same hum as my interstellar engine. When the platform noise changed volume and pitch, the Pentemor's engine followed suit. Both were linked by some force which I was unable to detect. The enormity of what was occurring began to dawn on me. I had initially thought that the glowing stone I found and subsequently used to power the transdimensional

259

engine had come from the Azdawns. Now I was not too sure that this was the case.

Peering out of the cockpit windows, I saw several white robed figures emerging from an opening in the side of the chamber where the Pentemor had come to rest. They were several meters away from my ship, but I could clearly make out their features.

The entity in the lead was over seven feet tall and humanoid in stature, but he had a gray cast to his skin. The other aliens had the same skin tone and humanoid features but were slightly shorter than the first. I descended the boarding ladder to find the outside air was cool, damp, and sweet to breathe.

When the group approached, I knew I was in the presence of a very highly evolved species.

"Durell," the tall leader said. "I am Alistar, and I represent the entire group present. We are the Kasdorians, and we have followed your journey from the time you found our artifact."

I was shocked to learn that the author of this entire adventure was not the Azdawns but rather the Kasdorians. Now, totally confused, I backed up toward my ship's boarding ladder.

Knowing that this entire group could read my mind, I thought, *I can no longer trust anyone. Why didn't you come forward sooner? I might have put my trust in someone who might be my enemy. So why don't you just state your case so I can decide who to trust?*

"Your sudden interest in utilizing the artifact to build an engine was in response to our injection of thought into your brain. We must apologize for the trauma you experienced during your first flight, but we were unaware that your body was so fragile. Thankfully, you were intercepted by the only person that could save you."

They must be referring to Atina, I thought. *I had assumed that she and her father were the inventors of the process that resulted in my rejuvenation. How many other entities are going to weigh in on this adventure?*

"The device she used to save your life was provided by us. We never thought that its use would be instrumental in saving our species. Although she was unaware of our intervening in her life, she has been followed just as you were, and her actions were greatly influenced by our mental directions. We will now call on you to assist us

UNIVERSAL EXTINCTION

in bringing the Azdawns' need for universal domination to an end. They have already taken the first steps to salvage their species by crossbreeding with a humanoid, your friend Atina."

"I know you most likely know a hell of a lot more about what is going on with Atina, but how am I supposed to put all my trust in the authenticity in what you have told me.? I cannot and will not believe that we have lost the child we created together. You'd better give me more than you have so far."

I assumed that Atina was still on Habordiz and pregnant with our child. I now wondered what had happened to her and how she could have agreed to such an insane scheme even to salvage this species. What had happened to my child? Had she totally abandoned our relationship and moved on to someone new? All these questions flooded my mind. Unknown to me, the Kasdorians present were aware of my thoughts and started to formulate a plan to resolve my fears.

Alistar spoke. "Durell, we are the overseers of this universe and will aid you in bringing about order. You were selected many millennia ago to serve as our emissary. We are going to grant you many abilities which will aid in bringing about order. You were given only a few of the powers which the Azdawns felt would not threaten their superiority, but now you will have the ability to cast a shadow on their capability to recruit other races to do their bidding."

"Now just wait a damn minute here. I have put up with all the crap the Drezil handed me, been bullshitted to the max by the Azdawns, and now you guys expect me to just lay down for you? Not gonna happen. You need to do something better than this to convince me that what you are saying is true."

"Durell, you had been convinced that the Drezil were defeated, but you were misled. The Azdawns have secretly made a pact with the Drezil which will allow them to rebuild their armies. This will allow the Drezil to assist the Azdawns in their desire to become the rulers of the universe. They must be stopped. Although you have already made a pact with the Earth forces, you will need to keep all that you have heard here to yourself. You will have the power, but you cannot divulge or openly use it. Do you agree to this plan?"

MICHAEL BRADLEY

All I could do was put my head in my hands and try to absorb what was happening to me. How had I ever gotten myself into this situation? I turned my gaze back to Alistar and pointed directly at him. "You are not going to drag me into another fight that I did not start. Go find some other sucker to lead this crusade."

Alistar answered, "Durell, you have every right to refuse this challenge. However, do not forget that all those who fought by your side as well as those who were killed in the last series of battles looked to you for leadership and courage. Do you really think you can turn your back on them during this critical time?"

I had not expected to be pulled back into an interstellar war which could determine the future of the human species. I knew that no matter what I said, I could never refuse to accept a leadership role and let someone else do my job for me.

"Alistar," I said. "I will, of course, try to aid in the protection of my species, but I do not know how I can possibly be of any use to you in this conflict. I know that we will all be in jeopardy if the Azdawns and the Drezil manage to combine their forces. They would be a formidable enemy, and the Earth forces I represent would not be able to win any conflict that might occur. Exactly what do you have in mind concerning my part in this plan?"

Without hesitation, Alistar replied, "The abilities we are giving you will allow you to form an effective group that will be able to match the Azdawn and their allies' every strength. Your mind will contain all the knowledge we have gained over the past many millennia. This information will include not only the resources you will need to build starships but also the ability to foresee any plans they may have for attacking you."

"Alistar," I asked, "how can I possibly do all the things you want of me? I can barely walk and chew gum at the same time, so I think you might be confused about who you are working with here. Without Atina's support, I am almost powerless."

"You have performed at an extremely high level since you rediscovered the artifact you found on Earth. Know now that the artifact you discovered was not provided by the Azdawns but came from our ancestors. It is not a stone but a biological being with which you can

262

UNIVERSAL EXTINCTION

now communicate. You stumbled across a colony of these beings on Alpha2, but they were not allowed to reveal themselves to you."

I could not recall any entity other than the Azdawns who were on Alpha2. I was getting a little pissed about all that had happened behind my back. I could not figure out who was friend and who was foe.

Alistar continued, "Anyone who does not share your DNA will never be able to approach the being as its defense mechanisms will shield it from any inspection. Only those who you approve will be able to work with it as a power source. You will feel a bit strange for a short period, but be assured that the abilities we give you will neither harm you nor be apparent to anyone. We will need to place you in a machine which will provide a conduit for our brains to yours."

Oh crap, here we go again. Another procedure that I have no idea what it's going to do to me. I guess I got in too deep to back out now. I shrugged my shoulders in resignation and waited for instructions on how we were going to proceed.

Alistar said, "The volume of information you will receive could be large enough to cause harm to you, so it will take some time for you to absorb all we offer to you. Are you willing to go forward with this procedure?"

After what I had been through, I decided that this next experience could be no worse than what I had already endured. "Let's get this over with," I replied. "I have many other very important things to attend to, and you have interrupted my trip to Habordiz."

I knew that Alistar and his cohorts could care less about my need to investigate the status of my lover, Atina. The only way I could join with them was to clear my plate of all the unfinished business I had left behind.

"I have a lady there who I believe is pregnant with my child, and I need to find her and bring her back to Earth with me. Although I am no longer sure how far my association with her will go, at the very least, I need to discuss our future with her. So I am ready to move forward with this process."

Alistar crossed to me and placed his hand on my arm. *Now what?* I wondered. "I did not wish to bring this news to you, but as you were on your way to Habordiz to meet with Atina, I think you need to know what has occurred since your departure from that planet. Atina is no longer there. She has been taken to the Azdawn's adopted planet, Simiri 86, where she was forced to give birth to two hybrid children which the Azdawns will use to rebuild their species."

I was stunned by what he was telling me. How could she have allowed her body to be violated by those assholes? I had seen some signs that she was beginning to detach herself from me, but I thought I was just imagining something because I was returning to Earth without her. Now what was I supposed to do?

"She was then moved to Emporia 8, where the Azdawns plan to leave her until she has totally recovered from the birth of the two children," Alistar said. "They then plan to repeat the impregnation process as many times as she can physically stand. Her only chance to escape this vile plan is to run and hide from these monsters. You will need to assist her in getting out of the grasp of the Azdawns and Dlano. Your ship has been rebuilt to include all the technologies we have to offer so you can easily make your way to Emporia 8. Now let us begin your transformation."

Chapter 52

Emporia 8 was a cold, dry, faceless planet. Atina was housed in a structure which stood above all others in the community she was to now call home. The planet's atmosphere was rich in oxygen. It was a bit too much for Atina's taste as it made her lightheaded. However, her mind was extremely clear, and she could finally have thoughts of her own without the constant flood of directions from Dlano.

They might have made a big mistake separating me from Dlano, she thought. *I can now plan for my escape without fear of discovery. This planet must have some means of travel, and I will find it as soon as I can. In the meantime, I will concentrate on the birth of the child that Durell and I have made.* Her stomach was swelling by the day, so any interaction she might have had with the Azdawns would now reveal her pregnancy. Looking at her distended belly, she vowed to keep her condition a secret for as long as possible. She dressed in loose-fitting clothing to help mask her changing body shape.

Atina peered out of the clouded glass of the window in her enclosure. She could see that the barren surface of this planet was scarred from many years of conflict which had ended with a fragile agreement to cease hostilities. The two opposing forces were facing each other for the first time and were attempting to forge a lasting peace which would allow them to rebuild their separate populations. One side was composed of a warrior species called the Sargins, who wished only to dominate this planet for their own use. The other side, known as the Teiugs, were a species of highly intelligent individuals who used their minds to formulate defensive plans to shield them from the Sargin's attacks.

265

One of the Teiugs, Rathen, had been assigned to watch over Atina just in case she tried to use her abilities to escape the Azdawn's clutches. He was a humanoid with large hands and a chiseled body. It was apparent that he possessed many of the attributes which Atina found desirable and was most likely completely human in all respects. The Azdawns had chosen this planet for Atina's recuperation because the unrest would make it impossible for her to escape. The scorched earth was testament to the battles that had taken place throughout the planet and the need to call an end to all the fighting. Atina began to formulate a plan for her escape. She would use her newly acquired resources to bond with the intellectual who had been chosen to ensure her safety and comfort during her stay on Emporia 8. Her current pregnancy had not caused any concern among her caregivers, so she was free to plot her escape. Any plan she formulated had to include the escape of both herself and her offspring. She was due to give birth to the child she and Durell had produced, so she would plan her escape to take place following that event.

Atina had carefully thought through her options for escape. She knew that her captors had vehicles capable of interstellar travel and that several were housed not far from her current location. With this knowledge, all she needed was to force her overseer to assist her in her escape. With that in mind, she summoned Rathen to her chambers. When he arrived, she immediately began to probe his mind with the intent of planting suggestions that he join her in planning her escape.

When Rathen first saw Atina, he was immediately taken by her beauty and her intelligence. *This woman,* he thought, *could very easily capture my heart. Whenever I am close to her, I feel as though she and I share some sort of real connection. It is as if she and I are one, our thoughts merging. I know she is in great distress, and I cannot ignore her cries for help. I am a dedicated citizen of the Teiug race and will continue to do my best to help bring an end to this insane war, but Atina's needs are now of more importance to me.*

Atina felt Rathen begin to invite her into his mind. She was overwhelmed when she began to sense Rathen's growing infatuation with her. She found him to be very wise, and he allowed her to begin to plant suggestions in his mind. Rathen, on the other hand, began

UNIVERSAL EXTINCTION

to feel Atina's presence in his mind and decided to allow her to roam through his memories.

I need to convince this woman that I pose no danger to her and am willing to help her in any way that I can, Rathen thought. *Those who placed her on this planet assumed that we are all so focused on the war that we will not question their motives. They were naive to think that we would follow their lead.*

Probing Rathen's mind, Atina found all the information she needed to proceed with her escape. She now had an ally who would assist in the actual implementation of her plan, even though he did not fully realize why. Any action on their part would have to wait because Atina was now feeling the first pains associated with childbirth.

"Rathen," she said, "although it has not come to the attention of the Azdawn, I am pregnant with a child which was fathered by a humanoid from the planet Earth. This child's presence will have a great impact on us all. I need to keep my pregnancy a secret because there are those who would wish to do harm to this child if they knew about him. Will you help me?"

Rathen thought, *I have no choice. I must help this woman. She has a hold over me, and I cannot seem to think for myself.* "Atina," he said, "I know you will need some time to deal with the birth of this child. However, we need to act immediately if you are escape unde-tected. You might have to endure your childbirth while we are in transit to another safe planet. If that is agreeable with you, I suggest we plan to leave immediately. I can get us to a spacecraft which I have permission to use if we leave now. Is it possible for us to proceed?"

Knowing that this would most likely be her only chance of escape, Atina said, "Rathen, whether you know it or not, we have both experienced a mental connection which cannot be broken. We are emotionally connected, and I know you have some deep feelings for me as I do for you. To keep the birth of this child and his heritage secret, I am going to ask you to marry me and become the adoptive father."

Atina knew that she was taking a risk asking Rathen to join with her. Her plan was to use him as a buffer between herself and Dlano.

267

She moved to his side and wrapped her arms around him and put her head on his shoulder. She became more insistent, hoping to seal the deal.

"Although this might not be a conventional proposal, considering the timing, it will have to do. I never considered a marriage to anyone but the child's father, but I have begun to have some intense feelings for you. This union will most likely put you in considerable danger, so don't take my request lightly."

Rathen was totally taken by the offer Atina had just made. "Atina" he said, "we have only known each other for a short time, but I know I am in love with you and hope you will feel the same sometime in the future. I will do as you ask."

Rathen led the very pregnant Atina out to a place that had been scorched by prior attacks. In the middle of the area was a small indentation which held a steel door. Rathen opened the door to expose a long corridor devoid of any doors except for one at the far end which had a light that could be seen shining through a small window embedded in its center. They moved quickly to the far end of the hall and opened the door. Beyond this exit stood a small silver ship which was pointed toward the dark sky. It appeared to be a very conventional ship which might have been constructed many eons ago. A ladder pointed the way up to an entry in the belly of the craft. Atina and Rathen moved to the base of the ladder and prepared to board.

"Rathen," Atina asked, "this ancient craft could not possibly provide a means of escape for me. I am sure we could find some more appropriate conveyance that will ensure that I successfully escape this planet."

Taking Atina by the hand, Rathen led her up to the entry port of the ship. Gesturing for her to board the ship, he led the way up the ladder. Once inside the ship, she was amazed by the level of the technology it contained. The inside somehow seemed much larger than it appeared from outside. A large control console occupied the center of the bridge area.

Rathen said, "Don't be deceived by the appearance of this ship. It is possibly the most advanced vessel in the entire universe. It can perform trans-dimensional intergalactic travel, and I intend to move

UNIVERSAL EXTINCTION

you to your home planet, Habordiz. I cannot tell you where or how I came into possession of such an advanced ship, but believe me, it will be your savior. When we reach Habordiz, you will be made comfortable so your labor will not be too intense."

Having apprised her of his escape plan, Rathen gestured for Atina to the craft and followed her up the ladder into the cockpit. Once they had settled in, the craft was put on a predetermined course to Habordiz and shot into the sky above the planet. The trip was completed in a flash of colored light, and they arrived in orbit above Habordiz, not knowing how this ship had performed so magnificently.

Atina knew the time for the birth of this child was approaching very quickly. Their tiny ship slipped out of orbit, and Atina saw the launching pad she had used so many times appear below their craft. They settled onto the pad. The engines shut down, followed by a hiss of air entering the ship as the hatch opened and the ladder extended to the ground. Atina looked intently at Rathen, who seemed to be unsure of what to do next.

"Rathen, please help me out of this ship. I know the time is short before I give birth, and I am looking to you to help me through this. I know you have saved my baby and me, and I intend to find some way to thank you for all you have done. I will direct you to our laboratory where all the medical equipment is stored. It will ensure that I have a successful labor."

Having developed a personal interest in Atina and her plight, Rathen scooped her up in his arms and made his way out of the ship and into the laboratory which had been shared by Atina and Dlano. Laying her on the raised bed which occupied the center of the room, Rathen left to find a physician who could assist in the birth.

Rathen had no idea where to go for help as he had never been on this planet. The birth process was totally foreign to him, but a woman was lingering in the hall outside the laboratory, and she offered to help. Rathen told her of his problem, and she offered to bring a physician to the laboratory. Having found the assistance he needed, he returned to Atina's side.

269

It was already too late. Atina was holding a normal human baby boy in her arms. The course of humanity had just been altered as this new superior being entered the world. The unique talents and gifts which Atina and Durell had passed on to this child would eventually be the catalyst for a new universal order.

Unknown to Atina, Durell had just arrived at Emporia 8, intending to spirit her away from her captors. He found no sign of her or their child but suddenly felt an overwhelming sense of loss as though Atina and his child had been taken from him. He would come to know that she had given birth to their son, and she was to be married to the entity who had saved them both. The two other children who were the product of her forced insemination by the Azdawn were a boy and a girl, one of which would prove to be an invaluable asset to humanity and one who would be their most powerful enemy. A new chapter was beginning for them all, one that would have a profound impact on the entire universe.

CPSIA information can be obtained
at www.ICGtesting.com
Printed in the USA
BVHW040227090822
644111BV00006B/60/J